NOW
YOU
SEE ME

BOOKS BY D.K. HOOD

D.K. HOOD

NOW
YOU
SEE ME

bookouture

Published by Bookouture in 2023

An imprint of Storyfire Ltd.
Carmelite House
50 Victoria Embankment
London EC4Y 0DZ

www.bookouture.com

ISBN: 978-1-80314-902-8
eBook ISBN: 978-1-80314-901-1

This is for my wonderful husband, Gary. Without him, I'd forget to eat and drink when I'm writing. He is the most tolerant, loving man I've ever met.

PROLOGUE

MONDAY

An ice-cold wind, straight from the mountains, cut through Maisy Jones' thin winter coat as she left the Triple Z Bar. Only a fool would walk through a parking lot in the dead of night in Serial Killer Central, but Maisy had no choice. The patrons had left and she'd cleaned the tables and stacked the chairs. It was after midnight and patches of ice cracked under her boots with each cautious step over the uneven ground. Heart pounding, she scanned the long shadows from the surrounding forest of tall pines. They met up with the dark patches shed by the rows of parked trucks, some of the vehicles glistening with frost. The thick cloud cover had threatened a blizzard, but for now only a sprinkle of snowflakes brushed her cheek, melting into cold rivulets and dripping from her chin. She brushed them away and headed hesitantly across the dimly lit parking lot toward her old Dodge truck, hoping that none of the men who'd been pestering her all evening would be lurking in the darkness.

Footsteps crunched on the gravel but stopped when she spun around to see who was behind her. Fear gripped her, stealing her breath. Had someone followed her from the bar? Grabbing her keys from her purse, she held them in her fist, with one key protruding from between her knuckles to use as a weapon, and hurried on, but the footsteps came again. The slow even pace was gaining on her. Someone was close by. She glanced around as a figure moved through the parked trucks. Uncertain, she froze. Too scared to walk to the end of the eighteen-wheeler beside her, she glanced back over one shoulder in the hope, if necessary, she'd find refuge in the bar. Her heart sank. The building sat in darkness, the proprietor had left already.

A shiver of uncertainty ran through her, and sucking in a deep, freezing breath, she crept back the way she'd come and slid around the truck parked two slots away. Her vehicle in sight, she broke into a run, wishing she'd parked closer to the bar. Fumbling with the keys in her freezing fingers, she wrenched open the door, climbed inside and locked the doors. The engine started, coughed and died. Trying to keep calm, she turned the key again. "Come on. Come on. Don't do this to me now."

As the engine shuddered into life, a big black pickup sped by throwing up dirt and skidded into the gas station outside the roadhouse. Maisy let out a long breath, filling the cab with steam. It had only been someone walking to their ride. She laughed, shaking herself. "Get a grip."

She bumped out of the parking lot and headed along Stanton. The stink of cigarettes and stale beer from the Triple Z Bar clung to her clothes. She figured the old building must have been there since the days of the Wild West and hadn't changed inside. It had the classic swinging doors and a long wooden bar. The tables surrounded by chairs seemed to spring up like mushrooms from the stained filthy floor. The tabletops, decorated with ring marks from a million spilled drinks, had names and dates carved into them by customers wearing cowboy hats or leather jackets and all openly carrying weapons. It sure was a fun place to work.

The Triple Z Roadhouse, on the other side of the parking lot, shone like a beacon for passing traffic. The flashing lights above the gas pumps with signs for a diner and motel appeared welcoming enough, but inside cracked vinyl seats lined the booths around stained tabletops. The place hadn't ventured out of the nineteen-sixties. Maisy couldn't believe her life had come to working in this dump. Heck, the Triple Z Bar wasn't the end of the earth, but she could see it from here.

The images she'd scanned online of Black Rock Falls had depicted an alpine paradise, but she guessed every nice town had its share of lowlife hangouts, and the Triple Z Bar must rate as number one. She'd missed out getting a job this winter at the ski resorts in Idaho's Pebble Creek, and after reading an article about the tourists flocking to Black Rock Falls to enjoy the Glacial Heights Ski Resort, she'd driven hours to hunt down a job. On arrival, the only work she could secure was the bartender position at the Triple Z Bar on the outskirts of town. Her first shift, from six through to midnight, had been exhausting, not from serving at the bar but from avoiding the unwanted attention of the customers. Being in her early twenties, the idea of staying at the Triple Z Roadhouse Motel with bikers, truckers and ladies of the night wasn't going to happen. She'd found the rates at the Cattleman's Hotel too expensive and eventually found a cold but clean room at the Black Rock Falls Motel.

It was only a ten-minute drive to the motel, but a few minutes along Stanton the engine coughed, spluttered and died. Steam poured out from under the hood. Aiming the truck onto the side of the road, Maisy stared at the gauges. The gas tank was three quarters full. She turned the key and the engine shuddered, refusing to start. She stared at the empty highway. The blacktop shimmered with ice patches and the snow was getting heavier. There was no one she could call for help. She hadn't joined an auto club. She rubbed her arms, wishing she'd added a few extra layers before leaving for work. All her things were at the motel, and if she stayed in the truck, she'd freeze to death. She had no option but to walk.

Stepping onto the dark road, she used her phone to light the way. She walked as fast as possible to keep warm, and when a vehicle's headlights lit up the blacktop, she increased her speed to a jog to take advantage of the light. Behind her, the beat of tunes playing loud surrounded her as the vehicle slowed. It was the big black pickup she'd seen before. The tunes stopped and only the roar of a powerful engine throbbed beside her. She glanced around as the window slid down.

"Wanna ride?" A man peered down at her from the cab, his face in shadow. "It stinks some—I've been hunting—but it's better than walking."

Unsure, Maisy stared at him. "I'm heading for the motel. It's not far. I can walk."

"It's more than five miles. You'll be a popsicle by then, and finding you frozen solid on the side of the highway wouldn't help our town's reputation, would it?" His mouth flashed in a white smile. "It's a few minutes away. Aw, come on. I feel bad just leaving you out here on your lonesome. The smell is not so bad. I have a Perspex divider between us and the back seat. It's to stop my hunting dogs from jumping all over me when I'm driving."

A few minutes. The seconds she'd been standing still had already frozen her feet, Maisy shrugged. "Okay, thanks." She went around the hood, the door opened and she climbed inside. The smell hit her in a wall of stink, and she swallowed the bile rushing up the back of her throat.

"Click in your seatbelt. I drive kinda fast." The man turned to look at her.

Maisy complied and the vehicle took off at high speed. She breathed through her mouth to avoid the stink. The man drove recklessly, swerving around patches of ice. She gripped the seat and kept her eyes on the road, willing the motel lights to come into view. Her heart sank when the pickup slowed and pulled into the curb. When the man opened the lid to the console, her hand went to the door handle. "Why are we stopping?"

"Oh, I forgot to introduce you to my friends." He pulled out a plastic bag and smiled at her, indicating with his chin to the back seat. "I'll turn on the light."

Maisy turned slowly and gaped in horror at three corpses sitting bolt upright and secured in seatbelts behind the Perspex divider. A man, a woman and a kid about ten years old stared at her with unseeing eyes. Her throat closed in terror as she tried to open the door. The man beside her was laughing, but she didn't care. She just wanted to get away. She pulled and pushed at the locked door, but it wouldn't move. "Let me out."

"Now that wouldn't be any fun at all, would it?" He inclined his head, looking at her. "I assume you don't like my friends?"

Screaming in terror, Maisy lashed out at him, but he grabbed one of her hands and slammed a wet rag into her face, covering her nose and mouth. The rag pushed down so hard, it ground her lips painfully into her teeth and squashed her nose. A chemical taste and smell burned her throat and stung her eyes. She held her breath and fought like a wild animal to dislodge the hand pressing into her face, but she had no hope against the strength of this man. Lungs bursting, she unwillingly sucked in a breath. Her arms became heavy and her gloved hand fell from his chest. His face blurred. Her chest tightened. She couldn't breathe and her heart pounded in her ears. *Someone help me.*

ONE

WEDNESDAY

Sheriff Jenna Alton leaned back in her office chair and stared at Deputy Jake Rowley. "So, you noticed the truck yesterday morning. Did you check it out?"

"Nope, not at the time." Rowley curled the rim of the brown Stetson in his hands and shrugged. "I did on the way home last night. I checked the doors to see if they were locked. I looked around for signs of a problem and couldn't see anything wrong, but when it was still there this morning, I ran the plates and it belongs to Maisy Jones out of Nampa, Idaho. I figure she might be a tourist, but the truck is an old Ford. Maybe she came here for work or she's in trouble."

Concerned for the woman's safety, Jenna nodded. "Okay, run a background check on Maisy Jones and see what you can find. Check her last known address and see if Nampa has issued a missing persons report for her. If not, hunt down her relatives and call them. Try and get a phone number for her. She might be holed up in town with a boyfriend. I'll go and look at the truck. How far is it from Triple Z Roadhouse?"

"Five minutes, I guess." Rowley nodded. "I'll get at it." He strolled out of the room.

Jenna's role as sheriff of Black Rock Falls had come about after being placed in witness protection five years previously. A former DEA agent, she'd brought down a drug cartel and put her life at risk by giving evidence to convict kingpin Viktor Carlos. Living in plain sight, with a new face and name, she'd fought for the role of sheriff in Black Rock Falls, a backwoods town in Montana. There she'd hired Dave Kane as deputy sheriff, only to discover sometime later that he was an ex-special forces sniper who'd worked in the White House as a member of the Secret Service. After a car bombing killed his wife and left him with a metal plate in his head, he'd been secreted in Black Rock Falls like her with a new face and name, but he still remained a valued asset to the government. Sometime later, Shane Wolfe and his family arrived in town and joined the team, becoming the medical examiner. Wolfe had only one secret and that was he was Dave Kane's handler, and both men could be called back into active duty at any time.

Jenna stood. "Dave, we need to check out this truck. What if Maisy Jones wandered off into the forest and has gotten lost?"

"Sure." Kane pushed to his feet and reached for his black Stetson. He glanced out the window. "It's snowing again." He took Jenna's coat from the peg behind the door and handed it to her. "Don't forget your gloves."

Raising her eyebrows, Jenna shook her head. "Forget the Stetson today. It's freezing out there." She opened her drawer and pulled out two woolen caps and tossed him one. She chuckled. "Oh my, it's not been a year yet and we sound like an old married couple."

"I like it." Kane grinned at her, pulled the cap over his ears and pushed on his Stetson.

Jenna rolled her eyes. "You're wearing your hat over the cap? Isn't that a little tight?"

"Nah, it's all good, Jenna. My hat keeps the snow from running down my neck." Kane shrugged. "I guess we should take Duke. It's not been snowing all night, so it won't be thick on Stanton and we might find something inside the truck we can use as a scent to track the owner." He patted his leg and the bloodhound came to his side to allow him to fit his coat. "Okay, we're ready."

At six-five and two hundred and seventy pounds, Kane had gained twenty pounds of muscle before winter this year and was even taller in his snow boots and wider in his puffy jacket. Jenna couldn't help admiring the handsome man she'd recently married and then dragged her eyes away to concentrate on the job at hand. She grabbed two survival backpacks from the closet, handed one to Kane and then headed for the door. At the bottom of the stairs, the sheriff's department was unusually quiet. Nobody waited in the foyer or lined up at the counter to speak to their receptionist, Maggie Brewster. Rowley was at his desk, as was Deputy Zac Rio, a gold shield detective from LA who'd joined the team a year or so previously. She went to Rio's desk. "We're heading out to check out a truck on Stanton. You're in charge while I'm gone. Rowley will bring you up to speed with the abandoned truck. See if you can find the owner, a Maisy Jones out of Idaho, in town. She might be in trouble or in need of assistance."

"Yes, ma'am." Rio nodded. "I'll see if I can hunt her down at one of the motels or the shelters."

Jenna nodded and, giving Maggie a wave, followed Kane out into the artic tundra. With Duke in his harness in the back seat, she helped Kane shift the ice from the windshield of the black tricked-out truck affectionately known as the Beast. Bulletproof and bombproof, it made the Batmobile look like a toy. She stamped the snow from her boots and climbed inside. "What were you working on when we left? Anything interesting?"

"It was an email from Ty Carter." Kane was referring to Special Agent Ty Carter, ex–navy Seal from the local field office out of Snakeskin Gully. "He's investigating missing persons reported in Blackwater and just letting us know he'll be stuck there for a time until the weather breaks. The visibility is bad over the mountains right now."

Wondering why the Blackwater sheriff's department would call in the FBI to chase down missing persons, she frowned. "Is Jo with him?" Behavioral analyst and Special Agent Jo Wells was Carter's partner.

"Yeah, and before you ask, an entire family—Mom, Dad and a kid—have vanished." Kane swung her a gaze as they headed along Main. "Dinner half eaten on the table, coats left in the mudroom, dogs not fed. It was as if they just walked out of the door and disappeared." A nerve ticked in one cheek. "Freaky."

A cold chill spilled down Jenna's spine. "An entire family? What else did Carter say?"

"That's it." Kane accelerated onto the highway alongside Stanton Forest. "He made it to Blackwater just before the blizzard hit last night and now they're stranded. He can't risk flying the chopper until the visibility improves."

Frowning, Jenna turned to him. "I understood that his chopper's engine was fitted with snow filters or whatever. The snow shouldn't be a problem, should it? We have choppers dropping people in and out of the ski resort all the time."

"Yeah, his chopper has the filters, but only a fool would risk flying over the mountain range when the visibility is low." Kane cleared his throat. "He doesn't plan on being splattered all over the mountainside anytime soon."

Jenna snorted. Carter was known to be fearless in the chopper and risked his life far too often. Maybe this was a side of him she hadn't met yet. "That's good to know."

TWO

As they drove along Stanton, Jenna kept her attention riveted on the forest. The pine trees dusted with the first powdery snow reminded her of Christmas as a child, and she wished her parents had been alive to meet the man she'd married. She figured they'd approve and pushed back the memories of finding gifts under the tree and scanned the forest for any signs of Maisy Jones.

"Up ahead." Kane lifted one finger from the steering wheel and pointed. "That must be the truck."

As Kane turned the Beast around and parked behind the truck, Jenna looked in both directions. The Dodge truck was parked in the middle of nowhere. On one side of Stanton was Stanton Forest and on the other the land spread out from back-to-back ranches. The only houses were the other side of the Triple Z Roadhouse and then a few closer to the motel before habitation joined the outskirts of town. It was unusual for hunters to leave their trucks on this side of the road. Most would park near a forest warden's station or drive a ways into the forest. The local council maintained a ton of off-road parking lots, placed at the beginning of marked trails for campers and hikers. It seemed unusual for a young woman to leave her truck so far from assistance. She climbed out and followed Kane to the vehicle. The truck was locked. Jenna walked a ways along the highway and then brushed snow away from the dirt on the side of the road. She found footprints in the frozen mud. "I had a hunch. If I decided to walk, I wouldn't walk on the road, not with eighteen-wheelers flashing by. I'd stick to the verge. The footprints are small and there's a chance they could belong to Maisy. Why would she leave her truck?"

"Maybe she ran out of gas." Kane shrugged. "Although she'd just passed the roadhouse, so that makes no sense." He turned to look at the truck. "I'll go take a look."

Jenna followed him. "It's locked."

"It's an old truck, getting into it will be easy." Kane pulled lockpicks from his pocket and went to work. "Okay, I'm in." He smiled at her and bent inside the cab, playing with wires.

The engine shook and rattled but didn't start. Kane straightened and walked around to the back of the truck and bent to examine the exhaust pipe. Interested, Jenna followed. "What are you looking for?"

"Sabotage. Someone wanted this truck to break down." He pulled on examination gloves and eased a wad of something wrapped in wire from the tailpipe. "I'm surprised it started at all, but the way this is made, rather than the exhaust shooting it out, it expands when hot, blocks the pipe and the engine dies."

Jenna went to the Beast to grab an evidence bag and held it open for Kane. "If someone did this to her, she's in big trouble."

"Yeah, typical serial killer ploy. Make the victim vulnerable and then lure them into your vehicle." Kane stared into the distance. "Unless they took her down between here and the motel, which is reasonable to assume because once there she'd be safe, Duke won't be able to track her in the snow. We'll have to search on foot."

Jenna pulled out her phone. "Rio, we need to search the

side of the road from the abandoned truck. Bring something to clear away the snow."

"*On our way.*" Footsteps echoed through the speaker. "*I have info on Maisy Jones. She is staying at the motel, but no one has seen her since Monday. I got the manager to check her room, and all her things are there. She took the room on a week-to-week, saying she had a job at the Triple Z Bar. I called them and the proprietor figured I was checking up on her qualifications. He insisted she was trained and had completed an online course to serve liquor here. He said she worked Monday night six till midnight but didn't show last night. The proprietor locked up when she left just after twelve Monday night and said she was heading for her truck.*" He cleared his throat. "*I asked what she was wearing. He said jeans and a black sweater. She had a jacket but it wouldn't have kept her warm in the snow. He mentioned it to her and she told him she had a thicker one back at the motel. I asked if she was carrying a purse and he doesn't recall.*"

Jenna nodded. "Good to know and it fits into the scenario we have here. Kane figures her truck was disabled, so she had to abandon it. She could be fine but I'm not risking it. We'll need to make sure she's okay. We have time. It's not as if we have a ton of work to do. Get here ASAP." She disconnected.

Jenna stared at the footprints frozen in the damp soil. "It snowed overnight. I went to the bathroom just after midnight and it was snowing, so this happened right after she left the Triple Z Bar."

"Would *you* accept a ride from a stranger, who just happened to come by after your vehicle died?" Kane removed the gloves and pulled on his thick padded ones.

Jenna considered the options. "If I was armed, yeah, but if not, out here? No way. I'd walk or jog to the motel. Maisy knew it was five miles or so down the highway. If she's from Idaho, she understands winter temperatures and keeping moving would be better than freezing to death in the truck. Remember it wasn't snowing when she left the bar. We have proof from the foot-prints." She stared ahead. "This is going to take all day."

"Not necessarily. We can assume she walked for maybe a mile. The snow would be getting heavier by then, and she would be cold. It would be a perfect time for a serial killer to become a knight in shining armor." Kane smiled. "Get into the truck. We'll drive a mile along the road and then check for footprints."

Unconvinced, Jenna shrugged. "You're surmising he planned an abduction. How could he when she only started work at the bar on Monday night? How would he even know her ride?"

"A six-hour shift." Kane slid behind the wheel. "He might have seen her arrive and spoken to her during her shift. She was one of the bartenders. If he was a regular, he'd know the bartenders' shifts are ten until six and six until twelve. I know and I don't drink there. Only the roadhouse is open twenty-four seven."

Jenna fastened her seatbelt and nodded. "Okay, we drive a mile and stop and check for tracks."

To her astonishment, the small footprints were still showing under the snow a mile along the highway. They went on another fifty yards and stopped again. She looked at Kane. "You're starting to think like a serial killer. I'm not sure if that's a good thing or not."

"I don't know, Jenna." Kane grinned at her. "One minute you figure I'm a cyborg, the next a werewolf and now a serial killer. I'm just a man, is all."

Shaking her head, and knowing it was Kane's way of relieving the tension of having another serial killer in town, she met his gaze. "One thing for sure, you've never been 'just a man' and the jury is still out on the cyborg theory." She searched through the snow, moving it to one side with her boot. "No foot-prints. We need to go back some and expand the search."

Glad to see Rio's sheriff's department truck pulling up on the opposite side of the road, Jenna waved them over. Rio was carrying a janitor's broom. The head was at least two feet wide with stiff bristles. "There are no footprints here. They started from the abandoned truck, so we came down here a ways and decided to walk back. We need to find where they stopped. Clear the snow along the edge of the road but be careful not to destroy evidence. If she climbed into a vehicle, the chances are the footprints will show she turned toward the road."

"Rowley has another broom." Rio's attention moved up and down the road. "It would be easier to search in ten-yard sections. From the last sighting of the footprints. If you start there, we'll work toward you." He shrugged. "It's more efficient."

Jenna appreciated Rio's unique abilities. He could mentally take in a complete crime scene in a few minutes, he recalled everything in perfect detail and he was able to see solutions at a remarkable speed. The day he showed for a position in her department as a deputy had been her lucky day. She nodded and took the broom from Rowley. "Okay, let's get at it."

It didn't take too long before they found the end of the footprints. Jenna waited patiently as Rowley cleared the snow from them before they noted the difference. Rio took a ton of photographs because the footprints revealed more than they'd hoped for. "What do you make of them, Dave?"

"She started off walking at a good pace, but by here"—he pointed to a yellow flag—"she started to run, not fast, just a slow jog, but the pace changes, and here, she turned around, looked behind her and then continued to walk on." He pointed to another marker. "I figure someone drove up behind her, maybe stopped to speak to her and to offer her a ride, and then they crawled alongside her as she walked. "Here she stopped and turned toward the road. She moved around some, maybe deciding if she should take a ride. The marks change direction.

So, she walked maybe to the hood of his truck, and from the angle of the prints, she either crossed the highway or rounded the hood and climbed inside." He looked at Jenna. "We should search the opposite side of the road in case she decided to take a stroll at midnight in the forest, but my bet is she took the ride."

A shiver went through Jenna and it wasn't from the bitter cold. Maisy Jones never made it back to the motel and had likely taken her last ride. "Okay and can you see any tire tracks alongside the footprints? Any blood—anything?"

"Nope." Kane handed Rio the broom. "I was hoping we'd find some trace of the vehicle but looking at where she stopped and moved around. If we surmise that she was talking to someone through the window, and then walked around the hood, it's too small for an eighteen-wheeler or too short for a van. We're talking about a truck the size of the Beast."

"Nothing over here." Rowley waited for vehicles to roll by before he crossed the slippery blacktop. "I checked straight ahead and on different angles. There's no sign of her. No smell of death in the forest and the snow hasn't penetrated it yet. There's a dusting at best on the trails."

The cold had affected all of her team. Rowley's nose was red and Rio's lips had turned blue. No doubt Kane's head was throbbing. It was bitterly cold out on the windy highway. Jenna nodded. "Okay, head to Aunt Betty's Café and stay for a time. You both look frozen. We'll go and check out her motel room and meet you there. I need coffee and my feet are frozen solid. Show Maisy's picture to Susie Hartwig and her assistant manager, Wendy, and ask if they've seen her. It's the first stop for most people, when they get into town."

"Yes, ma'am." Rowley banged the snow from the broom and tossed it into the back of Rio's truck. "I called the Nampa Police Department before I left town and they'll be calling back once they've located Maisy Jones' family."

Jenna pushed her freezing fingers into the pocket of her

jacket. "Okay, thanks. Let me know when you have something." She turned and followed Kane back to the Beast. She shook the snow from her boots and jacket and climbed inside. She rubbed Duke's head but he was snuggled under his blanket fast asleep. She looked at Kane. "I have that terrible sinking feeling again."

"Why?" Kane started the engine and headed back to town. "She might have gone back to his place. It happens, you know."

Jenna rubbed her temples. "Yeah, I am aware of one-night stands, Dave, but if Maisy had met a guy and decided to stay at his place, she'd need clean clothes at least, especially after working a shift in a bar. Most normal men would at least take her back to the motel so she could get changed. When someone goes missing in our town, they're rarely found alive. We have another killer in town, don't we?" She waved a hand toward the thick coating of snow building up alongside the blacktop. "He could be hiding bodies all over and we'd never find them in the snow."

THREE

Maisy came out of a foggy haze, struggling to open her eyes. Panic rocked her and she spun around looking for the man who'd drugged her. A wave of giddiness blurred her vision and bile filled her mouth. She gripped the side of the narrow bed and tried to calm her pounding heart. Cold seeped through her clothes and she shivered, teeth chattering. White steam surrounded her with each exhale of breath. Where was she and where was the hideous laughing man who'd kidnapped her? Disorientated, she turned her head more slowly this time to absorb her surroundings. The room was empty and only the sound of clocks ticking, drifted through an open door. The man had drugged her and the smell still lingered in her nose. She drew up her knees, clasping her arms around them. Dread gripped her and she looked down at herself, checking her clothing, but everything looked okay. He hadn't hurt her, so why was she here? She took in the room more closely. The cold dim room resembled a bathroom without the fittings. Chipped white tiles covered the floors and walls. The room held no furniture, apart from the bed. She ran her hands over the metal sides. It was an old-style hospital gurney, rusty and caked with dust. A sink sat against one wall, yet the normal paraphernalia she'd usually see in a hospital room were missing. The tiled floor held the dirt from many years of neglect. Trembling with fear, she pulled the rough blanket around her and listened.

Nothing.

She searched her pockets and, finding them empty, stared at the tiny stream of water spilling from the tap into the sink. It was as if the liquid was calling to her and, moving her tongue over dry cracked lips, she edged off the gurney, swayed a little and then, using the freezing-cold wall for support, made her way to the basin. The water running slowly from the tap appeared to be clean, although a rust stain in the bottom of the stainless steel bowl made her wonder how long it had been left dripping. Desperate to take a drink but aware someone might be watching her, she looked all around. Nothing moved in the other dim room. Instinctively she looked up, searching for cameras. She'd read about a serial killer who'd kept women prisoner in caves so he could murder them when he had the urge, but she found nothing but dusty spider webs deserted long ago.

Reaching out, she turned on the faucet and stared at the stream of water rushing down the drain. Using both hands, she scooped up a handful, sniffed it and tested it with the tip of her tongue. It smelled and tasted like pure mountain water. She drank deeply and washed her face, drying it on the arms of her coat. Her head had cleared and she rested her back against the wall for a few more minutes, assessing her situation. There was an open door at the end of the room and, moving slowly, she stepped toward it and looked inside. It was a bathroom, with a toilet and shower but no windows. She had to find a way out, get to the cops and tell them about the man in the black truck with the bodies in the back seat.

Still a little unsteady on her feet, she headed for the door. With each of her steps, the air became tainted with a bad smell. Covering her face with her shirt, she peered out of the door and blinked into the half-light. The room was huge and at one end hospital gurneys lined up against the wall. They were old-style. The wheels had spokes and didn't look quite right. She moved along the wall, searching for a door or window to escape. As she moved closer to the line of gurneys, the silver-colored tops came into view. She'd seen similar in TV shows: autopsy tables, but not new and glistening, old and decrepit.

Heart pounding, she moved past them, heading for the end of the room. Ahead, three gurneys sat close together and the sound of clocks ticking was louder. She searched the gloom but not a soul lurked in the corners. Her confidence grew and she walked straight down the middle of the hall. As she got closer, the bad smell increased and she gagged. Moving closer to examine the lumps on the gurneys, she froze unable to believe her eyes, and pressed a fist to her mouth to prevent the scream threatening to break through her lips. Three horrific bodies lay on separate gurneys, eyes fixed and staring into nothing, bodies blue and patchy. A machine sat beside each of them, hooking them up with tubes to both arms. On one side, a clear fluid was being pushed into the vein via a pump. She stared at the buckets beside each corpse. The ticking of clocks she'd heard wasn't clocks at all. It was blood draining from the corpses and dripping into buckets. She turned, running blindly toward the end of the hall, searching ahead for a door. Double doors loomed out of the darkness and she hurled herself at them. Bouncing off the unforgiving locked metal, she fell hard to the floor. She couldn't breathe and her heart pounded so hard she waited to die, gasping on the cold floor. There was no way out. No escape. The laughing man had trapped her in a room with rotting corpses.

FOUR

It was a short drive to Black Rock Falls Motel, and Kane parked outside the office. He scanned the parking lot. Only three vehicles sat piled with snow outside the doors to the rooms. It seemed that most of the tourists had headed for the ski resort. The snow on the mountains had come early this year and visitors were already enjoying everything Glacial Heights Ski Resort had to offer. Part of him wished he was up there, hurtling down the slopes with the rush of cold wind on his cheeks. It was almost like flying and he pushed his body to the limit to go as fast as possible, but the seconds he spent on the descent were never enough. He always wanted more. In those few seconds there was no time for thoughts, problems vanished and his mind relaxed. Like skydiving, nothing mattered until he pulled the cord to open his chute, and then gravity slammed reality back into him. He glanced up as an eagle spiraled overhead. *Now he's got an uncomplicated life, that's for darn sure.*

He let Duke out of the truck to stretch his legs and then followed Jenna inside the office. Cigarette smoke hit him in a wall of stink and the ceiling above the counter had a yellow hue from years of exhaled tar. This he found unusual as the

Montana Clean Air Act prohibited smoking in offices. He'd never smoked. Not after a particular grueling lesson about the dangers of tobacco products. He vividly recalled the shock of seeing the cross section of a smoker's blackened lung displayed beside the glass jar of tar they'd drained from his lungs after he'd died. He figured the dejected-looking doctor giving the lecture believed if he could prevent one kid from taking up smoking, he'd started to win the battle. Kane sometimes wished he'd run into him over his lifetime, to tell him it sure had worked for him.

He stood beside Jenna at the counter as she asked the manager about Maisy Jones.

"When did you last see her?" Jenna's pen was poised over her notebook.

"She drove out of the parking lot at about four-thirty on Monday." The man scratched the back of his greasy unwashed hair, spilling dandruff across his shoulders. "I don't ask my guests where they're going. I just happened to look out of the window. Her old truck is hard to miss."

"Was she alone?" Jenna made notes. "Did she have any visitors that you noticed?"

"Not that I saw and, yeah, she was alone." The manager wrinkled his brow. "She struggled some getting out her bags. She looked younger than her ID stated but the picture was the same."

Kane glanced around wondering how desperate someone was to stay at the motel in winter. "How did she seem when she arrived?"

"Normal, I guess." The manager shrugged. "Whatever that means. She seemed okay, not nervous or agitated. She just asked the price of a room and could she get a deal if she took one for a week. We negotiated a price and she paid in advance."

Kane imagined a young woman walking into a motel office to get a room. "How did she pay, cash or card?"

"Cash." The manager frowned. "Nothing wrong with taking cash. It's legal."

Moving his gaze over the man, he nodded. "Was she carrying a purse or did she pull the cash from her pocket?"

"A purse." The manager's eyes squeezed shut and he pulled a face. His eyes sprang open and he smiled displaying yellow stained teeth, with one or two missing. "I remember it was hanging over one shoulder, blue with a bright yellow flower on one side. Like kids draw, you know, with a smile in the center?"

"That's very helpful." Jenna folded her notebook. "We'll need to see her room. Has housekeeping been inside this morning?"

"Yeah, and when your deputy called and asked me to check if she was in her room, I spoke to Maria, the housekeeper. She told me that the bed hadn't been slept in but the towels were damp, so she changed them, wiped down the bathroom and vacuumed the floor."

Kane held out a hand. "Give me a key and we'll check it out."

"Don't you need a warrant to search her room?" The man's eyes narrowed.

Kane lifted one shoulder and stared him down. "Not if you give us permission as it's your place. Miss Jones is missing and we need to find her."

"Sure, I'll get the key." The manager turned away, grabbed a key from a hook behind him and handed it to Kane. "Don't lose it. It opens all the rooms. She was in room four."

Kane took the key, attached to a six-inch slab of wood with DO NOT REMOVE FROM OFFICE written in marker pen on both sides. He pushed open the door to the office and took a few deep breaths of fresh air. He turned to Jenna. "I've inhaled about six packs of secondhand smoke just being inside that room."

"Yeah, the last time we were here Rowley wrote him a ticket

and he paid a fine." Jenna frowned. "The back part of the office is his private residence, so maybe the smoke is drifting out from there."

Kane shook his head. "Nope, from the stains on the ceiling, he smokes at the counter." He headed across the courtyard and toward the line of motel rooms.

"Then I'll write him up again." Jenna flicked him a glance. "Getting bored? It's not like you to chase down illegal use of cigarettes."

Hiding a smile, Kane stopped outside room number four. "No, I'm just looking out for the health of the guests he has going into his office." He shrugged. "That's our job, to uphold the law." He slid the key in the lock and stood to one side. "After you."

"Okay, glove up." Jenna removed her thick mittens and pulled examination gloves from her pocket and snapped them on. "I want to go through her things. She might have a laptop or tablet with her and I sure hope we find her purse."

Kane stood in the doorway, scanning the room. He liked to take in the feel of the room and imagine Maisy Jones inside. A bag was open on the bed, clothes dragged out and tossed aside, another sat beside the closet. He walked into the bathroom, pulling on examination gloves. Personal toiletries sat on the vanity. An open makeup bag spilled cosmetics across the top. A pink toothbrush sat in a glass beside a hairbrush. She had seemingly arrived, showered, changed and left well before her shift. Where did she go?

A plastic laundry bag sat on the floor beside the door. The motel did offer laundry service, but as Maisy hadn't left it beside the front door with the pickup slip, he figured she'd planned to wait a couple of days and then send a bundle of clothes. He pulled evidence bags from his pocket. He carefully pushed the cosmetics back into the bag and, along with the hairbrush and toothbrush, added them to an evidence bag and labeled it. Next, he bagged the soiled clothes. He walked out of the bathroom. "The bathroom yielded enough DNA for Wolfe to identify her if she's a victim of crime." He dropped the bags onto the bed. "Find anything?"

"Apart from clothes, nothing." Jenna shrugged. "The problem is most people use their phones for everything now. I had hoped for a laptop but there's nothing here. There's a safe in the bottom of the closet. It's locked. I'll go to the office. They must have an override key."

Dropping down to squat in front of the safe, Kane looked at her. "What is her birthdate?"

"Just a second." Jenna scrolled through her phone for Maisy Jones' DMV record and gave him the date.

Kane entered the numbers and the door clicked open. He smiled at Jenna. "People use what's familiar to them. Usually their birthdate, one of their kids' or the date they married. It's a mistake criminals have been taking advantage of for a very long time."

"Yet you know." Jenna peered into the safe and then looked at him. "Is there something I need to know?"

Chuckling, Kane shrugged. "Tons but if I told you... Well, you know the rest."

"Interesting." Jenna fished out a passport and a large manila envelope stuffed with bills. She stood and tipped them out onto the bed. "That has to be twenty thousand. Who carries that amount of cash with them?" She looked at Kane, both eyebrows raised. "This case has just got interesting."

FIVE

Jenna led the way into Aunt Betty's Café, glad to be out of the cold. The wind had picked up and had seeped into every opening in her clothes. She thought it would be cold but hadn't bargained for it to be freezing. Sometimes when the snow came the temperature rose a little. Not this time. Ice was forming on top of the snow, and even with salt covering the sidewalk, there were icy patches. She'd be wearing thermal underwear from now on. Winter promised to be harsh this year and she made a mental note to ask Kane if he'd ordered extra supplies. Road closures meant no deliveries, and the horses needed to be fed and kept comfortable. She ordered her meal and followed Kane to the table at the back reserved for the sheriff's office to join Rio and Rowley. Both had their phones pressed against their ears. She smiled inwardly. It was so nice to see the office running so smoothly. She removed her gloves and coat and sat down beside Kane. After waiting for the deputies to finish their calls, she poured a cup of coffee from the pot on the table and added the fixings. "How did it go? Find any information on Maisy Jones?"

"Yeah, I found her family. I have Maisy's number. I called a few times but it went to voicemail. I'll send it to you." Rio's eyes narrowed and his mouth formed a thin line as his fingers moved over his phone. He looked back at Jenna. "Maisy recently split from her partner. She'd been living with him for a few years. She told her mom she needed to get away. Emptied the bank account and told her mom she planned to work at one of the ski resorts. She missed out on a local job, tried at Glacial Heights, but because of the early season, they were fully staffed. She secured a bartender position at the Triple Z Bar and, would you believe, drove here in that old truck to take the job."

"That has to be a twelve-hour drive." Kane frowned. "What was she running from? Why didn't she want to be traced?"

"What makes you believe she doesn't want to be traced?" Rowley leaned back in his chair.

"She's using cash." Kane sipped his coffee. "You know people's movements can be traced every time they use their cards. Maybe she was running from her ex." He turned his attention to Rio. "Did her mom mention anything about the split? Was he violent toward her?"

"I asked but she doesn't know. They argued is all she said. She thought he was cheating on Maisy but doesn't know for sure." Rio turned his coffee cup around in his fingertips. "I followed up with the Nampa Police Department. I asked if they could go and check if he's in town. If he is, he can't be involved in her disappearance."

Jenna smiled as Susie Hartwig delivered the meals and slices of pie for Rio and Rowley. "Thanks, Susie." She waited for her to leave and looked at Rio. "Maisy left the Triple Z at midnight on Monday. It's Wednesday afternoon. Her ex could have easily abducted her, killed her and be back home by now. Get back on the phone and explain the situation. See if they can trace his whereabouts since Maisy left town. Have them check his vehicle."

"I'm on it." Rio stood and headed outside to make the call.

"That would be a reason she'd get a ride." Kane bit into his burger, chewed and washed it down with coffee. "She might be mad with her ex but it would be better than freezing to death."

Jenna nodded and turned to Rowley. "We need a timeline. Did anyone see her before she arrived at the Triple Z Bar?"

"I spoke to everyone here and looked over the CCTV footage." Rowley swallowed a forkful of pie. "She came in before five and left about five-thirty. We know she arrived in time for her shift at six." He sighed. "That was the first time they saw her. Wendy recalls her purse. It's distinctive. It's a shoulder bag—my wife has something similar—about ten inches wide, with a flap on one side. Blue with a big yellow flower with a smile."

"Yeah, the motel guy mentioned it." Kane started on his peach pie. "I figure we have enough probable cause to get a trace warrant on her phone. She could be in trouble."

The horrible realization that something bad had happened to Maisy Jones drained Jenna's appetite and she pushed her plate away. "I'll do the paperwork as soon as I get to the office."

"I'll do it." Rowley pulled on his gloves. "I'm done here and there's Rio. We'll head back to the office."

Jenna nodded. "Okay." She looked at Rio as he stopped at the table. "What have you got for me, Rio?"

"The detective in Nampa said they can't locate Zander Hastings. Originally from Kentucky, he is a self-defense instructor and a fitness fanatic." Rio leaned on the back of a chair. "He's a no-show at his fitness center, and no one has seen him since last Thursday." He sighed. "After giving the detective our information, they're going to hunt down his movements."

Glad of an efficient team, Jenna nodded. "Okay, get that paperwork over to the judge and lean on him for a warrant. We're heading to the ME's office to drop by the evidence we collected today. We might need Maisy's DNA." She leaned back and sighed as they pulled on coats and headed for the door. She turned to Kane. "Oh, that reminds me, have we stocked up enough provisions for a long winter? It's come early this year."

"I have everything under control. We have a barn filled with hay and straw, and sacks of everything else, including dog food. It arrived by truck last Saturday when you were out with Sandy and the twins. Now eat." Kane pushed the untouched pie in front of her. "It's too cold to drop calories. You've been feeling better since you started the protein shakes, haven't you? Not so many headaches?"

Watching Kane wave to Susie for another slice of pie, Jenna picked up her fork. "Yeah, much better. You should drink them too."

"I don't need to. I'll just eat more." Kane shrugged. "Last winter, I dropped weight way too fast. That's my problem. I can't keep the weight on. I can lose it real fast and then my energy and strength suffer. This year, I decided to build more muscle bulk."

Smiling, Jenna dug into the pie. "Okay, I'll eat the pie." She frowned. "I don't know where to start looking for Maisy. She could be anywhere, even out of the county if she took a ride with a killer. I hope the warrant will come through today. My gut is telling me we need to move on finding her ASAP."

SIX

Blackwater

Special Agent Ty Carter stepped inside the neat compact ranch house in the beautiful suburb known as Paradise Falls and scanned the crime scene. Charlie Bridger; his wife, Clare; and eight-year-old son, Gavin, had vanished without a trace. A half-eaten meal sat on the kitchen table alongside two phones. The keys to the white Buick Encore in the garage sat in a dish by the kitchen door. Coats and hats hung in the mudroom. It was as if they'd been abducted by aliens. He turned to Agent Jo Carter and shrugged. "I figure we're wastin' our time here. I've been through the house twice now and there are no traces of anyone being here, apart from an overturned chair."

"Not even so much as a footprint." Jo shook her head. "What concerns me more than anything is that, whatever happened to them, they left in such a rush they didn't put a coat on their little boy. It's freezing outside and even under duress a mother would insist on getting him a coat."

Carter moved the toothpick across his lips, noticed Jo's annoyed expression and removed it. So, he'd start chewing gum again—anything for a quiet life. "That depends. What's missin' from this scene?"

"Signs of a struggle, blood, drag marks?" Jo huffed out a sigh. "What are you getting at, Carter?"

"Weapons." Carter waved a hand around, encompassing the entire house. "No gun locker, no rifles, I found no sign of a weapon anywhere. I figure this family had an aversion to owning weapons." He smiled at her. "So, if a guy walked in the back door wearin' a ski mask and wavin' a gun around, do you figure the mom would ask him real nice if she could grab a coat for her kid, or would she be too darn scared?"

"She'd be terrified and do what was necessary to protect her child." Jo raised both eyebrows. "They would have followed instructions."

Carter nodded. "Yeah, someone could have marched them outside and into a vehicle. The nearest neighbor is five acres away, the driveway shielded by trees. It's a kidnapper's paradise. One guy goes into the house. There's no forced entry, so they left the door unlocked and he orders them to leave. I figure he had a van with a driver. The gunman pushed them inside and then climbed in after them. Maybe he got the husband to restrain the others... Who knows? There had to be at least two abductors, or one of the family would have made a run for it."

"Maybe not if the kid was threatened." Jo stared into space like she did often when she was visualizing a crime scene. "If they held a gun to the kid's head, the parents would comply."

Taking in the scene again, Carter shook his head. "I don't think so. Look at the table. Dad sat here with his back to the door, Mom next to him, the kid next to her. The phones give their positions. The cover of the pink one, has the wife's name on it." He rubbed his chin. "This was a normal guy, not trained to protect himself, probably never got into a fight in his life, but

I've seen all types throw themselves at a gunman to allow their wife and kid to escape. It should have been a bloodbath." He sighed. "No one just walks out with a gunman."

"Maybe the chair was the only thing he could do?" Jo folded her arms over her chest. "I'd like to know why they were taken."

The same thoughts had been spinning through Carter's brain. He nodded. "Yeah, the reason behind the kidnapping is what we need to know. There's nothing for us here." He pulled out his phone. "I'll call the local sheriff and tell him first break in the weather we'll be heading back to Snakeskin Gully. We'll work on the case from there. We'll need background info on the victims. People don't just vanish like this unless they have value to someone, as in witnesses to a crime, drug syndicates, snitches. We need to know everything about them to find out who kidnapped them, and as no bodies have shown up, I'd have expected a ransom by now. Why is this family so valuable to someone?"

"If they'd witnessed a crime, the sheriff would have told us." Jo looked around the room. "The calendar says the kid had a dentist appointment today." She shook her head. "Witness protection?"

Carter rubbed the back of his neck itching to chew on a toothpick and looked at her. "I can call it in and leave details about the couple and when they went missin'. If there's a problem, we'll never know. They'll handle it." Giving up, he pulled a toothpick from his top pocket and tossed it into his mouth. He looked at Jo and wiggled his eyebrows. "Do you want me to start smoking cigars? I kinda like the smell of them."

"You hate cigar smoke, so that won't fly, Carter." Jo leaned against the kitchen counter and shook her head slowly. "I pulled a splinter out of your mouth, Ty. A splinter. That's one thing, but the wood must be wearing down your teeth. It's just replacing one bad habit with another. Have you tried hypnosis?"

Carter took one more look around the kitchen and then settled his gaze back on Jo. She was mothering him again. Darn, he wasn't that much younger than her, but he understood her lack of close family manifested in a need to nurture. He lifted one shoulder in a half shrug. "Yeah, and it didn't go well. I had a major flashback and found myself restrained by two psychiatric nurses and drugged up for days. That ain't ever happening again."

"Okay, I'll drive and you make the calls." Jo ducked under the crime scene tape on the front door. "Call Wolfe as well. His team did the forensic sweep of the scene when the family were reported missing. See if he's found anything." She headed toward the rental and looked up. "It's stopped snowing."

Carter stared at the bleak sky. "Maybe it's not snowing here and the chopper can handle light falls, but I'll need to know the visibility over the mountains before we leave. Head back to the motel. If it's a go, we'll take off without delay. The weather could close in again at any time." He smiled at her. "With luck, you'll be home in time to kiss your little girl goodnight."

SEVEN

A cold wind battered Billy Stevens as he headed home from work along Stanton. His job as a teaching assistant at Black Rock Falls High School often kept him late, and the walk home, so easy in summer, was dark and lonely in winter. He took the same route home every night: straight down Stanton and turned left onto Pine. He shared a house with three other men. They were a group of single doctors completing their residencies at Black Rock Falls Hospital. They were nice guys who had so many shifts someone was always asleep. He'd gotten used to creeping around and not making a sound. They all treated him well and, when they weren't sleeping, were good company.

The winding road snaked through a suburb covered with pine trees, and the smell of them filled the air more here than opposite the forest. Pine needles crunched underfoot and cones tumbled everywhere across the fresh dusting of snow. It wasn't snowing hard, just the odd snowflake drifting down, but the sky was heavy and it would only be a matter of time before winter came in full force. He hoisted his backpack over one arm and stuck to the blacktop to avoid the snowy shoulder. Along this road, the uneven edge had many holes and a gutter to prevent flooding. Walking on it during snow season was a recipe for breaking an ankle. The road became more remote as he walked, the houses set farther back from the road, secluded and surrounded by land. He glanced through the trees to the lights blazing from a massive house donated to the college for a fraternity. Murder had happened there some years previously and now the guys who lived there swore it was haunted. The tales about the house changed from year to year but seemed to make living there even more desirable for the college boys. He chuckled to himself. "Some people are just plain crazy."

As he turned the corner, his attention moved to the massive black truck sitting under the trees with the back door wide open. He'd seen the sheriff going by in something similar with her deputy at her side. He took in the light covering of snow and wondered how long it had been there. As he approached, he made out a figure sprawled on the ground. He ran forward, and found a man face down in the long grass. He stared at him for long seconds, waiting to see if his chest moved. He didn't look dead. Maybe he'd suffered a medical episode and collapsed? "Hey, are you okay?"

Nothing.

Not wanting to touch a corpse, if this was one, he reluctantly pulled off a glove, bent down and slid his fingers down the man's neck to feel for a pulse. It happened so fast. As his fingers touched the warm flesh, the man's elbow slammed into him, hitting him in the neck. Staggering, Billy gasped trying to force air into his lungs. The next second, his feet left the floor and he sprawled across the back seat. Stink filled his nostrils as the door slammed shut behind him. Shocked, Billy gasped in air and struggled to sit up. Panic gripped him and he slapped both hands on the thick Perspex divider between him and the man sliding behind the wheel. "Hey, what the heck do you think you're doing?"

Dark eyes shielded by a black Stetson peered at him in the

rear view mirror, but the man said nothing. The truck's engine hummed as the man turned the vehicle around and headed sedately back toward Stanton. Billy grabbed for door handles but found none. He lay down on the seat and kicked using both feet on the door and window, but nothing happened. "Let me out of here. Have you lost your mind? Stop the car, you jerk. I'm calling the sheriff."

The truck didn't stop and just kept heading out of town. Unease sank through him to settle in his bones as reality dawned. He wasn't getting out of the truck anytime soon. Looking around for his backpack, he shook his head in disbelief. It was gone, along with his phone. He pushed at the doors and windows and scanned all directions. Surely someone would see him? The driver slowed and his window buzzed down. Billy gaped as his backpack flew from the window and tumbled into a bank of snow. "Hey, that's my property. You can't do that?"

The man just kept driving, his eyes flicking back only occasionally to look at him. Freaking out, Billy smashed into the Perspex divider, using all the force he could muster. It didn't so much as creak. As he hunted the floor and under the seat for anything to use as a weapon, the cab filled with smoke and a strange smell. He slapped at the Perspex divider again. "Let me out."

He blinked. Acrid smoke poured out from under the seats. He waved it away but it was filling his lungs and stealing his breath. He pulled his shirt over his nose but his eyelids grew heavy. He couldn't breathe and the smell was making him nauseous. *He's suffocating me with carbon monoxide gas.*

EIGHT

THURSDAY

A flurry of snowflakes brushed Kane's cheeks as he walked from the stables. Underfoot, the frosted grass crunched. The temperature had dropped dramatically and he'd decided to leave the horses in the barn. They'd waited in vain for the search warrant the previous afternoon. The judge had been in court and, as it was quiet in town and they couldn't move on with the missing persons case, they'd come back to the ranch and taken the horses out for a trail ride. Although, they'd talked shop all the way and back. If something had happened to Maisy Jones, there would be a ton of suspects to wade through, seeing as she had worked a shift at the Triple Z before she vanished. He climbed the steps and wiped his feet on the mat outside the door before stepping inside the house.

A wave of warmth and the smell of hot coffee greeted him as he shucked his coat and hat and headed for the kitchen. "It's getting colder." He poured coffee and added the fixings and then used the cup to warm his hands. "If it gets any colder, it will be too cold to snow."

"It always snows and the ski resort is counting on it being a long season this year." Jenna smiled at him. "You weren't serious about having Pop-Tarts for breakfast, were you? I couldn't find any in the pantry."

Grinning, Kane washed up at the sink. "I happen to be partial to Pop-Tarts, but when it's cold like this I need protein. I'm thinking smoked ham, cheese and bell pepper omelets, and you can make the toast." He pulled the ingredients from the refrigerator. "You like?"

"You amaze me." Jenna opened the bread and dropped four slices into the toaster.

Kane beat the eggs. "Don't cook the toast yet. Slice up the ham for me and open the bag of shredded cheese."

"I saw a pile of this in the freezer." She frowned as she pulled it from the fridge. "It says it's made in the UK. What's wrong with American cheese?"

Pouring the eggs into a pan with melted butter, Kane smiled at her. "I had it on my travels. It's called English cheddar and the taste is quite strong. I like it, is all."

"Hmm, you have very expensive tastes." Jenna sliced the ham into strips. "Your own special blend of coffee, wine imported from New Zealand and now English cheese."

Kane laughed. "Well, everything else is one hundred percent American."

The phones both chimed at the same time. Kane raised his eyebrows. "You'd better get it. I'll finish the omelets."

"Hi, Jo, we're just having breakfast. What's up?" Jenna put the phone on speaker and took plates from the kitchen shelf.

"We thought we'd catch you before you left for the office." Jo yawned. *"It's been a crazy few days. We arrived home from Blackwater late yesterday. We had to wait for a break in the weather and then hightailed it in here this morning at five when the alarms in the building were activated."* She cleared her throat. *"You know that Bobby Kalo lives in the building, right?"*

"Yeah, you have mentioned it." Jenna recalled the IT whiz

kid inducted by the FBI and pushed down the toast. "So, what was the problem?"

"He went to the bathroom and one of the doors malfunctioned and he was trapped inside the passageway. No phone, nothing, so he had to smash the scanner beside one of the doors to set off the alarm." It was Carter's voice coming through the speaker. *"We have override codes if anything happens, but he was blue with cold when we got here. When the building goes into lockdown, it closes down everything including the heating."*

Kane loaded the plates and saved the toast from burning. "Is he okay?"

"He's cold, is all." Carter chuckled. *"He's giving me the stink eye now. I figure having me rescue him has bruised his ego."* He cleared his throat. *"This isn't why we called."*

After pouring fresh coffee Kane sat beside Jenna at the table and listened with interest about the missing family in Blackwater. He sighed and told them about their missing woman. "So, we're facing the same mystery. Vanished without a trace. We're hoping if we get the warrant this morning, we'll be able to trace her phone. Maybe she's holed up with a guy or something?"

"I'd be worried about the little boy." Jenna looked at him. "It's so cold and not wearing a coat. That sounds like an abduction to me. Did you ask Wolfe to do a forensic sweep?"

"Yeah." Jo's chair scraped. *"He searched for latent DNA as far as I'm aware. There's really nothing at all in the house. Like Carter said, it's as if they just up and left."*

Kane swallowed a forkful of omelet and shrugged. "We have frozen footprints going nowhere. They go from the grass to the blacktop and vanish. Unless we're having an influx of alien abductions, I don't have a clue."

"Have you hunted down everything you can about the family?" Jenna sipped her coffee, holding a piece of buttered toast in the other hand. "It's not unusual for people involved in crime syndicates to go missing."

"Yeah, Bobby is doing background checks and we're going to speak to family members if we can find any." Carter's voice carried from across the room and Kane could hear him stirring his coffee and tapping the spoon on the rim of the cup. *"I'm wondering if they were in WITSEC and have been discovered, likely kidnapped and murdered. We can put in a query but there's no chance we'll get a reply. They don't give out info. If Kalo tries to hack their files, he'll end up in the state pen."* He sighed. *"You know when you have the gut feeling it's homicide? I had that the second I walked into the house. Typical professional abduction, clean and fast."*

"Let's hope there's no connection between your case and ours." Jenna glanced at Kane. "Two cases where people just vanish in connecting counties is more than a coincidence."

Allowing the two cases to filter into his mind, Kane shrugged. "Maybe we'll know more later when we've hunted down Maisy's phone. Keep in touch. Your case is intriguing. What's the new sheriff's name in Blackwater? He called you in early when these people had just gone missing. That seems unusual."

"The new guy is Dirk Nolan." Jo sounded amused. *"He's unsociable. I'm not sure why people voted for him. I hope he'll be good at his job or we'll be getting calls from him every time someone's steer goes missing."*

"Maybe not." Carter chuckled. *"He asked me for a list of things he could contact us for if he needed assistance and I didn't mention cattle rustling."* He sighed. *"Okay, we better let you get at it. I wish we had Aunt Betty's Café here. Our local diner doesn't open until eight. We didn't have time to stop to eat this morning."*

Kane smiled. "Catch you later." He looked at Jenna. "What do you make of that?"

"Complicated." She pushed both hands through her hair and sighed. "No weapons in the house or signs of them. Seems to me these folks were sitting ducks, but why were they targeted? If they can get to the bottom of that, well then, they'll solve the case. Seems to me we both have the same problem. We don't have any evidence and missing people." She stood, collected the plates and smiled at him. "Great omelet, by the way, and I didn't burn the toast. It's going to be a good day."

NINE

They arrived at the office to find both deputies' vehicles and Wolfe's parked out front. As Jenna slid out of the Beast, the wind pushed its way down her neck and up her sleeves. Trying to avoid the icy blacktop, she edged around the door and leaned against the hood. The heat from the engine was a nice balm on her cold extremities. She inhaled the crisp morning air and took in the spectacular view. From the top of the mountain to almost halfway down the peaks and the forest had a thick coating of snow. A pale blue hue descended the slopes as thick bands of cloud rushed by. It was bitterly cold and trying to avoid the sheets of black ice on the highway into town had been a nightmare. Salt spreaders were out in force, but she expected her phone to be ringing nonstop with accident reports. She turned and her stomach sank as she stared at Wolfe's white truck. If Wolfe was here this early, he'd found something or someone.

"What's wrong?" Kane lifted Duke from the back seat and came to her side. "Cold?" He pulled her into his arms in a bear hug.

Jenna snuggled into him. Kane was always warm, as if he

had his own personal furnace tucked inside his shirt. "Cold, yes. I wouldn't be human if I wasn't cold in this weather. That's not the problem. Everyone is here. Something nasty has happened to Maisy Jones and part of me wants to turn back around and go home. Sitting in front of the fire drinking hot chocolate or snuggling in bed watching TV sounds like much more fun."

"I agree and we can do that when we've figured out what's happened to her." He rubbed her back. "With luck, Rio and Wolfe have solved the crime and Rowley has collected a ton of evidence." He stepped away and took her hand. "Come on, if we wait here much longer, poor old Duke will freeze to the sidewalk." He led her toward the steps. "The steps are slippery, hold on tight."

Blowing out a cloud of steam, Jenna looked down Main. "It's okay. They're spreading salt along the sidewalk. I'll ask Maggie to make sure they give the steps a good coating."

"Come on, Duke." Kane pushed open the door. He smiled at Jenna. "You go see the guys and I'll fill the coffee pot." He waved at Maggie and headed for the stairs.

The deputies and Wolfe were congregated around the kitchenette at the back of the office. After speaking with Maggie about salting the steps, Jenna headed toward them. "Morning. Any progress on the warrant?"

"Not yet." Rowley sipped from a steaming cup of coffee. "It shouldn't be long. I'm waiting on a call to go and collect it. The judge's secretary said she'd make sure he made a decision before court at ten this morning."

"There's a few things we need to discuss." Wolfe's expression gave nothing away.

"Yeah, I'll need to bring you up to date too." Rio pushed away from the counter.

Nodding, Jenna turned on her heel. "Okay, my office and someone please turn up the heat."

Standing at the whiteboard, pen in hand, Jenna glanced at Kane. "I doubt any other law enforcement office goes to such lengths to find a missing person. It's only been a couple of days. She could be back with her boyfriend by now for all we know."

"That's not going to happen." Rio leaned against the counter, his fingers wrapped around a cup of coffee. "Her boyfriend, Zander Hastings, was found dead on Tuesday morning. The local PD were reluctant to give out information as it's not our case, so I called Wolfe."

"I called the Idaho ME's office and they sent over the autopsy report and photographs of the scene." Wolfe's gaze narrowed. "The ME gave the cause of death as a heroin overdose." He dropped a folder on Jenna's desk.

Jenna made a note on the whiteboard and linked it with Maisy Jones. She turned back to Wolfe. "Do you think she left him and he overdosed?"

"They have his time of death as between late Friday and Saturday night." Wolfe raised both eyebrows. "Which means he died around the time she left Idaho."

"I've been hunting down his friends, clients and family." Rio sipped his coffee. "The one thing they all said about him was he was a health fanatic—organic food, vegan, protein shakes and the like. He never drank coffee or smoked in his life." He cleared his throat. "He had broken up with Maisy and was seeing someone else. They all said he was happy. There'd be no need to take his own life."

The room fell silent with the implications. Mind whirling with possibilities, Jenna returned the pen to its holder and picked up the folder. She laid out the photographs over her desk and peered at them. Hastings was in a vehicle, leaning back in the driver's seat, a strip of rubber tubing tied around one arm. A syringe hung by a needle from his arm. In her time as DEA Special Agent Avril Parker, Jenna had seen too many overdoses.

"Can you deliver this much heroin using a one-milliliter syringe?" Kane frowned at the toxicology report. "He'd pass out trying to reload the needle, wouldn't he?" He shuffled through the images. "This isn't right. There's no drug preparation paraphernalia in the vehicle."

"Yeah, y'all be familiar with the usual types of street heroin. It's a powder heated in a spoon and injected." Wolfe indicated to the images with his chin. "What I saw here sent up a red flag, so I looked a little deeper. I've asked for blood samples to run my own tests because there's something else that concerns me." He looked at Jenna. "I have the autopsy images. There's something there that might explain the amount of heroin in his system." He laid his tablet on the desk and scrolled through the images. "The family wants the body released for cremation, but I've requested more information. I asked for close-ups taken of the body after noticing something on the neck."

Everyone crowded around behind Jenna as Wolfe enlarged one image of Hasting's head turned to one side. "What are we looking at, Shane?"

"A needle mark on the neck, for one, and this man wasn't an addict. Apart from the lack of linear needle track scars, his body and internal organs don't show the results of an addict." Wolfe blew out a breath. "The problem here is, when people find someone with a needle in their arm, they usually test the residue in the syringe, and then log it as an accidental overdose. Many don't find their way onto an autopsy table. Hastings' parents paid for the autopsy because they wouldn't believe he'd taken his own life or overdosed." He sighed. "I figure what we're looking at here is liquid heroin. It's heated black tar heroin mixed with water and is easily used without the usual paraphernalia. The needle in the arm is clumsy. It may not have hit the vein but it wouldn't be necessary if someone administered five milliliters into his carotid artery."

Incredulity swept over Jenna as she stared at the images and then at Wolfe. "Do you think he was murdered?"

"Yeah, I do, and I think you're hunting down a missing woman who is more than likely the one who murdered him." Wolfe straightened. "I'll do what I can to prevent the cremation. I'll speak to Hastings' parents and offer to clear their son's name. I don't have jurisdiction in Idaho, but as we might be harboring his killer in Black Rock Falls, I could offer to fly the body here for examination." He looked at Jenna. "I figure it would be about a two-hour round trip. I'll be landing on the closest helipad, signing a few documents and flying back. No wait, no delay, but I'll only suggest this if you approve, Jenna."

Nodding slowly, Jenna tried to take it all in. "If you can get his parents to agree, I think it's the best course of action. You'll have to fly the body back to Idaho when you're done. Do we have funding for that?"

"Yeah, my budget is a little higher than yours." Wolfe smiled at her. "If you don't need me for anything else, I'll get at it."

"Thank you." Jenna returned the smile. "You're a genius." She waited for him to leave and turned to the others. "Rowley, head over to the courthouse and see if the judge has signed that warrant. Is there anything else I need to know?"

"Yeah." Rio placed his coffee cup on the counter and turned to her. "Maisy's prints were in the vehicle, but she'd ridden in his truck all the time. What caught my attention was that they didn't find prints on the syringe." He sighed. "Trust me, addicts don't wipe their prints off a syringe."

"Nope, with a dose that high he'd have been out in a few seconds." Kane stared at the report and then dropped it back onto the desk. "If Maisy killed Hastings, why did she tell people her plans to come here looking for work?" He scratched his cheek. "It doesn't make sense. If nobody knew she'd come here, she could hide off the grid forever."

"Really? You don't know?" Jenna shook her head in disbelief. "She left no evidence to indicate she committed the crime. It's all circumstantial, and if she went to trial, telling people where she was headed will be seen as a presumption of innocence. She'd get off on reasonable doubt. This is one smart cookie."

TEN

Pulling off his gloves, Rowley headed inside the office and handed the warrant to Maggie on the front counter. "Scan this into the files for me please and then I'll go tell Jenna the good news."

"Maybe you should take a look at this before I log it into lost and found." Maggie pointed to a backpack resting on the front desk. "Wendy from Aunt Betty's was on her way to work just before and found this backpack on the side of the road. It was about fifty yards from the Black Rock Falls sign heading in the direction of Blackwater. She picked it up figuring a kid maybe had dropped it on the way to school and then found a phone not two feet from it in the snow. She said she searched all around but there was no sign of anyone, no footprints in the snow, and she figures she'd have seen them as the snowfall we had yesterday is frozen solid this morning and the backpack was right on the top." She frowned. "Maybe it fell from the top of a vehicle, but with people going missing all the time in these parts, I told her to set it down right there on the counter and she placed the phone into an evidence bag. I've been waiting for the sheriff to finish her meeting. I didn't want to disturb her, but seeing as that girl is missing, I figured I shouldn't touch it."

Intrigued, Rowley pulled on examination gloves and, collecting the scanned warrant, evidence bag and backpack, smiled at her. "You did the right thing." He thought for a beat. "Was Wendy wearing gloves?"

"Oh, yes." Maggie nodded and her dark curls bounced. "She knows the way of things around here."

Rowley nodded. "Great. I'll take them up to Jenna." He headed for the stairs.

Seeing the images spread over Jenna's desk he paused at the door. When there was a break in the conversation, he moved closer to speak to her. "I have the warrant, and this backpack and phone were found on the side of the highway by Wendy from Aunt Betty's Café."

"Okay, Rio, call Kalo and ask him if he can locate the phone and send him a copy of the warrant. He'll be able to gather the information quicker than we can." She collected the photographs on her desk, tapped them into a neat pile and placed them in a folder. "Okay, now we're the lost-and-found department." She raised her brows and looked at him. "Can't Maggie log this into the system?"

Rowley's face grew hot. He guessed he should have dealt with the problem himself, but he recalled his wife's advice. She'd told him to go with his gut instinct with the twins. It had worked just fine raising them and he hadn't been wrong yet. He straightened. "As we have a missing person, I figured these might belong to Maisy Jones. I haven't opened the bag. I thought that would be something better left to you or Kane."

He listened with interest as Jenna brought him up to date with the case. "Ah, so our missing woman could have an accomplice?"

"Well, we haven't discussed the possibility." Jenna leaned back in her chair. "What's your take on this?"

Confident he'd worked out another scenario to the woman's disappearance, Rowley straightened. "Well if, like you say, she murdered Hastings, it would take some planning." He could almost see the crime in his head playing out step by step. "If she had an accomplice, she could tell everyone she was coming to Black Rock Falls, start a job and then vanish. Everyone would figure she'd gone missing never to be seen again, but really, her accomplice met her on the road and now they're in the wind."

"That's a thought." Kane poured a cup of coffee and handed it to him. "Almost the perfect crime."

"We'll follow her phone and see where she went." Jenna smiled. "It's hard for people to leave their phone behind and so many people have no idea they carry a GPS chip." She took gloves from her desk drawer and examined the backpack. "Let's see who this belongs to." Jenna found an iPad and a few notebooks. She held up a library swipe card. "Billy Stevens out of Pine."

Rowley frowned. "I know that name. I'm sure I've met him. He was dating one of Sandy's cousins before she left for college. As I recall, he is working as a teaching assistant at the high school. He took a gap year to save money to finish his degree. He used to live on Pine with a bunch of doctors, but that was after Christmas."

"The phone is likely his as well." Kane examined the phone. "It's locked, fingerprint protected."

"Okay, contact the high school and see if you can hunt down Billy Stevens." Jenna rubbed her temples. "Leave the phone in the evidence bag, just in case something has happened to this guy." She suddenly smiled at him. "Good thinking about the accomplice. I figure we have a new detective on our team."

Rowley grinned and picked up the backpack. "Thanks."

He headed downstairs and dropped the backpack beside his desk. One side of the pack was wet and stained from being on the wet ground. He looked at it more closely and frowned. The damage to one end and the grass stains would make him believe the bag was tossed from a moving vehicle. He'd seen people leave property on the top of their vehicles, left up there when they opened the door and then driven away forgetting the item. The property would often sit there for miles until the driver took a bend and it slid off. It would be difficult to find it again in a vast area like Black Rock Falls, but the stretch of highway where the bag was found was straight. He found the number of the school and made the call. His neck prickled when he discovered Billy Stevens was a no-show for work and he hadn't called in to say he was sick. The woman in the office said it was very strange because Stevens was very professional. Rowley thought for a beat. "Is he still living out on Pine? I'll drop by and do a welfare check."

"I'll check." A tapping of fingers on a keyboard and then the woman came back on the line. *"Yes, he is still living there, Deputy Rowley. Thank you. If you see him, please ask him to give me a call."*

Rowley disconnected and pushed to his feet as Rio walked into his cubicle. "Hey, Billy Stevens is a no-show for work. Not calling in is out of character for him, and as he only lives on Pine, I'm going to drop by to see if he's home."

"I'm waiting on Kalo to send through information on Maisy Jones, so I'll come with you." Rio grabbed his coat. "Although, if he lost his phone, he couldn't call the school, could he? I figure he'd still go to work. I wonder how his phone and backpack ended up halfway to Blackwater. Pine is walkable distance from the high school and in the opposite direction."

Rowley nodded and buttoned up his coat. After pulling on thick gloves, he gathered his things and they headed for the door. As he stepped outside, a blast of arctic wind hit him full in the face in an eye-stinging blast. "It's getting worse. The weather has gone crazy. Where has the gentle snowfall gone?" He tossed the bag and phone into the back seat of his sheriff's department truck and then pulled out his sunglasses and pushed them over streaming eyes.

"It's the same all over. You only have to watch the news, one-hundred-year weather events happening weekly. Europe is on fire, Australia is underwater and we had the flooding. Now it's our turn to freeze. Living in an alpine region, I guess we should be used to cold weather." Rio climbed into Rowley's truck.

It was slow going traveling the ten-minute drive to Pine. The line of vehicles stuck behind a salt spreader crawled along and Rowley was glad to take the turn onto Pine. He drove to a large house about halfway down the road and turned into a driveway that led to the front of the redbrick house. He climbed out and, after scanning the yard, noticed two vehicles in the garage. "It looks as if someone is home."

He followed Rio up the front steps and knocked on the door. They waited for a time and knocked again, before a disgruntled voice came from inside and the door flung open.

"Sorry, I was asleep." The startled man gaped at them as if they'd grown two heads. "I worked the graveyard shift at the ER last night. Is there a problem?"

Heat seeped from the house but carried the smell of stale pizza and dirty socks. Rowley took in the tousled man wrapped in a tatty robe. "I hope not. We're looking for Billy Stevens. His backpack was found this morning along with his phone. We're just doing a welfare check."

"Billy?" The young man frowned. "He should be at work. He's an assistant teacher at the high school."

"He's not there." Rio pushed his hands deep into his pockets. "Would you mind checking on him please?"

"Okay, but come inside and wait. All the heat is escaping out the door." The man turned away and headed for the stairs. Moments later he appeared again, shaking his head. "He's not in his room. I'll go and check the rest of the house." He took off with his thick woolen robe flying out behind him.

"This doesn't look good." Rio pulled out his phone and called Jenna. He explained the situation and waited. "She's talking to Kane." He listened for a time and then nodded. "Okay, will do." He disconnected just as the young man came back along the passageway.

"He's not in the house." The man ran a hand through his tousled hair. "He doesn't stay out overnight and always comes home and studies most nights. He doesn't have a girlfriend."

Rowley exchanged a meaningful look with Rio. "Are his things in the room? I mean he hasn't packed up and left town or anything?"

"No, his stuff is there." The young man blinked a few times. "He doesn't own a vehicle and walks to work and back. Maybe he fell or had an accident. Have you tried the hospital?"

"If he went to the ER yesterday afternoon, wouldn't you have seen him?" Rio stared at him. "You did mention working there last night."

"He might have, but we've been so busy, with all the ice on the roads and the fender benders, we had people lining up for treatment." He sighed. "I could easily have missed him."

Rowley pulled out a card and handed it to him. "If he shows, tell him to call or drop by the sheriff's office to collect his phone and backpack."

"Okay." The young man showed them to the door.

Rowley headed for the truck, moving down the slippery steps with caution. Once inside he fired up the engine and cranked up the heater. "What did Jenna say?"

"She's following up with the ER and will call us if he's there, but she suggested searching the side of the road from here to the school just in case he's slipped over on the ice. It's a wooded area. He could be lying somewhere." Rio waited until they left the driveway. "I couldn't see him anywhere alongside the driveway. Drop me here and drive up fifty yards or so. If we head toward each other, we'll cover the ground faster."

After one long freezing hour, it was obvious Billy Stevens wasn't anywhere alongside the highway between his home and the school. Rowley's nose was cold enough to shatter as he climbed back into his truck and turned to Rio. "Two people vanish into thin air in the same week. Only in Black Rock Falls."

ELEVEN

Snakeskin Gully

Agent Ty Carter strolled along the main street of Snakeskin Gully with Zorro on his heels. The cold wind pushed him along, lifting the back of his Stetson and whipping up dust and swirling it away. The main road stretched some forty yards wide, and the vehicles all parked nose in on an angle to the curb. It was a busy town. The stores lining the sidewalk sold everything a rancher could possibly need. He'd found Guns and Ammo had a surprising display of weapons and ordering anything wasn't a problem. He'd fit into the town with ease and had been accepted as the ex-military man in need of solace. The local minister and the sheriff had checked on him during his darkest days, bringing food for him and Zorro. The local sheriff had married a woman from Helena and moved recently. The new man, Dallas Knox, and ex-army major had won the election in a landslide.

After his partner, Special Agent Jo Wells, had spouted the

poetic about him, Carter figured it was about time he met the man. Jo wasn't easily impressed and she'd returned from town flushed and obviously taken by Knox. He reached the sheriff's office. Outside, three department vehicles sat in a line, their once pristine paintwork now covered in dust and patches of frost. The front steps had a liberal coating of salt and what could be ash, which crunched under his boots as he climbed the steps. He went to the front counter, where a deputy sat staring at a computer screen, and took out his cred pack. He hadn't met the deputy before and cleared his throat. When the deputy finally dragged his eyes away from the screen, he held out his creds. "Is the sheriff in?"

"Yeah." The deputy reached for the phone. "Sheriff there's an FBI agent out front."

Carter looked at the young deputy, who must have been twenty-one and no doubt a rookie. "And you are?"

"Flint Boone, sir." Boone tipped his hat and smiled. "It's nice to meet you. How good is it to work with Agent Wells? She's a behavioral analysis person, isn't she?"

Carter was about to answer when a man of his size and build, with fair hair and laughter lines around his brown eyes, emerged from behind an office door. "Sheriff Knox?"

"Yeah, you must be Ty Carter." Knox held out his hand. "Jo told me all about you."

Carter moved the toothpick across his lips and smiled. Knox was around forty, a twenty-year career army man, without doubt. "Not everything, I hope?" He followed him into a pristine office. The man was army all the way and Carter assumed his bedsheets would be tucked with military precision. He took the offered chair. "I'm dropping by to introduce myself. As you know, we run the field office for the FBI in the West."

"Yeah, I'm aware." Knox leaned back in his chair. It was an old captain's chair crafted with seasoned wood, rounded back with comfortable arms. "I've hired two deputies, so I won't be calling in no FBI to interfere with the law in my town."

The rebuff was there but delivered so smoothly that Carter didn't take offense. "We haven't been needed in Snakeskin Gully. Our work is usually farther afield. What made you decide to make this your home?"

"Born and raised here." Knox smiled. "My folks have been raising beef cattle here for generations, but it wasn't for me. I wanted to travel, so joined the army. Now I'm home. I figure it's not too late to find a wife and settle down." He lifted his chin toward Carter. "I hear you're a Seal. You're too young to be pensioned out of the service. What happened?"

As it was none of his darn business, Carter waved a hand dismissively. "I had a hankering to join the FBI, is all."

"Really? I heard tell you went AWOL and hid yourself off the grid in the forest." Knox towered his fingers. "You're bomb squad, right? Was that dog part of the team? He must be a valuable military asset." He stood and, leaning on the desk, glared at Carter. "Maybe you should take him back where he belongs. Stealing military property is an offense." He waved a hand toward the street and then slapped it back down on the desk. "I don't see no bombs around these parts."

Hackles raising, Carter sucked in a deep breath. What was this man's game? He'd come to be neighborly, is all. He barked a laugh. "The gossip must have been hot in town when you arrived. For the record, I was an agent when I took a year to recuperate after an on-the-job injury." He laid one hand on Zorro's head and to his surprise the dog's eyes fixed on Knox and his lips drew back to reveal sharp canines. "Zorro here, I raised from a pup. Yeah, he is an explosives detection canine. He's the only Doberman in the team. All the others are Labradors. He goes where I go, same as all the other handlers."

"The K-9 dogs are supposed to be friendly." Knox eyed Zorro critically. "He doesn't look too friendly to me."

Carter rubbed Zorro's ears. "He's a pussycat but he picks up on hostility." He stood. "I'd better get at it. It was nice to meet you." He turned as he opened the door. "If you need any assistance, you know where to find us. He fished a card from his pocket and tossed it on Knox's desk. "Keep it close by. Seems to me, Black Rock Falls was a sleepy little town before the serial killers made it their playground. You never know what might happen and Agent Wells is a specialist in criminal behavior."

Carter escaped out of the door shaking his head. He looked down at Zorro as they went back to the office. "What a jerk." When Zorro barked it was as if he were giving his two cents' worth. He laughed. "You can say that again."

With arms filled with takeout, Carter walked back into the FBI field office. They'd been working there for a time and it still resembled a bank, although Jo had added a few rugs to make it more hospitable. Jo was working at her desk and Kalo, surrounded by screens, was doing his thing running names through databanks. "I have food."

He dumped everything on the table in the small kitchenette, removed his gloves and refilled the coffee machine. "I met the sheriff."

"He's nice, isn't he?" Jo's mouth turned up at the corners. "He took me to the diner and we had coffee and pie."

Blowing out a long sigh, Carter removed his hat and coat and gave her a long stare. "In my opinion, he's a jerk. He gave me the third degree and told me he was in town to find a wife. It looks like you're on his list of potentials."

"Really?" Jo blushed. "Me? Well, that has to be a first."

Carter tossed her a bag containing her favorite blueberry muffins and turned to Kalo. "Did you hunt down anything on our missing family?"

"Absolutely nothing." Kalo peered into the bags. "He and the family are squeaky clean, not so much as a parking ticket."

"The only things I discovered is that he is part of the antihunting lobby and is against weapons of any kind." Jo shrugged. "There's a small group in town, not radicals or anything. They don't even protest, just send in the odd petition." She sighed. "That's not enough reason to kidnap them."

Carter rubbed the back of his neck. "If we can't find a reason for someone taking them, there is only one other choice, isn't there?" He looked at Jo. "I figure we go back to Blackwater before the snow gets any worse and get search and rescue out looking for bodies."

TWELVE

Black Rock Falls

Unable to believe her ears, Jenna snapped her fingers to get Kane's attention and put her phone on speaker. "Rio, are you sure? Have you checked his workplace and where he lives? Maybe he's at his girlfriend's?"

"Yeah, well we checked all that out before and he's single and doesn't have a girlfriend. .We walked the highway up one side and down the other looking for a body." Rio coughed and wheezed a little. *"Sorry, it's so darn cold I can hardly breathe. He's vanished the same as Maisy Jones. Apart from his bag and phone, there's no trace of him. We're heading back to the office. I'll bring you up to speed then."* He disconnected.

"If his backpack and phone were found on the way to Blackwater, maybe he got a ride with the wrong person." Kane stood and refilled the coffee machine. "What's the name of the new sheriff in Blackwater? I'll call him and ask him to put out a BOLO on Billy Stevens."

Jenna glanced at him. "Sheriff Dirk Nolan."

"Carter and Jo are working on a missing persons case in Blackwater." Kane shrugged. "I hope there's not a tie-in to this one."

Concerned about the implications of a potential kidnapper covering multiple counties, Jenna pushed both hands through her hair and stared at her casebook trying to think. "Why would Stevens take a ride? He was in walking distance of the school? I can't see a reason anyone would take a ride along Stanton when the distance between School Road and Pine is only one hundred yards. What's that, one to two minutes? He wouldn't be dawdling in the cold, that's for sure."

"Worst-case scenario, he was hit by a truck and dragged inside." Kane leaned against the counter nibbling a cookie. When Duke sat at his feet and whined, he smiled at him. "No more cookies for you today. Even though you get the vanilla doggy ones, the man in the white coat insists too many isn't good for your health." He tossed him a chew bone from a jar on the counter. "You'll like these. Suzie Hartwig says her poodle loves them." He turned to Jenna. "Getting back to the case. The same thing could have happened to Maisy. We might have a hit-and-grab psycho driving our backroads."

Shuddering at the thought, Jenna nodded. "Yeah, but where is he hiding the bodies? We have zip. Are these people really missing or are we chasing shadows?"

"Maybe Maisy and her mystery friend grabbed him?" Kane popped the last bite of cookie into his mouth and then folded his arms across his chest. "The probabilities are endless." He sighed. "We'll just have to wait and see if Kalo can track Maisy's phone." He glanced at his watch. "He doesn't usually take so long."

Jenna sighed. "He is hunting down background info on the missing family from Blackwater. I'm sure he'll get to it as soon as possible. I was able to get her last calls and messages from the phone company and there's nothing there. Her calls to Glacial Heights Ski Resort, the Cattleman's Hotel and the Triple Z Bar, and later to the motel, are the only ones before her disappearance. They all validate what we know about her. She called to find a job at the ski resort and worked her way down the list. There's no calls to Hastings, not for two weeks previously."

As Rio and Rowley came through her office door, the phone rang and Jenna held up a hand to silence the room. "Hi, Bobby, what have you got for me?"

"I've located Maisy Jones' phone. It's between Black Rock Falls and Blackwater. It's stationary. From what I can make out, it's right on the shoulder beside the highway, so it's not on her body or someone would have seen her. I've been monitoring it for the last hour and it hasn't moved. I'll send you the coordinates."

Jenna exchanged a glance with Kane and cleared her throat. "Is Carter or Jo today? I need to speak to them."

"Yeah, they're right here." The wheels of Kalo's office chair squeaked as he rolled away from his desk. *"Carter, it's Jenna."*

"What's up?" Carter sounded interested.

Searching for an explanation to explain her hunch, Jenna blew out a breath. "I might be grabbing at straws here but I'm starting to believe our cases are connected. We have two missing persons who seem to have vanished without a trace. The only indication we have is that their belongings were tossed alongside the highway heading for Blackwater."

"We've found nothing to indicate a reason for the family to vanish in the middle of dinner." Carter blew out a long sigh. *"No ties to anything illegal... zip. We're heading back to Blackwater first thing in the morning. I've asked the local sheriff to do a door-to-door and see if the neighbors have seen anything or heard rumors. It's all we have right now. If you figure the cases are connected, maybe we should join forces? Do you have room for three at the cottage? We'll bring Kalo with us this time."*

Jenna nodded. "Yeah, sure. We'll see you in the morning."

She disconnected and turned to her deputies. "Give me the rundown on what you've discovered about Bobby Stevens and then I'm heading out with Kane to locate Maisy's phone."

After listening to Rio and Rowley's report, she leaned back in her chair and sighed. "Okay, find his family and friends, check social media. You know the drill. Keep asking questions. Someone might be able to give us a lead." She stood. "First, take a break and eat. You both look frozen." She pulled on her coat, gloves and hat. "We shouldn't be too long."

As they drove along Main, Jenna pointed out a small wooden erection in the park. "Ah, now I know what it is." She smiled at Kane. "There's usually a Nativity scene outside the town hall but it looks as if the townsfolk are building one alongside the park. I noticed the building a week ago but now there's a crib and three figures. It's like an Advent calendar. A little of the scene is revealed each week. What a beautiful gesture."

"Life-sized too." Kane slowed to peer out of the window. "It looks good. I guess they'll be adding a few figures all the way up to Christmas Eve. That's where the local choir congregates to sing carols. It will be a nice backdrop."

Jenna thought for a beat as they drove past. "I'll ask the mayor if we can have a charity donation box placed out front. Winter is a big strain on the shelters." She glanced at him. "Will you be making a donation this year?"

"Don't you mean, will *we* be making a donation?" Kane frowned at her. "Those papers we signed combined our assets. What's mine is yours, including the income from the overseas companies and investments."

Swallowing hard, Jenna nodded. "Yeah, I know but it worries me... I mean, all that money between us. It's growing at a phenomenal rate. What if anyone finds out?"

"No one is going to find out. It's well hidden and taxes are paid." Kane chuckled. "It was set up for me by someone in Treasury. Part of my deal to come here, Jenna, and then there's the offshore bank accounts. We can afford to make generous donations to the needy."

A cold chill slithered down Jenna's back. "What if you're called back into service or something happens to you, or I have to disappear? How do we access our funds without being caught?"

"Getting the money will never be a problem, we're just numbers and codes, not names." Kane hit the on-ramp to the highway and blended into the traffic. "We're married now. If anything happens to either of us, we'll bale together. Even in WITSEC, we'll still be able to access our cash. Now stop worrying." He squeezed her hand. "We're coming up to the coordinates Kalo sent us." He pulled onto the shoulder and glanced at Jenna. "Maybe you should scoot over this side to get out. There's a convoy heading this way."

Eighteen-wheelers dashed past in a seemingly endless train, and the wind as they passed by rocked the Beast. Jenna scrambled over the center console and crawled across Kane's seat to the open door. Crawling across bucket seats was more difficult than she'd imagined. "I'm glad there's such a wide gap between the steering wheel and the seat. I almost got stuck." She held out her hand and Kane pulled her out and swung her to her feet. The bitter cold slammed into her and she caught her breath. "Thanks. It's freezing. How far away is this darn phone?"

"The phone is just along here." Kane was using his phone to pinpoint the direction but he hadn't moved.

Jenna moved to his side. "What's up?"

"From here I can plainly see the gully for at least one hundred yards and there's no lumps that would indicate a body." Kane turned, scanning the lowlands. "Unless she made it two hundred yards across the pasture and into the wheatgrass, she's not here. If you're planning on asking search and rescue to look for Billy Stevens, give them the phone coordinates just in case there's a body in the wheatgrass, but I don't see any crows and I've seen them picking at frozen carcasses, so they're not particular." He waved a hand toward Blackwater. "The phone is close by. If you prefer to walk in the gully out of the wind, I'll search on top."

As the wind lashed at her cheeks, tossing strands of hair across her eyes, Jenna fought to zip up her puffy coat and then pulled the hood over her woolen cap. "Thanks." She took his hand and he lowered her into the gully.

The frozen grass and puddles of moisture crunched under Jenna's boots as she moved along, avoiding the bottles and cans people had tossed from their vehicles. Kicking at the trail of garbage, she found an assortment of candy wrappers and squashed takeout containers, then a small clutch purse peeked out from under a burger wrapper. "I have something."

Bending down, she cleared the debris from around the purse and taking her phone from her pocket took a few photographs of the purse and its position from the highway. Picking it up in thumb and forefinger, she flipped it open. Inside was Maisy Green's driver's license. Before Jenna had the chance to tell Kane, the traffic noise grew louder, as if two powerful vehicles were racing along the highway. She cringed as the horns from eighteen-wheelers blasted and air brakes locked, bouncing the trucks' wheels as they fought to control tons of machinery. Engines roared and tires squealed in protest as they laid rubber across the blacktop. Jenna's heart leapt. Out of control, they were heading straight for Kane.

THIRTEEN

The deafening impact of metal on metal got Kane's attention, and with survival mode on full alert, he turned as a red pickup with metal strips trailing behind it spun end-over-end straight past him along the middle of the highway. A black pickup was spinning on its roof across the blacktop and two out-of-control trucks, a tanker and an eighteen-wheeler, headed straight for him. He ran toward them but at a forty-five-degree angle. The breeze from them lifted his coat as they bounced by, brakes locked and screeching. Duke was beside him and must have been barking, but all Kane could hear was the screaming of metal across the blacktop. Instinctively, he dove to the ground, one arm around Duke, and rolled them into the gully. Metal rained down on them and a spinning wheel flew over his head. The noise was deafening, car alarms sounded and a truck horn blasted in one continuous wail.

The smell of burning rubber surrounded Kane as he stood, coughing from the thick black smoke. *Jenna.*

He scrambled from the gully and gasped at the devastation before him. It resembled a war zone. He cupped both hands around his mouth. "Jenna."

Nothing ahead of him moved. No signs of life. "Jenna."

Grabbing his phone, he ran down the highway, searching the gully. "Rio, multiple-vehicle collision on the highway, ten miles from town, near Bedrock Flats, send everything."

He disconnected and stared in horror at the tanker on its side across the gully, with smoke pouring from the engine. A little in front of the truck, the back end of the black pickup was visible. It sat nose down, its wheels still spinning. In the middle of the highway beside the crumpled red pickup lay the body of a man, arms stretched with blood pooling around his head. Kane called Jenna's name again and, hearing nothing but the horns, headed to the injured man and bent to check his pulse. Dead.

As he straightened, people traveling in the vehicles behind the wreck were running to assist. He turned and waved his hands. "Go back, the truck might blow. Get back!"

Covering his face with a mask, he peered through the billowing black smoke looking in all directions, searching desperately for Jenna. He stared at the tanker and choked back the horror. Was she under the burning truck or trapped beneath the pickup. "Jenna, where are you?"

Running, he skirted the wreckage of the eighteen-wheeler. The driver was alive. "Can you walk?"

"Yeah, I'm okay." The man was holding a tissue to a cut on his head.

Kane helped him from the cab. "Get back a hundred yards or so. Tell everyone to keep back. Help is on its way."

The second driver wasn't so lucky and had been thrown from the cab. He skirted around the billowing smoke and checked him. Dead. When Duke barked and dived into the gully, Kane followed, running along the highway toward the upturned black pickup. He raised his voice. "Jenna."

"Here." A hand waved in the air on the other side of the pickup. "I'm here, Dave."

Heart racing, he followed Duke and slid into the gully beside her. Relief flooded over him and he pulled her to him. She was soaked in blood but appeared to be lucid. "Thank you, Jesus." He stared at her. "Where are you hurt?"

"I'm okay." Jenna held blood-soaked hands away from him and her mouth turned down. "I was trying to keep the driver alive, but he went through the windshield and pierced his jugular. He bled out in seconds." She leaned into him. "I was so scared. Last time I looked, you were right where they came off the road not moments ago. I called out to you."

Kane rubbed her back. "I was calling you too but, with the horns blasting, I didn't hear you."

"I've lost my phone. We need to call this in and get paramedics out here." She removed her gloves, tossed them onto the ground and pulled on a fresh pair. "Let's check the victims."

Kane sucked in a breath to steady his nerves. Losing Jenna was his worst nightmare and this time, he'd come too darn close. He pushed down the concern and concentrated on procedure. "I've called Rio. With this one, we have three dead and one walking casualty." He handed her a mask. "The smoke is much worse on the highway. We need to move away. The tanker might blow. I'll see if I can disconnect those darn horns." He held out his hand and climbed out of the gully. "We'll come back later and look for your phone." He stared at the damp patch spreading from the truck. "There's fuel leaking from the tanker. We need to get out of here. Right now."

"Did you find Maisy's phone?" Jenna ran beside him jumping over the debris littering the highway.

Kane nodded. "Yeah, just before the wreck." He patted his pocket.

"Maisy's purse is there too. It's likely under the pickup with my phone. I heard the truck coming and ran along the gully. It landed just behind me." She looked up at him. "Someone was watching over us today."

"I'm a doctor." A man waved Kane down. "The man on the road is deceased and the driver of the eighteen-wheeler has a suspected fractured collarbone and minor abrasions."

"Thank you, Doctor...?" Jenna stopped and pulled out a notebook.

"Dr. James Pringle from Blackwater." He eyed her speculatively. "Are you hurt, Sheriff?"

"No." Jenna indicated behind her. "Unfortunately, the victim in the upturned pickup bled out."

Kane grabbed her arm. "We can talk later. Right now, we need to get away from the tanker. It could blow at any second. Run."

As they headed to the line of vehicles blocking the highway, Kane waved back the people crowding toward the wrecks. "Move back, the truck could blow at any moment." He looked at Jenna. "Get them back. I'll stop the noise."

Running to what was left of the red pickup, he wrenched up the buckled hood and tore the horn wire from its moorings. He shook his head. His ears rang from the noise. In the distance he could hear sirens. Turning, he searched for Jenna. She'd reached the group of onlookers and was taking down names of witnesses. Beside her, Duke was sitting, leaning protectively against her leg. "That dog never ceases to amaze me."

The smell of gas came through the smoke. The fire was getting intense and had moved from the engine and now flames lapped around the tanker wheels. The fuel ignited in a whoosh. Jenna and the onlookers needed to be at least another fifty yards away to be safe. Kane swallowed hard and started to run. He waved his arms and made a pushing motion. "Get back. Get back now."

The explosion shook the ground before a wave of heat lifted Kane from his feet, tumbling him over and over. He landed on his back on the roof of a pickup and slid across the shiny top and landed on his feet in the bed. The momentum of the blast carried him forward and he staggered, falling to his knees before grasping the side of the truck. Coming to a halt, he stared at the carnage before him. People had been picked up and tossed around like rag dolls. The blast had pushed the row of parked vehicles together like an unfinished jigsaw puzzle. He turned his head to see a mushroom cloud rise up into the sky. Around the tanker, flames leapt and hissed, he stood in the back of the truck, searching for Jenna.

Kane choked back a gasp of fear. Through the smoke he made out the bright yellow writing across the back of her sheriff's department jacket. She must have been heading for the protection of the Beast when the tanker exploded. Chest tight with concern, he jumped down from the pickup and ignoring the falling debris, bolted toward the blood-splattered body sprawled across the hood of his truck.

FOURTEEN

Inside the horrific hellhole, Maisy Jones searched every square inch for a way to escape and found nothing. The only way out was through the locked doors. The dripping sound of blood from the corpses flowing into the buckets was like being trapped inside a clock store with every darn clock ticking at a different pace. She'd found a few blankets and a pile of discarded clothes and shoes tossed in a garbage pail. She'd taken a scarf and tied it around her face to filter the smell. The odor of rotting flesh hadn't increased, but now the suffocating smell of preservative she'd recognized as formaldehyde was choking her. The blood had drained from the bodies and now the chemical dripped into the buckets. She moved closer to the door, pressing her face along the cracks, trying to feel any breeze from the outside. Being so close to the dead people frightened her. She'd watched far too many horror movies and the silly notion that one might suddenly sit up was freaking her out.

A noise made the hairs on the back of her neck tingle and she stared all around, but the sound was coming from the other side of the door. Footsteps echoed in the distance and got louder with every second. A squeaky sound like an unoiled wheel accompanied the tapping of boots on tile. Terrified, Maisy ran back into the small room where she'd woken hours before and, heart thumping like the drum in a marching band, she hid behind the door.

Peering through the crack between the hinges, Maisy heard the grinding of the tumblers inside a lock and then the double doors swung inward, pushed open by a gurney. The man guiding the autopsy table was wearing scrubs, facemask, gloves and a wraparound rubber apron. On the table lay the body of a young man. The person pushing the gurney scanned the room, his gaze stopping on the open door. He'd seen her.

"You might as well come out." The man started removing the clothes from the dead body using a pair of scissors. "You can't escape from here and I have food and a hot beverage for you." He chuckled. "Don't worry, I'm not going to kill you. I need you fresh." He took a paper sack from the end of the gurney and placed it about ten yards from the bodies. "You have to eat, right?"

He sounded almost normal. Friendly even. Not like a man who'd drugged and kidnapped her and then left her alone with a bunch of corpses. She stared at the bag of takeout and, despite the stink, her stomach growled. It had been many hours since she'd last eaten. Trembling, she stepped out from behind the door and stood in the open. Acting tough was her only option. She lifted her chin and glared at him. "Why did you kidnap me?"

"I could have killed you." He went about removing a fluid line from one body, attaching it to the new one on the gurney. He started the machine and a rush of red liquid ran down the tube from the young man's arm and into a clean bucket. "I admit I'm a power freak." He looked up at her and shrugged. "Having you trapped in here, frightened and under my complete control, is very satisfying. I decide everything you do from now on. If you're good, I'll leave the lights on and feed you from time to time, but if you don't comply, I'll leave you in here in the dark, no light, no food, and just watch you die slowly." He pointed to a camera mounted high above the swinging doors. "It has an infrared function so I can see you in the dark." He pulled the tubes out of a middle-aged man and pushed him toward the door. "The rats are bad here and come out in the dark. Sooner or later, they'll eat you alive." He turned and peered at her over his mask. "Won't that be fun?"

FIFTEEN

Swiping at her face, Jenna blinked dust from her eyes and coughed. Somewhere behind her she heard Duke whine and the thump of his tail. Her head ached and her sight was blurry. Wherever she was, it was way too bright. She moved her fingers over her face and found an oxygen mask. Memory of the explosion came back in a wave of nausea. If Kane wasn't with her, something had happened to him. "Dave?"

She didn't recognize the gasping voice coming from her lips but was comforted by the unmistakable wetness from Duke licking her hand. The ear-shattering noise as he barked made her cringe. Blinking, she opened her eyes to see the dog six inches away from her face. His big brown eyes alert and his body shivering with happiness. Secured in his harness on the back seat of the Beast, he was trying very hard to stay. Dave must have given him the command. He must be okay but where was he? Her seat was tipped back almost horizontal. When Duke barked again, the door behind her opened.

"Jenna. Lie still, take deep breaths." Kane leaned over her. "Where does it hurt?"

Relieved to know he was okay, she grabbed his hand.

"Thank God, you're okay. I just have a headache and my ribs are sore, not broken just bruised. Oh, and my shoulder hurts a little. How long have I been out?"

"Maybe half an hour. You have a cut on your hairline. It bled like crazy, but Wolfe sutured it right here in the Beast. I cleaned you up best I could, but you have blood caked in your eyebrow and it's all down the neck of your shirt. Your eyes look fine, but you need to lie still for a time. Wolfe will come by and check you again soon. He's kinda busy right now." His fingers went to her pulse and then he brushed the hair from her eyes with gentle care. "Your blood pressure dropped out and it needs to be checked again before you move. So don't be a hero. There's nothing you can do out here at the moment, okay?"

Jenna couldn't see him properly. "Can I roll onto my back or sit up? I feel okay."

"Okay." Kane removed the blanket, unclipped her seatbelt and offered his hand. "Sit up nice and slow and I'll move the seat." He pushed up the back of the seat. "Keep the oxygen mask on." He pushed the blanket around her. "I'll go back and help Wolfe." He reached into the back and handed her a bottle of water. "Promise me you won't leave the truck."

Jenna swallowed hard and nodded. Dust and blood covered Kane's black clothes, he had small cuts on his face that hadn't been tended and dried tears of blood had run down his cheeks. His concerned expression moved over her and she gripped his arm. "What about you? Are you okay? You look like hell."

"I'll do." Kane smiled at her. "Seeing you awake has taken the edge off the stress level. I didn't want to leave you, but the casualties out here are overwhelming. Once Wolfe had stopped the bleeding and assured me you'd be okay, I went to help the team. Everyone is out there. I've been coming back to check on you every five minutes and I told Duke to watch over you and he did. He barked the moment you were awake."

Jenna waved a hand behind her, found the dog's head and scratched his ears. "He is a very good boy."

"I'll be close by. Don't move, you have a nasty head injury that needs attention and other injuries. Wolfe believes there's no internal bleeding, so please, just for once, do as you're told. If you get sick, sound the horn." Kane kissed her and shut the door silently and walked into the swirling smoke.

Outside, the highway was littered with bits and pieces of vehicles, clothes, shoes and other personal items. Bodies lay on the blacktop and the injured were being triaged. The entire team was there: Wolfe, Emily and Julie Wolfe, Colt Webber and her deputies, working alongside paramedics from Black Rock Falls and Louan. She watched Kane go to a blonde woman who was wearing a mask and examination gloves. The woman listened and then nodded, and after attaching a green label on the person sitting alongside other injured people, picked up her bag and turned to look at Jenna. As she came over, Jenna recognized her as Dr. Norrell Larson, the forensic anthropologist who had joined Wolfe's team. She'd met her at the Halloween Ball, but her occupation meant she was in demand across Montana and was often away. She'd instantly liked her. Warm and friendly, she had slipped straight into the team. Jenna couldn't miss the way she looked at Wolfe and hoped her dear friend had at last found someone to share his life. Wolfe's daughters Emily and Julie liked her and Anna thought she was a fairy princess. The door opened and Jenna looked at her. "Hi, Norrell, please tell me I'm okay, so I can help out."

"No can do, sorry." Norrell took a small flashlight from her pocket and flicked it over Jenna's eyes. "You've had a significant head injury and you were unconscious for forty minutes. You need an MRI just to make sure you haven't damaged your skull or neck. Moving around right now could be fatal. Brain swelling, for instance." She attached a blood pressure cuff to

Jenna's arm and waited for the reading. "We were concerned about internal injuries. You were thrown a long way and ended up on the hood of the Beast. Your blood pressure is okay, so that's a good sign." She frowned. "I know as the sheriff you feel duty-bound to be out there with your team but they are very capable. Kane called in assistance from Louan, and as the explosion crossed the country line, the Blackwater sheriff is here with his deputies. They're detouring traffic around the accident, collecting information and dashcam footage. The Blackwater sheriff is Dirk Nolan. He's apparently new, so I'm not sure if you've met him." She grimaced. "It was a mess out there for a time, but we had help. The team of auto accident forensic investigators from Helena was in Blackwater and arrived by chopper to evaluate the scene. They worked fast to get the highway cleared. There's trucks backed up for miles. Just before they gave permission for the wrecks to be removed. This is too much for Wolfe and his team to handle. The victims of the wreck are going to Helena and we're dealing with the victims of the explosion." She patted Jenna on the arm. "Just sit tight. We've already moved the critical patients and we're waiting for the ambulances to return to take the others who need medical attention to the ER. We've spread out the casualties between three counties."

Jenna peered out of the window. "How many dead?"

"Three from the initial accident, another seven from the explosion." Norrell frowned. "Three at this end of the highway and four on the Blackwater end. All were outside their vehicles sightseeing when the tanker exploded. If they'd remained in their vehicles, they would still be alive." She shook her head. "Twenty or more casualties. The Blackwater sheriff has been working his end of the highway, transporting people to Blackwater. He arrived with a team of paramedics and two doctors and around six deputies, so you don't have to worry. Your team have everything under control on this side. Wolfe will be taking the dead to his morgue for identification. As it's classed as vehicular fatalities, even the explosion, all of them require autopsies. I'll be able to assist, and since the new wing was opened for my use, we have double the capacity for bodies." She pulled a large medical notebook from her bag, opened it and tore off a page. "Here, give this to the ER when you arrive. It's a request for an MRI. Shane said he'd have taken you to the morgue but it's too crowded. The moment we have everyone triaged Kane will be driving you to the hospital. It won't be much longer." She raised both eyebrows. "Don't argue. Doctor's orders."

Right this moment, Jenna could hardly move. She ached all over and had the headache from hell. Staying in the Beast and allowing her team to take over seemed like a good idea. "Thanks, Norrell. I'll be good. I promised Dave."

"Good, and see that he gets his wrist X-rayed. He has the request in his pocket, but that man is more stubborn than you." Norrell tucked the blanket over her and shut the door.

Jenna frowned. Dave had been hurt and never said a word. He just went straight out to help others. She sat up slowly and peered in the rear view mirror at the bandage on her hairline. Blood matted her hair and she was filthy. Smoke still surrounded the Beast and she scanned the area searching for Kane. She found him, working beside Wolfe, and as if he'd felt her looking at him, he turned and looked over to her. She waved but he didn't see her behind the tinted windows and turned back to assisting Wolfe, lifting a body bag onto a gurney. He looked exhausted and she knew instinctively his head was hurting. No matter what she tried to do to make him leave, Kane wouldn't move from the scene until Wolfe no longer needed him. He knew she was safe and would work until he dropped from exhaustion. It appeared that most of the victims had been removed in the last few minutes. A few of the people with minor injuries still waited, sitting along the grass beside the highway. From what she could see, fire and rescue had cleared the highway of debris and tow trucks were removing the damaged vehicles. Foam covered the blacktop around the toppled tanker and the eighteen-wheeler had been dragged onto the side of the road.

All Jenna could do was wait, but she could put this alone time to good use. Although her body ached, her mind was working just fine. She had two people missing, seemingly vanished from her town without a trace. The fact Carter and Jo had a similar case in Blackwater was too much of a coincidence not to believe the cases were linked. Especially when Maisy Jones' phone and presumably her purse had been found on the connecting highway between the two towns. It could only mean one thing. Whoever was responsible had a very wide comfort zone. If they were looking at multiple homicides, where were the bodies?

SIXTEEN

Blackwater

After checking the weather, Jenell Rickers gathered up the leashes of the four dogs in her care and headed out the door of her doggy daycare center. She'd moved from Indiana to Blackwater the previous year and had quickly established her business. She'd started by dog walking and ended up turning her home into a registered kennel. It wasn't the usual type of kennel, with pens in rows. Her establishment catered to social dogs. She now employed two people and together they walked, groomed and entertained dogs from near and far.

It was a beautiful day, sunny with a light but freezing breeze, and winter had brought with it a delightful change to the scenery. From a summer of vibrant shades of green, the forest still held tightly to its fall mixture of green, yellow and gold. The colors peeked through the dusting of snow like precious jewels. In the shelter of the trees, late-flowering wild-flowers filled the air with bubbles of perfume. As she walked along her usual path with the dogs out in front, their coats changed color as the beams of sunlight from the canopy above washed over them. She walked the half mile to a fenced one-acre block of cleared land she'd purchased. Here the dogs could do as they please, and as they got closer, they pulled hard at their leashes in anticipation of running free. She carried a selection of toys with her to help keep them active. She could toss a ball or Frisbee for them to chase, but most times they enjoyed running in circles until they came back to the water trough to drink. Leaning her back on the gate as the dogs scurried madly in all directions and then chased each other in circles, she heard a muffled cry behind her and turned around. A man came rushing out of the forest in obvious distress. She frowned at him. "Are you okay?"

"It's my dog." The man pushed an agitated hand through his hair. "He caught his leg in a trap and every time I go to release him, he tries to bite me. Can you help me, please?"

Without hesitation, Jenell nodded. She hung the leashes over the top of the fence and, glancing at the dogs tearing around behind her, opened the gate and walked through. "Where in the forest is it?"

"About one hundred yards along the trail." He pointed to the leashes hanging over the fence. "You might want to grab one of those to tie around his muzzle. He is only a small dog, but he has a nasty bite."

Jenell patted the fanny pack at her waist. "I have a first aid kit in here. I'll be able to dress the wound, but you'll have to take him to the vet." She grabbed one of the leashes. "Let's go."

She followed the man along the trail at a run. When they reached a small clearing, he stopped and scanned the forest. She stared at him. "How much farther?"

"I've gotten turned around. I think it's through there." He pointed into the trees. "He isn't whining now. I hope he's still alive." He gave her a horrified look. "Can you help me find him?" He cast his gaze around. "Maybe if we split up?"

Concerned for the poor dog, Jenell peered into the forest. "Can you recall which direction he went?"

"Yes, he ran off to the left of this clearing." The man was staring at her. "I ran in about ten or so yards when I hurt him yelping." He wiped a hand down his face. "He likes to run through the trees and always comes back. It's like a game to him. I bring him here all the time and no one has laid traps here before."

Angry that someone could do such a thing, Jenell shook her head. "No, they don't. It's illegal and irresponsible as kids play in this part of the forest too." She stared through the trees but saw nothing. "I didn't see you ahead of me on the trail when I arrived. Which way did you come in?"

"I parked on the fire road over yonder. I come here every day to walk my dog." He was looking all around. "I heard your dogs barking, so I knew someone was close by. I was so glad to find you. I rarely see anyone around these parts." He stared behind her. "I heard something. Over there." He pointed into the forest and ushered her forward. "If you give me the leash, I'll stop him biting and you can try to release the trap?"

After listening, Jenell did hear a noise behind her, but it could have been anything. She turned and headed in the direction he'd pointed. She'd walked about ten yards through the trees but heard nothing other than the usual sounds in the forest, birds singing and the wind rustling through the pines. Behind her, the man was breathing heavily, sending clouds of steam into the air. A sudden wave of fear gripped her. Being alone in the forest with a stranger didn't feel safe. "I can't see your dog. I'm sorry. My clients' dogs are in my care and if anything happens to them while I'm away, I'm responsible. I'm heading back."

The next moment the leather leash fell over her head and

landed heavily on her shoulders. "Hey, there's no need to do that. You could have just handed it to me."

One end had been slipped through the loop handle and before she could get her hands up to grab it, the noose tightened around her neck. Gagging, she clawed at the leather leash digging into her throat. Why was he doing this? She had to get away from him. Lifting up one booted foot she dragged the heel down the man's shin. When he yelped in pain, the noose slackened and she grabbed hold of the end of the leash and bolted. Running blindly through the trees, she plowed through bushes and dead vegetation. In fear of her life, she tried to pull the leash free but only managed to loosen it a little. He was crashing through the brush behind her, his footsteps pounding only a few yards away. She needed help now and dragging air into her lungs, she screamed but no one would hear her. The sound wasn't loud enough. Something had happened to her throat.

Desperate to escape the swearing man crashing along behind her, she zigzagged between trees. Snow slipped from branches and slapped at her face, but she kept running, slipping and sliding on the icy patches underfoot. She couldn't hear him behind her and risked a look over one shoulder. Her feet tangled in dead vines and she tripped falling hard to her knees. Winded, she crawled to a tree and, hugging the rough bark, dragged herself up by the sheer will to live and kept running. Breathing was so painful. Each breath sucked freezing air into her lungs. It was like having a heart attack, but she forced her legs to keep pumping and ignored the brambles and low branches tearing at her clothes and dragging at her like quicksand. Footsteps came closer and the next second, her head jerked back and she crashed to the dirt. He'd caught hold of the end of the leash and was wrapping it around his hand. Panic gripped her and she lowered her chin as the noose tightened. He was reeling her in like a fish on a hook. Forcing out her words as she struggled to breathe, she glared at him. "Please, stop. What do you want?"

"You're coming with me." He gave a low chuckle. "I enjoyed chasing after you. It makes it so much fun, but you can't outrun me. Playtime is over. Be a good girl and do as I say."

Confused and gasping for every breath, Jenell slid the fingers of one hand under the noose and pulled hard, but it didn't budge. She was under his control and right now he decided if she lived or died. Staying alive was her priority. She had to negotiate with him. It was her only chance of survival. "I can't breathe. If you want me to walk, you'll need to loosen it some."

"No can do." He dragged her to her feet as if she weighed nothing and gave her a shove in the back. "Move. Straight ahead to the fire road. We're going to take a ride. My truck is just up there. Be good now. If you scream again or kick me like a mule, I'll knock you out and carry you over my shoulder. It's your choice—the hard way or the easy way. What's it to be, princess?"

Jenell stared into his unyielding expression. She'd be able to pick him out in a lineup and memorized every inch of his face. "Okay, okay. I'll do as you say, just don't hurt me."

Others might be using the fire road and if she got into his vehicle, he'd have to go along a highway. Someone would hear her if she screamed, and she might be able to escape. She bit back the wave of terror gripping her and moved ahead on trembling legs. Maybe if she talked to him, he'd let her go. "Why did you choose me?"

"I've been watching you for a time." The stranger wrapped his hand around her long hair and sniffed it. "You're perfect. I like an angelic face. It makes it all so much better."

Horror gripped her. Was he planning on raping her or keeping her locked up as a sex slave? Heart pounding in her ears, she staggered forward. She could smell him and the odor coming from him was like death. As they broke through the forest, ahead of them the fire road stretched out wide and deserted. On one side sat a large black truck. When he pushed her forward, she hung back terrified of what might happen. She flicked her eyes both ways, but no one walked in the forest. She must do something and, pretending to faint, collapsed to the ground.

"Stupid woman. Didn't you figure I'd know all the tricks in the book by now?" He dragged her up by the hair. "Get up or I'll hurt you real bad. I have a knife. Do you want me to cut your throat? Stand up. I'm over being nice to you."

Trembling, she staggered to her feet. Shaking with terror, she fought back the tears streaming down her face. "Okay, what do you want me to do?"

Pushed hard toward the back of the truck, she stood motionless as he opened the hatch. Inside was lined with plastic and she turned to look at him over one shoulder as the stark realization that there'd be no escape hit her in the pit of the stomach. She turned and punched him hard in the ribs, lashing out, once, twice, three times, but it made no impression on him but sent pain shooting up her arms. It was like hitting a brick wall. In desperation, she kicked at his legs, but he pulled her closer.

"Is that all you've got?" His face cracked into a wide smile. "You're like an annoying fly."

When she lashed out with her nails, he ducked away, laughing just as the leash around her neck tightened. Spun around, his hand came down hard between her shoulder blades and her chest struck the metal tray. Air rushed from her lungs and she couldn't take a breath. Desperately gasping small sips of air as the noose tightened, she fought for survival. The next moment, he was on her with his knee pressed into her back. Pinned like a butterfly on display, she dug her nails into the slippery plastic to gain a hold. Unable to breathe, her body jerked. The noose cut deep, sending white-hot shards of pain into her head. Behind her, she could hear him, humming a Christmas jingle. As her sight slowly failed, her thoughts went to the gifts so lovingly wrapped under the Christmas tree. The pain had gone now and all she could see in her mind was a twinkle of light, like the star on the top of her tree.

SEVENTEEN

On the drive back home from the hospital, Kane glanced at Jenna. She'd been more concerned about him than herself. When he'd seen her covered in blood and sprawled across the hood of the Beast, he thought his heart would burst. Memories of losing Annie, his first wife, in an explosion flashed into his mind. He'd lost both his wife and unborn child that day. The pain had come back in a wave of nausea as he ran blindly to Jenna. She'd been out cold and he'd just held her until Wolfe peeled him away from her. He couldn't let her go, too afraid if he did, she'd die.

"Headache any better?" Jenna squeezed his thigh. "You haven't said two words to me since we left the hospital."

Kane covered her hand and sighed. "Mine? Yeah, I'll be fine, but your head must be sore. You took a beating, Jenna. You could have died in the explosion."

"It's not like you to dwell on things, Dave." Jenna turned in her seat to look at him. "We've been through worse than this and it's not the first time we've been blown up. I'm fine, the MRI was clear and I'm glad you haven't broken your wrist. It's all good."

Holding back a sudden rush of emotion, Kane swallowed hard. "What if you'd been pregnant, Jenna? A baby wouldn't have survived." He glanced at her. "We need to rethink how we're going to work around a pregnancy."

"I know this brings back bad memories, Dave, but I can't live my life worrying every second what might happen." Jenna squeezed his hand. "Have you considered I might not be able to carry a child? I'm not getting any younger. I asked Wolfe and he gave me the name of a doctor in Helena. We'll go and see her and then we'll know for sure. Wolfe says I should be optimistic. He figures women in their forties have babies all the time, so I should have plenty of time yet." She looked at him. "I know you want us to have a baby and I feel as if I'm letting you down."

Shaking his head, Kane stared at the road. "That's not what's worrying me, Jenna, and by all means, see a doctor if you need answers. I'm more concerned about you being pregnant on the job."

"Don't go there." Jenna pulled her hand away. "We've discussed this before and made plans. I have a team to step in when necessary. I'm not stupid. Do you honestly believe I'd risk the life of our child?"

Turning the Beast into their driveway, Kane waited for the gate to slide open. "You're stubborn and I can just imagine the week before our baby is due you'll be hunting down a serial killer wielding an ax." He glanced at her. "I know, even after what's happened today, if I insist you take a shower and go straight to bed, you'll refuse."

"Me? Why don't you take a long look at yourself, Dave. You're exhausted and in pain. I know you too well. You can't hide it from me. You're in no shape to tend the horses." Jenna stared at him. "I intend to help, and as you haven't eaten for hours, I'll make dinner. I've been resting and you haven't stopped since the wreck."

I might be hungry and in pain, but I could keep going for

hours if necessary. Kane blew out a breath and drove into the garage. "See, you never take good advice. I can handle the horses. The new system with six stables makes life easier. I just move them out of one stall into a prepared clean one and then I can leave the mucking out for the morning. Five minutes and I'll be inside. There's a casserole in the freezer and I'll pop it into the microwave. There are mashed potatoes left over from yesterday." He turned and looked at her. "We're both battered and bruised, Jenna. Let's not argue."

"I'm not arguing but I'll need time to soak in the hot tub before dinner." She stepped from the Beast.

Kane opened the door for Duke to jump down and then went to her side. "I'll walk you to the house. You'll need to shower to remove the blood from your hair before you climb into the hot tub."

"What about getting the wound wet?" Jenna ran her fingertips over the bandage on her forehead.

Kane pushed back her hair and smiled at her. "Wolfe said he covered it with a waterproof bandage, but I'll redress the wound when you're done."

"Okay." Jenna cupped the back of his head and kissed him. "There, Mr. Grumpy, is that better?" She sighed and looked into his eyes. "I'll feed the animals and head for the shower. You don't need to walk me the twenty yards to the door. I'll manage just fine. I have Duke as a bodyguard." She gave him a wave and headed for the house.

Kane stared after her. "You'll be the death of me, Jenna."

After tending the horses, Kane walked back to the house. His phone chimed and he checked the caller ID. "Yeah, Carter, what's up?"

"I heard about the wreck on the highway and the explosion. Are you and Jenna okay?"

Kane snorted. "We were both tossed around like leaves in the shockwave, and Jenna has a cut on her head. She was knocked out cold. We've been checked out at the ER and we're fine. She'll be sore for a few days, is all."

"*That's good to know.*" Carter's boots clattered on tile. "*We're in Blackwater and walked straight into a report of another missing person. I'm at the sheriff's office now. This time it's a woman, Jenell Rickers, in her mid-twenties. She runs a doggy daycare center in town and took a few of her dogs to an exercise yard owned by the business in Broken Wolf Forest. It's a regular part of her day. She walks six or so dogs through a trail in the woods and lets them run around for an hour or so in an enclosed corral. The other workers at the center became concerned when she didn't return and set out to look for her. They searched all over. The dogs are all in the exercise yard, one of the leashes is missing, but there's no sign of Jenell Rickers.*" He huffed out a sigh. "*As Sheriff Nolan is snowed under and we're involved with the Bridger case, we headed out to take a look and couldn't find a trace of her. The light was failing, so we'll be heading back out in the morning.*"

Kane stopped on the porch and stared into the endless dark sky. The stars seemed close enough to pluck out of the sky. He leaned against the front doorframe and thought for a beat. "We've made no progress on our missing persons cases either. We located Maisy Jones' phone and Jenna did see a purse fitting the description of the one she carried, but that was just before the explosion. I fell on the phone when I landed on the top of a truck, so it's pretty messed up and where the purse was located is a hole in the ground." He cleared his throat. "Nothing more on Billy Stevens. We've spoken to his housemates and colleagues at work. He walked home the same way every night. If someone was planning an abduction, he'd be the perfect choice."

"*I figure we should work together.*" A door opened and closed and Kane could hear conversation in the background. "*Run it past Jenna. We have Kalo with us and he'll be able to extract information from the phone. We really need Duke on this one. The snowfall in the forest is light and he might be able to pick up a scent on the trail and find our missing woman. At the moment, with everyone still out investigating the wreck, I can't ask the only remaining deputy to shut the office and assist us."*

Kane rubbed the back of his neck. "Sure, it makes sense to join forces. You'll need to convince Sheriff Nolan to give us jurisdiction if we need to arrest anyone. I'll discuss it with Jenna. Right now, she's exhausted and in the hot tub. I'll call you in a while."

"He won't be a problem. He called us in because he believes the Bridger family are victims of a serial killer. If Jenna agrees, I'll come and collect y'all in the chopper. Kalo can work at the cottage." Carter paused a beat. *"It would save you the time of driving back and forth to Blackwater."*

Kane smothered a yawn. "It would make more sense for you to move into the cottage now, so we're all together. I'll talk to her first thing in the morning. Not tonight, not after a head injury, or she'll be over there making up beds. You know Jenna. She never takes a break."

"I wouldn't expect you to and we can make up our own beds. We're staying at the Blackwater Motel tonight." The disgust in his voice was evident. *"Jo isn't impressed. The walls are paper thin and it's colder than the morgue."*

"And smells just as bad." Jo's voice came through the speaker.

Laughing, Kane pulled open the front door and stepped into the mudroom. "Okay, I'll talk to you soon."

EIGHTEEN

Maisy Jones pulled the rough blanket around her as cold seeped through her clothes. She'd dragged on anything she could find that was reasonably clean to ward off the freezing temperature. She sat in her room staring at anything other than the bodies on the gurneys dripping blood into buckets. A trail of ants carrying unrecognizable things above their heads, had become a fascination. They worked as a team, moving their burden from one to another in a line that went across the floor and up one wall to disappear through a tiny hole. How they maneuvered the tiny object of their attention through the hole had been her entertainment for the entire day. She'd needed a distraction. Morbid curiosity had drawn her to look at the young male corpse the Smiling Man had wheeled in earlier. His pale face had once been handsome and she wondered why he had murdered him and the young boy. In the middle of the night, her captor had returned with another corpse, this time a woman, and he followed the same ritualistic procedure with her. He removed the clothes and then sponged the bodies in what she realized was a preservative, and then drained the blood. Now that her mind was clearing from the shock of being kidnapped, she concluded he must be embalming the bodies for burial. Perhaps he was just an undertaker or maybe working for one? She rubbed the goosebumps on her arms. So why had he kidnapped her?

She'd gone hungry all day and must be adjusting to the stink because her stomach was cramping with starvation. If she was lucky, he brought a small meal once a day, but this time he didn't so much as acknowledge her when he rolled the woman into the room. He went to work, singing Christmas jingles. It seemed like an insult and hearing him made her angry, yet she sat on her gurney and remained quiet. She hated the thought of actually looking forward to his visits. Perhaps seeing a living person gave her hope of finally getting out of the room. She wondered if he was controlling her with food or she'd started to suffer from Stockholm syndrome. Shaking her head, she pushed the thoughts out of her mind. He terrified her, so how could she possibly like him? Concerned for her sanity, she scrubbed both hands down her face and smelled the stink of searching through clothes, some bloody or stained with what might be blood. She had water to wash her hands but nothing to dry them on and the water was ice cold.

The door to the room opened with a whine and she crept from the gurney, careful not to make a noise. It was the Smiling Man. He was carrying something and walking toward her. As his footsteps came closer, she moved to the corner of the room and brushed away cobwebs heavy with dust. Heart thumping in her chest so fast she couldn't breathe, she cringed away. Had he come to kill her and drain her blood like the others? He'd kill her. Trapped and alone, nobody would know. No one would come to help her, or even notice she'd gone missing. She brushed a cobweb from her arm, the occupants long gone and only the husks of a few flies left behind. The sight of a fly tangled in a spider's web had always horrified her. Trapped alive and wrapped in a cocoon just waiting for the spider to eat it was chilling. In that second, she'd become the fly. Caught and secured and the spider was heading her way.

NINETEEN

FRIDAY

Every inch of Jenna ached as she staggered back to the house. Her insistence to help Kane tend the horses had drained every ounce of energy from her. They'd cleaned the stalls and moved the horses to the corral only, so they had time to muck out and set up the spare stalls in case they were delayed again. It was a good idea but meant a double workload each morning. The exertion had eased some of the tightness in her bruised body, but the moment she'd finished she headed for the hot tub. Ten minutes and some stretches would ease her pain. "Breakfast can wait. I need to soak my aching body."

"Me too." Kane followed her into the mudroom and shucked his coat and boots. He pulled out his phone and smiled at her. "It will give me time to bring you up to speed about Carter's case."

Jenna led the way through the door leading to the space under the house that held their extensive gym, hot tub and cellar. She made her way along the passageway, through the gym and into the warm room that held the hot tub. "When did he call?"

"Late last night." Kane closed the door behind them and

undressed.

She gasped when Kane turned his back to her. Purple and red bruises covered his back. She must have been blind not to have seen them last night. She'd seen the cuts on his cheek and his bruised forearm, but they hadn't spoken about the explosion, just eaten and fallen into bed exhausted. "You're covered in bruises. What happened to you?"

"I landed on the top of someone's pickup." Kane climbed into the hot tub and sighed. "Slid down into the back and scared the hell out of the driver." He smiled at her, winced and touched the small cuts under one eye with his fingertips. "I'm fine, Jenna. I was lucky."

She shook her head. "Not so lucky, looking at your back." She placed her phone beside a towel, climbed into the deliciously hot water, leaned back and hit the control for the bubbles. "Okay, what did Carter want?"

As Kane finished, Jenna's phone buzzed. "It's Wolfe." She put the phone on speaker.

"How are you both this morning?" Wolfe yawned. *"Any headaches, blurred vision?"*

Jenna shook her head. "We're okay, battered and bruised, is all."

"That's good. With everything that happened yesterday, I didn't get the chance to tell you about Zander Hastings." Wolfe sighed. *"I went to see the body. I had permission to bring it back here for autopsy, but we had a jurisdiction problem. I spoke to the state medical examiner and explained the situation. They allowed me to examine the body and it's definitely homicide. The needle stick wound to the neck was dissected, and swabs taken indicated positive for heroin. As the needle in the victim's arm was a different gauge, it proves beyond doubt someone else administered the lethal dose via the carotid artery. The case has been handed over to the local law enforcement and the body sent to the state ME for further investigation. I was returning when I*

heard about the wreck. Before you ask, you were in no shape to discuss cases last night, Jenna."

Jenna nodded. "I agree. So one of our missing persons, Maisy Jones, might be a killer?"

"That part of the puzzle y'all have to work out." Wolfe yawned explosively. *"Sorry, we worked right through last night. I'm going to grab a few hours shuteye and then get back at it."* He paused for a beat. *"I know you're listening, Dave. Take the meds I gave you. They'll help with your pain and won't affect your work. Just an anti-inflammatory, is all."*

"I will." Kane smiled at Jenna. "Thanks, Shane."

"Take them with food." Wolfe disconnected.

Jenna listened with interest as Kane brought her up to speed about Carter's call. "The cases are similar. It could be the same person."

"So, what do you plan to do about Carter's idea of working together?" Kane sunk up to his neck in the hot water. "The cases are similar, people up and missing without a trace. It's as if someone is collecting them. Human trafficking, maybe?"

The idea had entered Jenna's mind, and she nodded. "Yeah, that's something to consider. Finding suspects is a problem if we don't have any evidence of a crime, apart from finding property."

"Well, if the cases are linked, then we can make up a list of probable suspects." Kane rested his head against the side of the tub. "We have a wide comfort zone, between Blackwater and here, and if we include Maisy Jones as a victim, it makes the parameters wider because she vanished on a highway. This would mean the kidnapper moves from one of the counties north of town. Louan, maybe, or as far as Paradise Falls."

Running professions through her mind, Jenna looked at him through the haze of steam. "Who moves between towns? Drivers, and they'd have a truck to hide a person."

"I'm not inclined to agree with a driver." Kane emerged

from the water and grabbed a towel. "If they wanted to kidnap someone, it would be hitchhikers. It would be easy to drug a drink beforehand and there are a ton of people at truck stops waiting for a ride. Hitchhikers are easy targets because they usually have little or no money and would take an offered drink." He dried off and wrapped a towel around his waist and stretched out his back. "I'm more inclined to think our man is a contractor or a delivery driver, a mailman, someone who moves in a circle of all four towns."

Jenna stood and reached for a towel. "Yeah, I agree. Someone who moves around unnoticed and blends into the background."

"Exactly." Kane nodded. "I'll get dressed and start breakfast. Don't forget to stretch now." He headed for the door.

Jenna drew an imaginary circle on the map in her head of the surrounding counties. The advertisements on TV and social media often had contractors who listed areas they serviced. Plumbers, real estate agents, courier services, auto club mechanics, tow truck drivers. She pursed her lips thinking as she headed for the bedroom to dress. All these professions would move around without gaining a second glance from the townsfolk. Why? Because they were frequent visitors or lived in town.

The smell of coffee drifted down the hallway, and when she entered the kitchen, two cups sat on the table. She walked up behind Kane and gently slid both hands around his waist and raised up on her toes to kiss the back of his neck. "Need me to burn the toast?"

"Nah. I'm good." Kane grinned at her over one shoulder as he turned the strips of bacon.

Jenna sat at the table and sipped her coffee. The rich hot brew slipped over her tongue in an instant burst of energy. She sighed and gave him her thoughts on her possible suspects. "If we had Kalo here, he'd be doing all the grunt work: searching for persons in the various occupations, who travels back and forth in the comfort zone and at what time. Most of the contractors work for a company. Where they worked would be logged online. Kalo could get the information we need and leave the rest of us to work the cases. The biggest problem will be treading on the toes of Sheriff Nolan. He'll have to give us jurisdiction to hunt down suspects in his county, same with anywhere else we need to go."

"Carter figures that's a given and I'd imagine Sheriff Nolan has his hands full with the wreck yesterday." He slid plates stacked with hotcakes and crispy bacon on to the table. "Many of the people involved are out of Blackwater, and as he offered to assist the auto accident forensic team, he'll be out interviewing witnesses and going over phone and dashcam video. I already told Rio and Rowley to collect what information they could from everyone on scene and to hand copies over to the forensic team. Before we left yesterday, I had everyone in the same loop. The forensic team understand we're tied up with possible homicide cases and are more than welcome for Rio and Rowley's assistance. So between them, they've split the witness pool with Nolan. This leaves us free to join up with Jo and Carter and try and untangle this mess of missing persons. That's if you want them staying at the ranch. I wouldn't just go and invite them before running it past you."

Nibbling on bacon, Jenna thought for a beat. Yeah, she did have the wreck and explosion to consider but everything had been handed over to the investigators. With Rio and Rowley gathering evidence, there wasn't anything more she could do. She'd just be stepping on toes if she got involved. She nodded. "Yeah, give them a call. We can set up the cottage as a command center and Bobby can feed us information as it becomes available."

"Sure, but we'll leave Kalo to set up a command center when he arrives. It's what he does best. I'll call Carter." Kane raised one eyebrow. "After I've eaten."

TWENTY

Special Agent Ty Carter dropped his bags inside his bedroom in the cottage and then gave his Doberman, Zorro, a rub on the head. "Go play with Duke."

He smiled as the dog's entire body wiggled with happiness and he took off at such high speed he almost collided with Kane coming along the hallway. "Zorro has been cooped up for a time in the motel."

"So it seems." Kane stared after the dog. "He can run free here." He indicated with his thumb toward the door. "Do you need to unpack? I want to show you something while Jenna is fussing over your rooms."

Grinning around a toothpick, Carter nodded. "You're starting to sound like an old married man." He chuckled. "Sure, where to?"

"It just so happens I like being married." Kane led the way toward the new garage. "I've finished the Harley."

Impressed, Carter walked past the Beast parked inside and admired the workbench with just about every tool known to man attached to a board on the wall. The place was immaculate and showed Kane's attention to detail, likely from his military background. His eyes settled on a motorcycle: a Harley-Davidson knucklehead. Since Kane and Jenna married, they'd made extensive improvements to the ranch. The garage, the extension on the barn and more. The security around the home was impenetrable and the additions expensive, and yet Kane came from a military background and he knew darn well it didn't pay that well. His gaze moved over the motorcycle. Kane had built it from the frame up using genuine parts and it would have cost a fortune. Where had the money come from? He walked around the Harley and whistled. "Man, she is beautiful. How did you get the parts for a 1941 1,200-cc knucklehead? It would be like finding hen's teeth."

"I found the frame and the engine a few weeks after we came back from our honeymoon." Kane grinned. "Wolfe has been helping me in his spare time."

Carter bent to examine the engine and ran a finger over the chrome. He straightened and looked Kane straight in the eye. Some questions needed answering if there was to be trust between them. "Excuse me for askin' but between you and me, how the heck are you paying for all this? The motorcycle, the garage? The Beast was modified this year as well, not to mention the security and other improvements. Did you win the lottery?"

"Nope." Kane took a cloth and slowly polished the Harley. He raised his gaze and straightened. "You're not suggesting I'd do anything illegal are you, Ty?"

Not wanting to ruin a hard-fought friendship with Kane, Carter removed the toothpick from his mouth and stared back into a face he thought he knew, but at this moment the man's expression had hardened to almost a mask. "Now, I never implied that, Dave. I've known you long enough to know you're honest. I shouldn't have asked. It's your business. Look, man, it's a beautiful motorcycle. Maybe we should get back to the cottage?"

"You might have noticed that I don't mention my family." Kane tossed the cloth on the pristine workbench and it looked out of place. He let out a long breath. "That's because they've all passed and it's too painful. My parents died first and then my grandpa. My sister was murdered six years ago. All had substantial estates and insurance policies. I inherited a ton of cash and two overseas investment portfolios. I also received compensation from two head injuries in the line of duty." He rubbed the tip of his nose. "Truth is I'm loaded. It's not something I like to advertise. I'm sure you understand?"

Carter tipped back his Stetson and nodded slowly. "Yeah, I do. Sorry for bringing it up. It's the detective in me. It never sleeps."

"Not a problem." Kane grinned at him. "Do you want a Harley? I'll build you one. It gets boring out here when we don't have a case."

Astonished, Carter laughed. "You do know it's against the law to bribe a federal officer?" He chuckled. "Although, the idea of a project to pass the winter is a good idea. I'm kinda sick of whittling."

"Maybe we can work on it together?" Kane glanced toward the cottage. "Jenna is talking about starting up a quilting circle. Emily and Julie have been making quilts for years. They show them at the fairs." He blew out a breath. "While I admire the quilts, it's not something I aspire to join, so I was planning on going fishing or hunting, but I'm not planning on freezing my butt off in the snow all winter. I need something to do."

Following Kane from the garage, Carter nodded. "Sure. We could start hunting down parts. There's a ton of old barns in Snakeskin Gully. I visited one recently that had a Model T Ford rusting away under the straw. I'd bet a dollar to a dime there's Harley parts all over."

"That sounds like a plan." Kane pressed a button on the control panel on the side of the garage and a door slid down into place. "Once this case is solved, we'll get at it." He laughed. "If Rowley and Rio get involved, we'll have our own biker gang."

An hour later, after Jenna had contacted her office and given her deputies their instructions, Carter landed the chopper in Blackwater and they climbed into a rental. As he drove, he glanced in the rear view mirror at Jenna. "I've spoken to Sheriff Nolan and he's given you jurisdiction in his county to investigate."

"That's good to know, although we could be here as FBI consultants. We've done that before." Jenna moved Duke's head from her shoulder.

"This way would cut the red tape." Jo peered out of the window. "The weather has gone real strange this year. Snowfall is different in each county. They haven't had much in Blackwater at all but the trees along Main are all decorated." She made a humming sound. "Oh, look, they've built a Nativity scene. Do they do that every year?"

"Yeah, it's the same in Black Rock Falls. They light candles and sing carols around it on Christmas Eve. It's nice. The one in our town is in the park. It's where they have the bandstand, on the cement slab. They've completed the building. People have been hanging lights on the outside and adding the animals. It's a community tradition. Everyone helps out."

As they reached the outlying parts of town, Carter glanced at Kane riding shotgun. "The trail through the forest is just ahead. I can park on the road or go up aways and come in via the fire road."

"Which way would Jenell have walked?" Kane peered ahead. "We'll need to follow her path if we have any chance of finding her."

Carter slowed and drove onto a gravel stopover area beside the road. "We can walk from here."

When they arrived at the corral where Jenell Rickers exercised the dogs in her care, they split up and searched all around for any trace of a struggle or disturbance. Finding nothing of consequence, Carter pulled an evidence bag from his pocket and handed it to Kane. "These socks belonged to Jenell Rickers. Jo collected them from her laundry basket last night. Duke might be able to pick up her scent."

"Can Zorro follow a scent?" Kane whistled Duke to his side and took the bag. "You trained him, right?"

Shaking his head, Carter smiled. "Not for tracking people, no. Not unless the missing woman was carrying explosives. Zorro's nose is trained to identify hidden IEDs, C4 and other types of explosive components."

"Okay. We have a chance. If it had snowed again last night, things would be different." Kane opened the bag and held it to Duke's nose. "Seek."

Carter fell into step beside Jo. "Now you're up to speed on the Black Rock Falls cases, do you have any insights I should be aware of?"

"I'm leaning toward a more personal occupation than a driver." Jo pushed her hands inside her pockets and shivered. "Someone people would usually trust. Although we found nothing in the Bridgers' home to suggest the need for a contractor."

Carter tossed a toothpick in his mouth and heard Jo's moan of distaste. The chewing on wood helped him to think or maybe it had become a nasty habit like Jo kept insisting, but what the heck. He'd given up everything else in his life: chewing gum and drinking great quantities of liquor came to mind. He still enjoyed a beer but kept within the limits. Allowing the Bridgers' home to come into his mind's eye, he nodded. "Yeah, that makes sense because they allowed him to go inside. They had sturdy locks on the doors and a peephole in the front, so why open it if they weren't expecting him?"

"Make a note to check the Bridgers' phone records. He might have called a few contractors to bid for work he needed doing." Jo lifted her chin. "The idea his work revolves around a house narrows the playing field. If we have the Bridger family as the center point, we can assume he planned their abduction for whatever reason. This would make me believe the same for Jenell Rickers." She waved a hand around her and pushed it back inside her pocket. "This place is isolated and we know Jenell walked the dogs here daily. I figure he was working close by and saw her leave every day around the same time. Maybe he followed her a few times to see where she was going and planned her abduction."

Carter rubbed his chin. "Hmm, then they're not connected to the Black Rock Falls cases? They all appear to be opportunity grabs."

"I disagree." Jo looked at him. The end of her nose was bright red with the cold. "Maisy Jones' vehicle was disabled. Yeah, she might have been an opportunistic kidnapping, but he made it happen, didn't he? He tampered with her vehicle and Billy Stevens took the same way home every night. They're all screaming 'organized psychopath' to me. I figure they're all dead. We haven't found any bodies because an organized psychopath would have likely dug the graves deep in the forest or wherever weeks ago before the ground froze. Or he's keeping them in a trophy vault somewhere."

Swallowing bile, Carter stared at her. "Trophy vault? That's a first. How did you come up with that doozy?"

"Not in a case." Jo smiled at him. "I went on a tour of Europe some years ago and we visited tombs. Generations of kings and queens all inside vaults under churches and the like. People have them here as well in graveyards. I figured it was only a matter of time before we find something similar here. The climate is perfect and there are so many survivalists no one would notice anyone building a bunker underground." She shot him a glance. "Would they?"

Mind spinning with the implications, Carter nodded. "I get

your point. You figure, after not finding a body, this guy is keeping his kills as trophies."

"It's a thought." Jo huffed out a cloud of steam.

"Duke has picked up a scent." Jenna had stopped on the trail and waited for them.

Carter brought Jenna up to speed and waited for her to process the information.

"Yeah, that's possible. Although many types of people are sold into slavery, they usually fit into one particular type or another." Jenna shrugged. "Mostly kids and good-looking or young men and women. Why did he take the Bridgers? Apart from their son, Mr. Bridger and his wife would be too hard to sell. If he'd killed them and made off with the son, he'd have done it at the house. Why drag them all over the county, and parents will fight to the death for their child. I'd like to examine the crime scene, but from what I could see, it looks as if they went willingly."

Carter snapped his fingers. "A firefighter maybe? If he'd arrived at the door and told them there was a gas leak, they might get into his truck." He followed Jenna into the forest, scanning back and forth looking for any signs of evidence.

"Possible." Jenna pointed ahead. "Dave has stopped. He must have found something."

Carter stared through the trees. Kane was pulling an evidence bag from his pocket. "Duke is one great tracking dog."

"You can say that again." Jenna took off at a run.

TWENTY-ONE

Moving with care, Kane scanned the area, making sure not to disturb anything. He took out his phone and recorded the area with a commentary and then took photographs. After pulling on examination gloves, he plucked hairs from the low-hanging branches of a pine tree and bagged them. Duke was still sitting, indicating the scent was strong and he smiled at him. "Good boy. Stay while I collect the evidence."

He heard Jenna running toward him and held up one hand. "Hold up. I have evidence here. Don't come any closer."

"Okay." Jenna moved from one foot to the next. "What have you got?"

Kane held up the evidence bag. "Hair and evidence of a struggle."

With care, he separated branches, peering into the distance, and not five yards ahead spotted the tip of a pink painted fingernail. He took a series of images and then, not risking the chance of destroying DNA evidence, he took a small box from his pocket. It was a first aid kit and held sterile disposable tweezers for holding swabs when cleaning a wound. He took out a pair, tore open the packet and carefully lifted the nail. He dropped it into a plastic jar and screwed on the top. He straightened and waved Jenna and the team forward, stepping away from the evidence to explain what he'd found. "So we're looking at an abduction."

"Or a fight with her boyfriend, if she has one." Jenna peered around the clearing.

"He'd have to be pretty violent to pull her hair." Jo bent to look at the marks in the dirt. "He'll be the first person we hunt down."

"Looking at the way the ground is churned up, she was fighting for her life." Carter peered through the bushes. "Is that a partial footprint in the dirt?"

Kane nodded. "Yeah, there's a couple, none deep enough to make a cast but I have images. Wolfe can work with images as long as we have a scale. I used my own foot beside them in a few shots to give the scale. There's more. Duke stopped here, sat down, then wanted to head deeper into the forest. She wasn't carried. I figure she got away and ran for her life."

"I think so too. This woman had guts." Carter marked the area with crime scene tape. "Let's go."

Pushing the evidence into the pockets of his jacket, Kane offered the scent to Duke again. "Seek."

Duke took off, nose down and tail wagging as he zigzagged through the forest. Kane slowed when he noticed another disturbed patch. "Duke. Wait boy. Sit."

He turned to Jenna, following beside him. "Look here, she fell to her knees. See the imprints on the ground?" He pointed at the churned-up pine needles. "Something happened here. The ground is disturbed again. "Keep going?"

"Yeah." Jenna turned to Carter. "If you mark this area and take photos, we'll keep moving."

"Gotcha." Carter pulled out the tape. "Stay in sight or we'll lose you in there."

Kane led the way to Duke. "Okay, boy, seek."

The forest opened out onto a fire road. Kane stopped on the perimeter and waited for Jo and Carter to catch up. "Look, Duke is sitting over there. That's the end of the trail or he'd be barking."

"Dammit, how many people have we lost on roads?" Jenna let out a long sigh. "Somehow, he got her into his vehicle and drove away. End of trail."

Moving with care across the snow- and ice-covered road, Kane examined the area where Duke was sitting. More disturbed ground but no distinct footprints, but he discovered the outline of two tires frozen into the disturbed snow. He pulled out his phone and took photographs and turned to Jenna. "I know that pattern. He's using the same snow tires I use on the Beast. The pattern is distinctive. They're RunFlat snow tires. They aren't usually stocked locally. I had to order them." He grinned at Jenna. "If he ordered them, we'll have a name." He smiled. "I'll give the local stores a call."

"Where does this road come out?" Jenna stared into the distance. "If there's mud on the end of the road, we'll be able to get the direction the truck turned."

"I know where it comes out." Carter looked at Jenna. "Why don't you go and see if there's any prints or evidence on the road and we'll head back and get the truck? We'll meet you at the end of the fire road." He stared into the distance. "I figure it's about the same distance either way."

Kane turned to Carter. "Sure." He whistled to Duke. "Check it out, boy. Let's go."

"Hey, wait for me." Jenna ran to his side and took his hand. "I'm coming with you." She grinned at him. "All alone in the forest, you might need my protection."

Kane heard Carter snort with laughter as he disappeared into the forest with Jo. He squeezed Jenna's hand. "There goes my reputation."

"Oh, that was ruined the day you married me." Jenna

leaned into him. "Jenna Alton, the cyborg slayer." She laughed. "That's what Rowley calls you but that's my fault. I let it slip once that Wolfe treats you in the morgue because you're a cyborg. I was joking but he's got a long memory."

They walked the fire road, following the projected path of the truck. It could only be a large truck similar to the Beast to be fitted with that size snow tires. That alone narrowed the search down. He kept scanning the perimeter of the forest for any signs of the missing woman. "The disturbance in the dirt was between the tire prints. I figure we won't find anything she might have tossed into the vehicle because the evidence shows she was pushed onto the tray in the back, so we're looking for a vehicle like mine, with a hatch or a covered pickup. Maybe a GMC Yukon or similar." He thought for a beat. "He'd have tinted windows if he's carrying bodies or incapacitated people."

"His feet are big, almost as big as yours." Jenna squeezed his hand. "That narrows the search down too. I don't know many small men with size-fourteen boots." She suddenly giggled. "Unless he's a giant garden gnome." She looked at him and her eyes rounded. "A garden gnome with an ax... Now that would be nasty."

Finding it strange for Jenna to make jokes when they were searching for a potentially murdered woman, he stopped walking and stared into her eyes, checking her pupils. "You feeling, okay? No headaches or blurred vision?"

"Now you're sounding like Wolfe." Jenna walked backward and dragged him along the road. "Just because I make a joke to break the tension of a terrible few days there's something wrong with me? I'm fine."

Kane slipped his arm across her shoulders, enjoying the warmth of her against him. It was bitterly cold and ice crystals crunched under his boots on the dirt road. "I wonder if Bobby Kalo would be able to infiltrate a local sex slaver site on the dark web? He's one of the best hackers I've ever known. Wolfe is good, but Kalo has the ability to slide in backdoors and move around without anyone noticing. If slavers are involved, we should be looking into that angle."

"I just can't see the value to a slaver of taking the family. The son maybe, but my jury is out on the others, Dave. From what cases I know about during my time in the FBI, the focus was on young kids under ten and twelve- to fourteen-year-olds for the sex trade. That is the biggest market. Women and men in their late twenties, unless they were stunning, wouldn't be considered. The money wouldn't be worth the risk." She shook her head. "We've been along this road so many times. You know as well as I do that these missing persons are all dead. This is an organized serial killer. You've described this type so many times to me, Dave, and it's what I'm seeing here. He planned to take these people and by now he's had his fun. He could have buried the bodies in any one of a million places between here and home. Our chances of finding them is close to zero."

TWENTY-TWO

Jenna sat in the back of the rental as they drove to the Bridgers' residence. She waited for a pause in the conversation. "Did the local cops preserve the crime scene?"

"Yeah, there was no call for assistance. It was a normal patrol doing a welfare check when the family went missing." Carter stopped outside a ranch house surrounded by trees. "Seems like it was normal for the family to park their vehicle out here. The Bridgers' SUV hasn't been moved. The garage door was open. When nobody responded to the knocking, the local deputies broke the side window and opened the front door. They did a check of the house and left. They mentioned the upturned chair in the kitchen and backed out. They didn't touch anything, wore gloves but not booties."

"That's understandable." Kane blew out a breath. "They didn't believe they were entering a crime scene until they got inside." He glanced over at Jenna. "Why? Is there something specific you figure we should look for?"

Jenna nodded. "Yeah. To move a family the man who abducted them used his vehicle, right?" Jenna pointed to the garage door. "The garage is open and maybe he backed his vehicle inside. We need to look for tire marks and footprints. Also, is there a way from the garage to the house?"

"If there is an entrance into the house from the garage, why didn't Mr. Bridger park his vehicle in there, out of the weather?" Jo climbed out of the rental and peered at the house.

Making her way carefully around the perimeter of the driveway, Jenna stared into the garage. Inside, a clothesline had herbs tied in bunches and set out to dry. Many were scattered on the floor of the garage and squashed into piles of dust. "There's the reason. They dried their own herbs. I'd say they were gathered before the first frost. It takes weeks to dry them."

"Look here." Kane had moved inside the garage and was pulling out his phone. "It's a small impression but it will do." He took photographs. "The tire squashed something green, basil by the smell of it, and left a nice clear imprint. It's the same guy." He walked out of the garage and waved to Carter. "Check the tires on Bridger's truck. Is it fitted with snow tires?"

"Nope, just regular tires." Carter straightened. "Nothing over this side, no tire tracks, nothing at all."

Excited they'd found evidence, Jenna smiled at Kane. "Okay, now we have a tie-in, we need to correlate everything these people did over the days before they went missing. We need to see if they match up with the missing persons in Black Rock Falls."

"This is what I like about you, Jenna." Carter smiled around his toothpick. "I'm one heck of a detective but you see things at different angles and Kane here is technical. He finds things others overlook—the minute details."

"Yes, there has to be a link." Jo stared into space. "A contractor is what I'm thinking. Someone they expected to come to the house." She shrugged. "Although backing into the garage, the family would hear him and complain, wouldn't they?"

"Maybe not." Carter folded his arms across his chest. "The

deputies first on scene mentioned the TV was turned on in the kitchen. The family had been watching TV during dinner. Maybe they didn't hear him drive in?"

"Look at the slope into the garage." Kane pointed with his chin. "Unless he revved the engine, he could have rolled the truck inside almost silently. I figure he drove in, climbed out and went straight through the door to the mudroom by the kitchen and took them by surprise. He'd have been armed for sure." He puffed out a cloud of steam. "The crime scene photographs show an upturned chair, which means he surprised someone. He probably, ordered them to leave. They went without their coats. It happened very fast."

"So he gets them to the vehicle and makes them climb inside." Carter stared at Kane. "You figure they just sat there waiting to die?"

Jenna shook her head. "Say he holds a gun to the kid's head. He orders the wife to secure the husband with zip ties, maybe the kid as well. He marches them out to the vehicle. She puts on the seatbelts and then the abductor secures her. It's been done before and a woman would do anything to save her child."

"I recall a similar case where the killer placed plastic bags over their heads and they all suffocated." Jo's face had drained of color. "Can you imagine how terrified they'd have been?"

Unwanted images flashed through Jenna's mind. "Unfortunately, I can. Seen enough out here?"

"Yeah. I think Carter has covered everything." Kane headed for the front door. "Then I figure we head back home and get started on a suspects list." His phone chimed. He looked at the screen and held up one finger. "Okay, thanks for your help." He looked at Jenna. "I called Miller's Garage and the tire store in town. I was the only person in Black Rock Falls to order RunFlat snow tires. The store in Blackwater was the same. Our abductor purchased them somewhere else. Or they came with his vehicle."

Rubbing her temples, Jenna shrugged. "This case is a collection of dead ends." She looked at Carter. "You good to go once we've done a walkthrough of the crime scene?"

"Yeah, but we'll need a personal vehicle to use if we're stayin'." Carter smiled. "Can we use your ride, Jenna?"

Jenna nodded. "Sure, but it's back at the office."

"Drop me in town and I'll drive it back to the ranch." Kane raised both eyebrows to Jenna. "I'll swing by Aunt Betty's and grab us some takeout." He laughed at her eyeroll. "It's lunchtime."

Jenna nodded. "Okay, but I'll come and keep you company. Only because I need coffee and whatever it is that comes out of the airport machine doesn't come close."

"Aw, Jenna." Kane hugged her close. "I know it's just because you can't be apart from me. You don't have to make excuses." He chuckled.

Laughing, Jenna pushed him away. "The truth is if I leave you alone in Aunt Betty's, you'll never leave." She pushed him toward the house. "Go, we have work to do. All this talk about food is making me hungry."

"Is that how married folk act all the time?" Carter followed behind them. "Or is it a new type of syndrome that affects newlyweds?"

"I have no idea." Jo shook her head. "My ex was too busy having affairs. I figure they're just in love."

TWENTY-THREE

The house revealed no hidden clues to how the people were abducted and Jenna climbed back into the rental. "We've collected all the evidence that's here. I figure we're just wasting our time in Blackwater. Can we head back to the airport now?"

"Sure." Carter slid behind the wheel. "Next stop, Black Rock Falls."

They headed back to the chopper and less than fifteen minutes later Carter dropped them on top of the ME's office and took off for the ranch. Jenna led the way downstairs to drop the evidence bags into Wolfe's office. She was surprised to see him, still working. He looked exhausted. "I feel guilty bringing these to you today. You really need to take a break, Shane."

"I'll take one soon. I'll need a DNA profile from Jenell Rickers' next of kin, to establish if the hair and nails belong to her. Have the local doctor in Blackwater send them here by courier ASAP." Wolfe's face was etched in fatigue. "I'll do a DNA profile as soon as they arrive." He wiped a hand down his face. "It's been a tough morning. Some of the victims were kids. We had two die in the hospital last night from their injuries." He sighed. "It's been a bonus having Norrell here. She's been a great help."

Jenna squeezed his arm. "I'm sorry to hear about the kids, Shane. That couldn't have been easy."

"Just doing my job. The kids' parents shouldn't have to wait. It's hard enough losing a child as it is." Wolfe covered her hand with his own warm palm. "I just need to get some rest. I'll take a couple of hours after lunch."

"You haven't slept at all since yesterday?" Kane shook his head. "Mistakes happen when we're exhausted. What happened to the two hours' sleep you said you'd take this morning?"

"That's when we heard about the kids' deaths overnight." Wolfe gave them a somber look. "I couldn't sleep and I owed it to the parents to get the autopsies over and done with. Honestly, if it hadn't been essential for the investigation and insurance purposes, I wouldn't have bothered, but I owed it to the kids. They didn't deserve to lose their lives because a driver was high on dope. Nor did any of the other casualties." He cleared his throat. "I'm glad I was on scene to collect the drivers' blood samples."

Jenna glanced at Kane and then back to Wolfe. "Have you finished for now?"

"Yeah, I need to write up the findings, is all." Wolfe yawned explosively. "I'm not sure about Norrell. She went home late and came back around ten this morning. She's working in the other wing with her team."

"Go home and get some rest." Kane slapped him on the shoulder. "The reports can wait until the morning when you're rested. The investigation will take forever to complete. There's no rush for the autopsy reports."

"Yeah, I will." Wolfe locked the evidence bags inside a refrigerated drawer. "I'll tell Webber I'm heading home. He can handle the store while I'm away."

Jenna nodded. "Great!" She turned to Kane. "We'll need to drop by the office so I can speak to Rio and Rowley. It will give you time to call Aunt Betty's with your takeout order."

"Okay." Kane headed for the door. "Let's hope we get home before it snows again."

They hurried back to the office. Along the way, Jenna admired the Christmas decorations springing up all over town and laughed at a mechanical snowman singing "Jingle Bells." They headed inside and she ran the day's events past Rio and Rowley. They were processing information and handing it off to the forensics team, but no new leads had come in about their missing persons on the hotline.

"We've had the usual hoax calls. The current one is they saw Santa's sleigh picking up stray elves on his way to the North Pole." Rowley shook his head. "I've hunted down workmates, friends and family of Billy Stevens. I followed up and made a few calls to get more information on him." He leaned back in his chair, twirling a pen in his fingers. "They all say the same thing. He never mentioned a girlfriend. The friends he had are the students he lived with. They all say he was a quiet guy. No one recalls him mentioning going anywhere or planning to meet anyone before he went missing." He shrugged. "There's nothing more on Maisy Jones at all."

Happy the case was in the forefront of their minds, Jenna nodded. "We'll be heading back to the ranch now. Kalo has set up a command center in the cottage, so we'll be working from there for a couple of days. I'll update you daily. With four cases of missing persons over two counties, we're waiting for the bodies to show." She pulled on a pair of warm gloves. "It's so cold outside. Maybe if it snowed again, it would warm up some."

"Yeah, and the trees are starting to crack. I keep thinking it's gunshots. I've never known it to be so cold." Rio stood and collected coffee cups from the desks. "If there are bodies dumped out there, they'll be frozen solid. We won't smell them and there won't be much left after the critters get to them."

"Ah, Maggie is waving at you." Rowley nodded toward the front desk. "And there's a man walking this way."

Jenna turned slowly as a strikingly handsome man walked toward her, dark eyes twinkling and his smile just about blinded her. "Any idea who that is?"

"Never seen him before." Rio placed the cups back on the desk and moved closer to Jenna. "FBI?"

Turning to face the visitor, Jenna smiled. "Are you looking for me? I'm Sheriff Jenna Alton."

"It just happens I am." The man pulled off his glove and held out a hand. "Troy Leman. I'm the anchorman for MVTVN, the new twenty-four-hour news channel. We've had some interesting footage of the explosion come in yesterday, and as you were involved, can you give me a story?"

Raising both eyebrows, Jenna shook her head. "Deputy Rio is our media person. I rarely have the time to do TV interviews."

"Well, how about we go for a cup of coffee at Aunt Betty's and you just give me the lowdown on how it happened? What it was like to be in the middle of the action. My viewers would love that." Leman raised one eyebrow and cleared his throat. "If you're too busy now, dinner perhaps at the Cattleman's Hotel tonight? I'm staying there for a few days. Room twenty-three if you need to think it over. We could work out a suitable time and I'll get the crew down here to record an interview. You don't need to be nervous. I'll look after you."

The name of the company didn't ring any bells and Jenna frowned. "MVTVN? I've never heard of it. What does that stand for?"

"Mountain View TV News, is all." Leman flashed his white smile again. "So, are we on for tonight?"

Jenna glanced past him and straight into Kane's eyes. He'd

come down the stairs without Jenna noticing. It was obvious from his predatory stare and the nerve twitching in one cheek that he'd heard every word. He'd moved up behind Leman and placed two to-go cups of coffee on the filing cabinet and then leaned against the wall listening. It was apparent from his expression that he didn't appreciate Leman hitting on her, but jealousy wasn't in Kane's rulebook. This was the first time she'd seen him react. His gaze rested on her, and then when he looked back at Leman, his combat face slid into place. Trying not to react, she returned the reporter's smile. "I'm sorry, Mr. Leman. I'm tied up with the FBI for the next few days. Like I said, Deputy Rio will be more than happy to give you a copy of the press release. If you ask him nicely, he might agree to a TV interview."

"Ah, but I want more than a press release." Leman leaned closer. "I want the inside scoop of what actually happened and what it was like to be at ground zero when the tanker exploded." He chuckled. "Come on, Jenna, give an anchorman a break. I'll make you famous." His grin widened. "You'll like me when you get to know me and, with what's been happening in this town, I need you on my side to give the viewers what they want. Come on. I'll pick you up at eight. What do you say?"

Jenna shook her head. "It has to be no, Mr. Leman. Like I said, Deputy Rio is our media liaison. I only poke my head out if it's necessary to give the townsfolk a message or warning. If I was out there all the time, they'd get used to seeing me and I need them to take me seriously. I'm sure you understand?"

"Then forget the interview and just come to dinner. You have to eat, right?" Leman grinned at her like some demented baboon. "And call me Troy, Jenna. We're going the be friends, right?"

Figuring it was always nice to have the media on her side, Jenna nodded. "Yeah, but I'll stick to Mr. Leman if you don't mind, and around here I'm Sheriff Alton." She could hear

Kane's stomach growling from starvation. He sounded like a huge teddy bear.

"You about ready to go, Sheriff?" Kane handed her a to-go cup of coffee and stared down his nose at Leman but didn't utter a word.

"Ah, there you are." Jenna smiled at him and indicated to Leman. "Dave, I'd like you to meet our new media contact, Troy Leman. This is Deputy Sheriff David Kane, my husband."

"Oh, good to meet you." Leman's eyes widened as he tipped back his head to look up at Kane and then held out a tentative hand.

Jenna took the coffee and smiled at Kane's expression. His gaze moved up and down Leman and settled on his face. He ignored his offered hand and nodded slowly as if deciding which part of him to detach first. When Leman paled, Jenna figured fun time was over and smiled at Kane. "I'm good to go." She turned to her deputies. "Keep me updated if anything comes in on the hotline."

Following Kane out to the Beast, she sipped her coffee and waited for him to place Duke in the back seat. "Did you see that guy's face when I introduced you?"

"Not really." Kane straightened and shut the door. "I was deciding if I should ignore his hand or risk breaking his fingers."

"Ha!" Jenna laughed. "You're jealous. Now you know how I feel when women drool all over you."

"Uh-huh." Kane looked at her and shook his head slowly. "I trust you and I'm not the jealous kind, Jenna, but I admit seeing a guy hitting on my wife was a new experience, especially when I had to play nice and not wipe the stupid smile off his face." He turned to look at her. "Not that I needed to. You handled him just fine."

Jenna put her arm around him and squeezed. "I kinda like it that you were jealous."

"Uh-huh, you don't need me to get jealous to prove my love for you, Jenna." Kane frowned. "Do you?"

Surprised by his serious expression, Jenna shook her head. "Not at all."

"That's good." Kane chuckled. "I thought I might have to go back inside and bring him into line but now I won't need to wash his blood from my hands." He searched her face. "Well, not this time. He knows we're married, but next time I might not be so accommodating."

Jenna laughed. "Trust me, there won't be a next time."

TWENTY-FOUR

Footsteps coming closer raised the hair on Maisy Jones' arms. Was the Smiling Man back already? He'd dropped into a routine, coming by to leave her food once a day. Last night, he'd arrived with hot food, towels and a selection of clean clothes— her clothes. The way he'd treated her had startled her and made her aware he was trying to get her to like him. As if! She'd stared at the clean towels and the pile of clothes for some time before venturing into the bathroom to turn on the shower. Water orange with rust had washed the grime from the shower recess, dead cockroaches and rat scat had circled around the drain and vanished in a gurgle. To her surprise, the dirty water had cleared and hot water streamed out. She'd stared all around, and not seeing any cameras, had taken advantage of the chance to be clean again. He'd supplied everything she needed, including a hairbrush and mirror. After, she'd slept in small bursts, waking with a start at any noise.

Hunger had finally woken her and she'd washed her face and walked around. Living in perpetual light and not knowing the time was driving her insane. Hearing the footsteps, she stood, unsure what to do. Had someone come to rescue her or was the Smiling Man coming early today. It had to be a new day, or had she slept longer than she'd realized? She pressed her ear to the crack in the door, listening. Her heart pounded in her ears as the footsteps came closer. She ran back to her room and slid into the shadows just as the door to the massive room whined open and he walked through, casting his eyes over the decaying bodies and then heading straight for her. With nowhere to hide, she edged around the room and sat on the gurney. Trembling as his slow and steady footsteps echoed through the emptiness, she stared at the door. Her questions always went unanswered. He didn't indulge her with his plans, he didn't touch her. *Why am I here?*

The door to the room pushed wide open to allow him to enter. His frightening gaze moved over her and the corners of his mouth curled up to show a flash of white teeth. He always had a smile. Chills scampered down Maisy's back as he came closer. She gripped the side of the gurney, helpless against an untrustworthy living portrait of a sinister clown: all smiles and hiding a knife behind his back.

"It's nice to see you clean." The Smiling Man dropped a takeout bag, placed two cups of coffee onto the counter and stared at her. "This is my way of making life easier for you, Maisy."

The use of her name startled her. This was a different side to him. Usually, the madness came to the surface and threats tumbled from his lips. She'd watched movies about people like him. He was like two sides of a coin in the same body. He leaned against the counter, and even with the stench of decaying corpses in the other room, the smell of the coffee and food made her stomach clench. "What time is it?" She indicated to the clock on the wall. "That hasn't worked since I arrived."

"A little after two." He picked up a to-go cup and takeout bag and then walked toward her. "I'll get you a timepiece and bring you food tonight if you agree to do something for me."

Peering into the bag and seeing the container, obviously untouched since he'd purchased it, she lifted it out. Inside she found hotcakes dripping with butter and maple syrup. A plastic knife and fork wrapped in a paper towel sat in the bag. Unable to stop herself, she dug in, filling her mouth. After swallowing the first delicious bite she looked back at him. "What do you want me to do?"

"First, I need a frontperson to speak to someone I need." He watched her eat, his gaze following each bite into her mouth. "Do it and you'll have a more comfortable room. I've prepared a better room for you inside this building. This first favor will be a test. The second one will be more demanding, but after that, I'll release you in time for Christmas."

Words spilled out of her mouth before her head had thought them through. "What makes you think I won't go straight to the cops?"

"And say what?" The Smiling Man shrugged. "You got into my truck voluntarily and I gave you a room and fed you. I haven't hurt you, have I?"

Incredulous, Maisy gaped at him. "What about the bodies?"

"They'll be long gone before you leave." He snorted and shook his head. "I went to your motel room and got your things." He smiled like a wolf. "I've read your diary. You murdered your boyfriend, so you're not going to say a word, are you?"

Shaking her head, Maisy stared at him in disbelief. He couldn't have broken her code, the journal on her iPad was encrypted and in code. It was notes on her life as she traveled around the US. She hadn't actually admitted to killing Zander but hoped he'd overdose with heroin after leaving her for a stick-thin blonde with needle tracks up one arm. "You couldn't have read anything."

"Ah, but I did." He folded his arms across his chest. "I have a mind that can decipher things. I've been doing puzzles since I could read. Your iPad took me all of two seconds to crack. Hidden files are my specialty." He smiled at her. "You'll go down for his murder. Staging an overdose for a guy obsessed with eating healthy is crazy. He'd never kill himself with heroin. That was your first mistake, especially with all the supplements these people buy and make into shakes. I mean some of them buy caffeine and add it to their shakes. Do you know how dangerous caffeine is in high doses? If you'd wanted to kill him without suspicion, you could have loaded his shake up with caffeine and just walked away. All this information is on the internet. When you're planning on killing people and getting away with it, you need to do your research."

Her journal was for her eyes only and nobody should have found it. It made no sense that he broke into an encrypted file and then deciphered her code. She stared at him. "Caffeine? Yeah, he used that, but it can't kill you. It's in coffee and a ton of sodas."

"Too much speeds up your heart and increases your blood pressure. Most people stroke out or have a coronary." He narrowed his gaze at her. "So, are you planning on helping me or would you like to join my other friends out there?" He indicated with his thumb toward the corpses.

Maisy eyed him over the rim of her to-go cup. He wasn't smiling now, and if he did turn nasty, she wouldn't stand a chance. He was big and muscular, with hands like dinner plates. "Okay, what do you want me to do?"

"There's a woman in town. I need you to contact her and offer to buy one of her paintings, is all." He smiled again. "You don't have to meet her, just tell her your husband will be around to collect it from her studio, he'll pay the full amount in cash."

Confused, Maisy stared at him. "You want a painting? Why not arrange to buy it yourself?"

"Because women who live alone don't like a stranger coming by, and her studio is in the forest." He chuckled. "They trust women, and if it's a husband picking up a painting, well, it's okay."

Maisy nodded. "I'll need more information. She'll ask me questions and if I mess up, she'll know."

"I have that covered. I'll show you the painting, so you can wax lyrical about it and offer her a substantial amount over the price." His face had become animated and he grinned at her. "I know what she is asking. She exhibits in the Black Rock Falls town hall and I dropped by to do my research. I listened in when someone asked for the price of a painting. It doesn't matter to me which darn painting you buy. I just need an excuse to get her alone."

Suddenly his intentions for this woman slammed home and Maisy chewed on her fingers. "I'm not very good at negotiations."

"You won't need to be. She'll jump at the figure you offer her, especially when you mention it's cash." He sighed. "It will work out just fine. She has a garage on the side of her studio. I'm hoping she'll allow me to back in and load it up from there. It's a substantial piece, but you'll say it will fit in the back of my truck."

Aghast, Maisy gaped at him. "Do you think I'm going to persuade her to do that, so you can kill her and bring her here like the others? I'm not like you. I can't do that."

"Unless you want to take her place, you will." He stared at her. "You'll mention the weather and worrying about the picture getting damaged when I carry it to my truck. I've been watching her for weeks and the paintings are like her babies. I'm sure she'll allow me to back my truck into her garage for loading. It will work out just fine." He slid a hunting knife from the sheath at his waist and ran his thumb down the lethal serrated blade and then lifted his gaze to her. "Will you, do it—or not? You or she will be next for embalming out there." He tipped his head toward the door. "Either one of you will do just fine. It's your choice. Live or die."

Trembling, Maisy nodded her agreement.

"We'll go over the spiel a few times until I'm satisfied, but when we do this I'll be right beside you listening to every word." He leaned in closer staring into her eyes. "Don't mess with me. Say one wrong word and I'll break your neck like a twig."

In a split second the detestable monster had returned. His eyes had changed to dark soulless depths and the Smiling Man had slipped behind a demonic mask.

TWENTY-FIVE

The wind picked up, dusting Jenna with snowflakes as she hurried from the garage to the cottage with Kane loaded up with takeout close behind. Confused, Duke ran around in circles, expecting them to be heading for the house. Quickly pressing the code to the entry panel, Jenna juggled her iPad and Kane's laptop and pushed open the door, only to be greeted by Zorro. Carter's dog was standing at the entrance, the skin around his mouth drawn back to display long white canines. The dog's low warning growl and frightening expression made Jenna stop in her tracks. "Zorro, it's me, Jenna." She looked around. "Carter, where are you?"

"I'm right here." Carter strolled into the family room and grinned at her. "That there is my first line of defense. He doesn't care who owns the place. When I'm here, he's on guard and nobody gets through the doors."

Not seeing the dog take a backward step, Jenna nodded. "I'm sure he is but do something or the food will get cold."

"Zorro is doing what he's been trained to do, Jenna." Kane eased inside the door. "Call him off, Ty. It's freezing out here."

"Zorro. By me." Carter smiled and waved them inside.

"Coffee is ready, and we've set up in the kitchen. I've taken out steaks for dinner."

"Good, I'll take them back to the house." Kane dropped the box of takeout on the kitchen table. "I'll cook." He looked at Jo. "Do you want to make the sides?"

"Sure." Jo smiled at him. "Something hot. Potato bake, maybe? Honey roast pumpkin?" She nodded. "I could make that ahead of time and reheat it in the oven?"

Jenna looked from one to the other. "That sounds like a plan. I can cut vegetables."

"Now you've all discussed the meals, can we get down to work?" Carter passed around coffee cups and then dropped into a chair. "Bobby has a list of possible suspects we need to discuss, although this will be the first time I've hunted down suspects for missing persons disappearances. I assume we're listing all the disappearances as abductions?"

Jenna sat at the table and nodded. "From the evidence, we have to assume foul play. Someone is either collecting or killing these people. We have five missing now. Someone is to blame and I need to hunt them down before anyone else vanishes."

"Yeah, I went through everyone I figured is a possible." Kalo gave her a boyish grin. "Thanks for having me along, Jenna. When the guys are away the office is kinda lonely."

It had been some time since Kalo had joined the team, but until recently he'd remained in the office, away from any danger. Bobby Kalo's story was sketchy, and Jenna had been given the essential details about him from Jo and Carter. She understood he'd had a rough childhood and lived on the streets for most of his young life and gotten himself into trouble with the law on many occasions, but here he sat surrounded by law enforcement as a crucial member of the team. She pushed the carton of takeout toward him. "Grab something before Dave eats it all."

"Hey, there's plenty for everyone and then some." Kane munched on a burger.

Turning back to Kalo, Jenna nibbled at a bagel and cream cheese. "I speak to you on the phone all the time but know nothing about you. Do you have friends in Snakeskin Gully?"

"Nope." Kalo selected a burger and fries and unwrapped the bun slowly. "I'm a big-city gaming nerd and they're cowboys. We don't have anything in common, and I know we all speak the same language, but I've tried talking to the locals and it's as if they don't understand a word I say. There is a computer store in town with free Wi-Fi and not many hang out there. In the city it's a great place to hang out, use the equipment and access the dark web."

Jenna sipped her coffee. "Is that how you got into trouble?"

"Using the dark web? Not really. Hacking the Pentagon and the DOD and not giving myself a backdoor was a mistake. Someone like me recognized a code I'd added and the Secret Service dragged me away." He indicated to Jo. "Jo was involved in research about hackers. She and a zillion others grilled me for months and then they gave me an offer I couldn't refuse. Work with them or be in the federal jail system for the rest of my life."

Listening with interest, Jenna nodded. "So did you go to Quantico? You're an FBI agent, right?"

"Nope, I'm an FBI consultant. I'm not permitted to be armed or carry a badge, but I do have FBI creds in case I'm arrested." Kalo chewed his burger slowly and washed it down with soda. "This is why I've been kept in the office. "

Finding his treatment, a little harsh, Jenna frowned. "You must have been very young when you joined the team at Snakeskin Gully. Where do you live?"

"I live at the office. I have a room." Kalo hunched his shoulders. "I like it there. At first, I had a room in a house with an old lady. She was a little deaf and had the radio on so loud I couldn't think straight. Carter made arrangements for me to move in to the office. I like it there. It's like having my own place, plus I can use all the equipment whenever I like. I can play games all night and nobody cares."

Raising her eyebrows, Jenna stared at him. "You were only fourteen when all this happened, is that right? Do you go back home to your family for the holidays?"

"Jo and Carter are my family." Kalo smiled at her. "They're good people. I go fishing and hunting with Carter. Well, I'm along for the experience. I don't like to fish or hunt. Well, I can't kill anything." He laughed. "We all spend the holidays together and have Christmas dinner at Jo's place, things like that."

"He couldn't come with us before, because he was too young." Carter leaned closer to Jenna. "He's eighteen now, so he can come along with us. Before when we were away on a case, he stayed at Jo's place. He has a room there and adult supervision. We do take care of him, Jenna."

"That's good to know." Jenna, smiled. "So how did you become so good with computers?"

"The first time I saw code, I understood it. I was about seven or eight. I wanted to know more and went to libraries and then started to steal books from stores." Kalo shook his head. "I know it's wrong but I was just a little kid. It was like an obsession and still is. I needed to know more. I could understand everything and discovered I could write new codes."

"What he is"—Carter's expression was serious—"is a lethal weapon. He's classified as a genius, and with his skills, it's better to have him, and kids like him, working for us. Most of them just need a break. Their curiosity got them into trouble. When Bobby hacked the Department of Defense, he didn't do anything, just left a smiley emoji, which was his downfall." He smiled. "He designed a new program to prevent hackers like him breaking into the system. He's with us to keep him safe, and the peace and quiet of Snakeskin Gully doesn't stifle his creativity. He has all the resources he needs."

Surprised that Carter was so involved with Kalo's well-being, Jenna nodded. "That's good to know. Talent should be nurtured." She stood and collected the trash from the table. "If everyone has finished eating, we'll get down to business."

"I've uploaded the list of possible suspects to your devices and phones." Kalo opened his laptop. "I'll go through them with you so everyone is on the same page. I selected all possible types of employment that had the following criteria." They looked at his list:

1. *Works with the public.*

2. *Has a profession that would enable him to move around unnoticed.*

3. *Works within a radius that encompasses Black Rock Falls and Blackwater.*

4. *Has a suitable vehicle for transporting kidnapped victims or bodies.*

5. *Lives alone.*

6. *Lives in a secluded area or owns property in a secluded area.*

7. *Male.*

8. *First priority is a man approximately five-ten to six-two, size-twelve boot.*

9. *Worked in the local area at the time of the abductions.*

"I added 'possible scratches from previous victim' as a reminder to be aware that Jenell Rickers could have scratched him."

Impressed, Jenna opened her iPad and scanned the files. "Okay, have you sorted them into highest probability?"

"I sure have." Kalo leaned back in his chair and sipped on his soda. He indicated to a jar on the table filled to the brim with candy. "Candy anyone?"

Jenna scanned the files. "No thanks, I'm good." She

frowned. "Only two live in Black Rock Falls. Lance Barker, plumber out of Clawed Rock, and Matthew Oakley, an auto club mechanic who works from his home out at Winding Alley in Lower Stanton Forest."

"The Blackwater suspects are Joshua Sage, an IT tech out of Hollows Ridge, and Wiley James, a realtor out of Bison Ridge, Blackwater." Carter looked at Kalo. "A realtor? Don't they usually stick to their own counties?"

"Nope, once they've passed the Montana licensing requirements, they're good to go statewide." Kalo gathered some candy from the jar and smiled. "This guy has an office but works mainly through an online site. He is a liaison between buyer and seller, meets people at the properties or their homes." He grinned. "So many things online now, the going-into-the-office daily routine will be a thing of the past soon."

"I see that most of these people would easily gain access to a person's home. Joshua Sage is a computer technician who works for IT-Fix-R-US and lives out at Hollows Ridge." Kane glanced up at Kalo. "Have you considered how these people would have been able to cause a problem for them to be called out, and why would the home owners choose these particular contractors?"

"*Why* is easy." Kalo popped candy into his mouth. "*How* is your problem, apart from the IT guy. I could cause problems for anyone online by hacking into their computer, no doubt, so could he, well, enough for someone to call in help." He shrugged. "Why these people? Because unless you use a certain contractor, what do you do? You run a search on your phone for someone to fix your problem. Everyone I've given you has ads running. So, when you search for, say, a plumber, up comes Lance Barker's ad because he fits the usual search requirements. He services your area, is a plumber and he adds an inducement, for instance ten percent off the first job, or work guaranteed. People usually go straight to the ad that appeals to them."

"A realtor wouldn't need an excuse to go to a person's

home." Jo looked at Jenna over the top of her laptop. "I've had them drop by and ask if I planned on selling my house, or one of their clients was interested in buying in the area. So, he'd be on the top of my list."

"So, then Matthew Oakey is a fit because we already know whoever abducted Maisy Jones pushed something up her exhaust pipe to stop her truck." Kane leaned back and smiled. "Case closed. He tampered with their vehicles, then showed and abducted them."

"There's not enough room in a tow truck to abduct an entire family." Carter tossed a toothpick into his mouth. "This guy drives a tow truck for work, but does he own a pickup or similar?"

"Not that I can see. He drives a tow truck with a logo on one side." Kalo scanned his screen. "It has one of those hooks hanging from the back for towing." He turned around his laptop to display the ad. "See, there's a picture of his ad: 'day or night, just call and I'll be there.'" Kalo grinned. "I love this part: 'I'm your knight in shining armor with a wrench.'" He met Jenna's gaze. "I checked him out. He was arrested for a misdemeanor in college and walked away with a fine."

Jenna listened with interest. "Plumbing could be tampered with as well. Most people who have gone missing are away from home some of the day and no one would take notice if a plumber or any of these men made a visit."

"I rest my case." Kalo grinned.

TWENTY-SIX

Blackwater

It was one of those perfect days. Ginger Vaughn straightened a picture on the wall inside the town hall and turned to smile at some of the people wandering by. The current exhibition had been a huge success. She held one in the town hall once a month along with other local artists and made a decent living from the sales. After selling two of her paintings in the last hour, out of the blue she'd received a phone call from a woman who'd offered her an exorbitant price for one of her pieces. The picture wasn't one of her personal favorites, which made selling it all the better. Not that she'd ever given negative opinions about her artwork. In fact, it was the complete opposite. She'd tell the clients how she could hardly bear to part with them. For some reason, the idea she loathed to sell her paintings made the clients more enthusiastic to buy them.

Ginger checked her watch. She needed to slip away and crate the painting. The client would be arriving at her studio at six. Well, not the client, the client's husband, who was dropping by on his way home from work. Of course, she rarely conducted business in her studio. Buried deep in the woods, it was her sanctuary—a place where she wouldn't be disturbed. The client's inability to collect the painting from the exhibition had been a problem, but the substantial offer and the fact it would be paid in crisp one-hundred-dollar bills made anything possible. How much inconvenience could a woman's husband collecting a painting possibly be? She waved over one of the gallery assistants. "Ellen, I need you to speak to anyone who comes to ask about my pictures." She thrust a list of prices into her hand. "Try to negotiate for more than the list price and I'll give you your usual commission. Come and get me if they need to speak with me. I need to get one into a crate for a buyer and get it into my truck for delivery, and I'm running out of time."

"Yes, of course." Ellen reached for her radio. "Tim, can you come and help one of our artists with her painting? Yes, in the storeroom." She smiled at Ginger. "Tim will be right along to help you load it into your pickup."

Ginger couldn't get away fast enough. She drove through town and then hit the highway at high speed. Sleet hit her windshield and ice caught on the wiper blades as she left the highway at the Broken Wolf Forest exit and took the dirt track to her studio. She wouldn't be able to work at the small cabin for much longer and had already packed up, ready to leave. Once the snow became heavier, she'd be isolated and the snowplow didn't come out her way. She'd move her unfinished paintings to her house in town and work from there over the long winter.

The sleet turned to snow as she bumped along the road and coated the way ahead with powder. She couldn't risk unloading the picture in the snow, so she backed into her garage. Not wasting any time, she jumped out of the truck and ran around the back, opened the hatch to the tray cover and slipped out the painting, dropping it carefully to the floor. Letting out a long breath, she leaned it against the back wall and checked her watch. Dammit, her client would be five minutes behind her. She ran back to the open door of her pickup and jumped inside. As she drove out of the garage a huge black truck came through her gate and stopped, steam pouring from it like a snorting bull.

Happy to see the client's husband had arrived on time, she parked in the driveway outside her front door and jumped out. The tinted window in the truck buzzed down slowly and a man looked at her. She smiled at him. "Have you come to collect the picture?"

"Yeah." He looked up at the sky. "I'm not happy about carrying it to my truck in this weather. It might get damaged and my wife won't be happy. You know what they say about a happy wife and all, don't you?"

Waving a hand in dismissal, Ginger pointed to the garage. "Yes, of course. Don't worry, it's in there all crated up and ready for you. I collected it from the gallery. If you back into the garage, we can get it inside your truck without getting it wet."

"Okay." The man nodded. "I have a roll of bills to give you as well." His gaze moved over the garage. "Can you go inside and guide me in? I don't want to damage anything. It looks kinda small."

Nodding, Ginger ran into the garage and waited for him to turn the truck around. She waved him toward her as she backed into the garage. He followed her inside leaving the front of the truck half out of the garage, opened the door and climbed out. He was a big man and very intimidating. A sudden shudder of worry slid over her. Would he take the painting and disappear without paying her? She pulled her invoice book from her pocket as he walked toward her. "You'll need the paperwork to say you purchased one of my pictures."

"Yeah, my wife was very clear about that part." He pulled a roll of bills from his pocket and handed it to her. "It's all there."

Ginger stuffed the bills into her jeans pocket and writing fast, made out a receipt. "What name is it?"

"John Smith." The man looked at her and inclined his head. "This it over here?" He indicated with his chin to the crate.

"That's it." Ginger held out the receipt. "I hope the crate won't damage the interior of your truck.

"Hmm, that is a problem." The man ignored the receipt and stared at the painting. "Can you jump inside and guide it in for me? I can lift it okay, but it might scratch the paintwork. The truck is wide enough for you to crawl out beside it."

Peering into the dark interior, Ginger swallowed the fear bubbling to the surface. The reason to stay and help this quiet yet daunting man was battling against her need to run inside and lock all the doors. Dragging in a breath to calm her agitated nerves, she forced herself to look at the whole picture. He was someone's husband, she had his money, he hadn't threatened her or even looked at her in a strange way and it was a simple request. She nodded. "Okay. Can you lift it okay?"

"Uh-huh." His gaze moved over the crate. "You climb inside and come up to the front. I'll lift it and take the weight and you guide it in. Okay?"

After climbing into the back of his truck and turning around she crawled toward him but he just stood there staring at the crate. "Is there a problem?"

"Yeah. This wood is rougher than I expected. Just a moment." He moved to the open door of his truck, leaned in and dragged out a roll of thick black plastic. "Maybe spread this out in the back?" He rolled it toward her. "Grab the end of the roll, kneel on it and then roll the rest toward me."

Ginger did as he said and then crawled toward the opening. "There. Is that okay?"

"Yeah, that's perfect." He smiled at her but the smile didn't reach his cold calculating eyes.

Fear gripped her and she crawled forward, attempting to

escape. The punch came so hard and fast she didn't see his hand move. Pain blurred her vision as she fell face down on the plastic. "Why are you doing this to me?"

"Just go with the flow, Ginger. Don't fight it. I don't want to damage you. I've never had a redhead before." He pushed the hair from her face almost gently. "Just relax, it will all be over real soon."

His large hands smoothed her hair, warm and almost comforting. The next moment, something slipped around her neck and tightened. Pain shot through her head like daggers and she couldn't breathe. Dizzy, her sight blurred and then everything around her slid away to a pinpoint of light that faded to black.

TWENTY-SEVEN

SATURDAY

Black Rock Falls

At breakfast the following morning, Carter couldn't help noticing the bruising on Jenna's face had turned a nasty shade of purple and Kane's bruising didn't look any better. He stacked the dishwasher and stared at her. "It would make it easier if we split the suspects list. We can handle the two suspects out of Blackwater. Kalo hacked into their appointments calendar. As far as we can determine Joshua Sage, the IT tech out of Hollows Ridge, should be at home, and Wiley James, a realtor out of Bison Ridge, Blackwater, will be in his office in town."

"Okay, that sounds like a plan." Jenna smiled at him. "I'll need to go and see how Rio and Rowley are getting along with the investigation into the explosion. I'm hoping the auto forensic team will have everything they need from us by now so we can get our full team back together. Then we'll go and see Lance Barker, the plumber. He works for Local Plumbing here in town. They'll give me his whereabouts and I'll call George at

Miller's Garage. I figure Matthew Oakley, the auto club mechanic, must work there. If not, he's not far away out at Winding Alley."

Not sure how to approach Jenna to ask how she was feeling, he thought for a beat. He'd tried real hard to act and speak around women in a way they'd not take every word he said as sexist. He sucked in a breath and weighed his next words carefully. He took a plate from her and added it to the dishwasher. "The injury to your face looks painful. We can cover for you both if you need time."

"Oh, don't worry about this." She touched her face. "I'll cover the bruises with makeup before I leave. I'm fine. The stitches sting if I frown, so I'll keep happy today." She smiled at him. "Thanks for being so considerate, Ty. I appreciate your concern."

Carter chuckled. "Good to know. Is Kane doing okay?"

"Kane is doing just fine." Kane dropped the silverware into the dishwasher. "Although, I figure I'll leave the makeup to Jenna. Then the servers at Aunt Betty's will feel sorry for me and give me extra pie." He turned away to wipe the table.

"He is not getting extra pie." Jenna rolled her eyes at Carter.

"I heard that." Kane came back to the sink and rinsed the cloth. "I've lost two pounds this week. I'm practically wasting away."

Carter smiled as Jo came back into the room. She'd been on a video call with her daughter. "All good with Jaime?"

"Yeah, she's fine. Clara is taking her to see a friend's puppies and she's so excited. It's so good to have a nanny like Clara. She's more like a grandmother." Jo smiled. "What are we doing today?"

"You're heading to Blackwater and we're staying here." Jenna looked at Kalo. "Bobby is doing deeper background checks on our suspects and trying to trace any properties they may own anywhere in the area of the missing persons."

"It's going to be difficult proving any involvement without bodies." Jo rubbed her forehead with her index finger. "So many people vanish without a trace each year. I often wonder how many of them are victims of serial killers."

"Yeah, they're outsmarting law enforcement all over." Kane leaned against the counter. "The more information that's available on the web, the harder it is to find victims."

Carter nodded. "Okay, let's get at it." He turned to Jenna. "I'll call if we get anything interesting."

"We will too." Jenna handed him a Thermos and a paper sack of sandwiches. "Stay warm."

Half an hour later, Carter put the chopper down on the helipad on the Blackwater Sheriff's Department roof. He'd made prior arrangements to have the space available and a cruiser for their use. As they took the stairs down to the office, Sheriff Dirk Nolan opened the door to greet them. "Mornin', Sheriff."

"As you're here, I figured you'd discovered clues on the whereabouts of the missing family?" Nolan tipped back his Stetson and held open the door against the blasts of freezing wind.

"Not yet." Jo hurried inside. "We have a couple of possible suspects, is all. We'll go and speak to them today."

"No clues?" Nolan looked defeated.

Carter shook his head. "We have zip. The possible suspects we're chasing down are just men who meet a suggested profile for someone who might abduct people. We're really chasing shadows and hoping something comes up." He followed him into the squad room. "How are things progressing with the explosion?"

"Slowly." Nolan lifted his hat to run a hand through his hair and then pushed it back on his head. "The people carrying ID were easy, but identifying the truck driver has been a nightmare. We believed it was one guy and sent someone to speak to his wife, only to discover he was sick at home and someone else took out the tanker." He held up a hand. "We've since notified the next of kin. The auto forensic team is very slow, so I have all my deputies working around the clock to help them pull all the evidence together. I know Sheriff Alton has her team on it too."

"Yeah, and she was in the explosion." Jo turned around to look at them. "Both of them are banged up but they're still out there chasing down the abductor."

"That's good to know." The sheriff went to a desk and pulled out a set of keys and then tossed them to Carter. "The cruiser is out front. I'll leave you to it." He tipped his hat to Jo and walked away.

Carter stared after him and then looked at Jo. "Okay, you navigate. I'll drive. Who is first on our list?"

"Wiley James, the realtor. He has his office here in town." She checked her phone. "It's the other end of Main. We'll drive. It's too cold and windy to walk, unless Zorro needs to pee?"

Carter rubbed his dog's ears. "He'll tell me if he needs to stretch his legs." He walked beside her to the door. "I hope this cruiser doesn't stink like the last one. It smelled like a trash can."

"Yeah." Jo grimaced. "I had gum stuck to my jacket too but that was when the last sheriff held office. Maybe this one sends his vehicles through the carwash and spends a little time cleaning out the garbage."

Laughing, Carter pushed his shoulder against the door and carried the Thermos in the hand without the car keys. "We can live in hope."

They found the realtor easily enough. He had a twelve-feet tall pink blow-up figure out front that waved and jiggled, its long ribbons of hair moving wildly to get attention. Carter pulled into the off-street parking area and they climbed out. The wind gusted around them in a flurry of snowflakes and sent a freezing chill through his clothes. He grabbed his hat just in time before it was ripped from his head. "Remind me to wear more layers when we go out tomorrow. It's colder than I expected." He headed for the door, noticing icicles hanging down between the blue and yellow flags attached to the gutters.

"Fasten your jacket. It will help." Jo pulled down her knitted cap snugly over her ears. "Oh, look at that, even Zorro wants to stay in the cruiser."

Taking her advice, Carter pulled up the zipper on his jacket and then stared at his unmoving dog. It was unusual for Zorro to not want to go with him. "That's strange. He never usually worries about the cold. He'll be fine in the cruiser. I'm glad I put on his warm coat this morning. I don't blame him at all for wanting to stay inside the cruiser." He rubbed Zorro's ears and then closed the door. "Let's see what this guy has to say for himself." He led the way to the office.

Concerned, Carter glanced behind him, suddenly worried about his dog. Having a constant companion for so long, the thought Zorro might be getting old tore into him. They'd faced death so many times together and come out on top, and during his time off the grid, Zorro was his only companion. He stopped walking and touched Jo's arm. "What if Zorro is sick?"

"He doesn't look sick." Jo's glance flicked back to the vehicle. "His eyes are bright, he's alert, eating, and he has a wet nose." She squeezed his arm in a comforting gesture. "Animals are like us. As we age, we feel the cold. He has a thin coat, and because he is inside all the time with you, he'd feel the cold just like we do." She smiled. "We'll take him to Duke's vet the moment we touch down in Black Rock Falls to give you peace of mind. How old is he?"

Carter thought for a time. He should know but time went so fast. "Maybe six. I had him during my last year of deployment. I'll need to check his papers."

"His last checkup was good and that was only a few months ago." Jo cleared her throat. "I'm sure they live longer than six years. Let's get at it, as he is not in any danger, and get back to

Black Rock Falls ASAP. I'll call ahead and make an appointment when we're in the air."

Carter nodded and tried to force his mind back to the case. "Just a minute." He hurried back to the cruiser, slipped inside and started the engine. He cranked up the heater and looked at Zorro. "There you go. It will be nice and warm in here for you soon." He leaned over the back and rubbed him all over. Tears stung the backs of his eyes at the thought of losing his best friend. "Stay, I'll be back soon." He reached into his pocket for a doggy treat and gave it to him. "Good boy."

Following Jo inside, he glanced around the comfortable room. A desk out front and to one side a sofa and chairs around a coffee table. Images of properties lined the walls. The man behind the counter, tall and broad, wearing a cowboy hat and holding a cup of steaming coffee greeted them with a wide smile. It was obvious not many people had dropped by today. Carter reached inside his pocket for his cred pack and held it up. "Special Agents Ty Carter and Jo Wells. We'd like to ask you a few questions."

"Me?" The man placed his cup on the counter, spilling the coffee on the polished top. He mopped it up with tissues.

"Yes, are we speaking to Wiley James?" Jo held out her creds.

"Yeah." James cleared his throat and his gaze flicked from one to the other. His cheeks pinked like the blush on a ripe apple. "I hope this isn't about any of the properties I've sold. I've paid my taxes. I always report all my income. This place is legit."

Carter had a list of things to ask him. First up he needed to know about his ride. "We're not with the IRS. This refers to missing persons."

"At this time, we're hunting down people who work in a certain radius of where the people went missing, mainly to discover if they noticed anything unusual." Jo made a show of slowly taking out a notepad and pen from her inside pocket. "Establishing people's movements will assist us in working out a timeline around the missing persons."

"Ah, okay." James avoided Jo's gaze and then shrugged. "Shoot."

Carter pushed up the rim of his Stetson to better see the man's face. He figured this guy was taller than Kane. "What vehicle do you own?"

"A Ram 1500 Classic Express truck, with quad cab." James tossed the tissues in a bin. "Why?"

Running the image of the vehicle through his mind, he nodded. It would be large enough to carry the missing family. "I'm asking the questions, Mr. James." He narrowed his gaze on the man. "Do you run a RunFlat system on it with snow tires?"

"Yeah, I go all over in my truck and take clients with me." James blew out a long breath. "I can't risk getting stuck somewhere, especially with snow threatening daily."

Carter nodded. "Yeah, everyone is using them these days." He indicated with his chin toward the computer on the desk. "Do you keep a record of where you go to see clients?"

"Yeah, I keep records." James sat down on the office chair behind the counter. "What do you want to know?"

"Did you happen to be in the vicinity of Paradise Falls on Friday night last week?" Jo lifted her pen and stared at him. "Around suppertime?"

"No, I haven't been out that way." James sighed. "It's a sought-after area and there's nothing available."

"What about Broken Wolf Forest yesterday morning?" Jo stared at him.

"I did drop by a cabin out that way yesterday." James rubbed the back of his neck and his Adam's apple bobbed up and down as he swallowed. "I often drive around looking for properties for sale and I approach the owners. Many are more than happy to deal with me. I have a good turnover of properties here and I tell them how to make their homes more appealing to buyers."

"Do you know the Bridger family?" Jo was watching him closely.

"Yeah, just so happens I do. I sold them a ranch house in Paradise Falls." James heaved a sigh as if finding something positive to say was a relief, but he kept his expression congenial. "Nice couple."

Carter glanced at his notes. This guy was being a little too cooperative, too nice. His neck prickled and he exchanged a meaningful stare with Jo. Had she picked up the unusual vibe from him too? He turned back to James. "What about Jenell Rickers, she runs the Doggy Daycare Center in town? She purchased land for an exercise area for her dogs not long ago."

"If she's the woman who walks a ton of dogs, yeah, I've seen her go by, but I don't know her." James shrugged. "I'm not the only realtor in town."

"What about Maisy Jones?" Jo looked up from her notebook and gave Carter a barely perceivable nod. "Or Billy Stevens out of Black Rock Falls?"

"Can't say that I do." James looked from one to the other. "Have you interviewed all these people too? Did they say they'd seen me?"

He is fishing to find out what we know. Carter shook his head. "Nope. Did you go to Black Rock Falls on Monday or Wednesday?"

"It just so happens I did go and see clients on both those days." James stared at his computer screen. "It was late, and I went to my first appointment at five. I signed up a client and dropped by Aunt Betty's for a bite to eat and then went out to sign up another client on Stanton at eight."

"Do you have the contact details of the people you visited?" Jo looked up from taking notes.

"Yeah, I do, but I'm sure if the FBI contacts them, they

won't be hiring me anytime soon." James' eyes flashed in annoyance and he rubbed the back of his neck, clearly agitated.

"We would call but they wouldn't know it was specifically about you." Jo smiled at him. "For instance, we might say we had a call about a prowler on Wednesday night around the time you were there. Then we'd ask them if they had any visitors, so we can eliminate unknown vehicles in the area."

"Oh, I see." James took a pen from a cup on his desk and scrawled on a piece of paper. "There you go."

"Thanks." Jo took the note and pulled out a card.

Carter's phone buzzed, and seeing it was Sheriff Nolan, he excused himself and went outside, leaving Jo to finish up with James. He accepted the call. "Carter."

"We have a problem. One of our townsfolk, a local artist by the name of Ginger Vaughn, is missing. She lives in town and I've sent a deputy by to do a welfare check, but she hasn't been seen and her neighbor seems to be the busybody type. I went into the town hall to speak to the person who reported her missing. Ellen Cartwright said she mentioned meeting a client out at her cabin who was going by to collect a picture last night at six. Vaughn was due at the gallery at eight this morning and didn't show. No one has been able to reach her."

Carter scratched his cheek and stared at the cruiser, seeing Zorro staring at him through the window. "Hmm, maybe she went to see her boyfriend?"

"Nope, he was the first person Cartwright called but he hasn't seen her for a week. They have a casual relationship. Both are artists and it's not serious. Vaughn might have switched off her phone and be sleeping at her cabin for all I know. Sometimes these artists go missing for days. It's not the first time someone in my department has gone by and found her asleep."

Wondering why this case involved them, Carter shook his head. "Haven't you been out to the cabin to check on her?"

"Nope, I have the auto forensic team breathing down my

neck right now and I'm needed here. This is the problem with the explosion occurring on the county line, both sheriff's departments are involved. I'm between a rock and a hard place here with the auto forensic team on my back all darn day."

Carter rolled his eyes. *Was this guy for real?* "With people vanishing all over your town, don't you figure you should prioritize this case? It's duty of care to at least check out the cabin."

"This is why I'm notifying the FBI. If something has happened out at her cabin, and it's linked to the other missing persons cases, your ME wouldn't want my deputies messing up a crime scene. I'll send you the coordinates. Maybe Sherriff Alton can provide backup, if necessary, as her team is already involved." Sheriff Nolan disconnected.

Carter let out a long sigh and pushed his phone back inside his pocket. "Life just became a whole lot more complicated."

TWENTY-EIGHT

Black Rock Falls

As luck would have it, when Jenna called George Miller from Miller's Garage, he was more than happy to help. He explained that Matthew Oakley, the auto club mechanic, had his own rig but took the garage's callouts when his mechanics were busy, which he did frequently. In his downtime, Oakley often worked between calls at Miller's Garage. Oakley lived out at Winding Alley but just happened to be at the garage working on a Toyota. She disconnected and turned to Kane. "Head straight to Miller's Garage. Oakley is working there today."

"That makes life easier." Kane turned onto Main and headed for the garage.

Jenna's phone buzzed. It was Carter and she put the phone on speaker. "Is there a problem?"

"I'm not sure. We're heading for a cabin somewhere in Broken Wolf Forest to hunt down a missing woman." Carter gave them the rundown of the case. *"We were interviewing*

Wiley James, the realtor, when Sheriff Nolan called. James is a possible suspect and has a pickup with run-flat tires. He was in the general area of the abductions. It seems to me Broken Wolf Forest is this guy's hunting ground. The problem is it was a gold-mining area and it's treacherous. There are uncapped mineshafts all over."

"A perfect place to dump bodies." Kane grimaced. "Some of those shafts go down a long way and there are hundreds, maybe thousands, all over."

"So I hear." In the background the engine roared in Carter's vehicle. *"We're coming up to the gate now. I'll keep you updated. If this is a crime scene, I'll call you."* He disconnected.

Jenna thought for a beat. "We have to assume this guy is abducting the people and then transporting them alive. If he had a kill area deep in the forest, we'd never find it with all the wildlife roaming around. This time of the year everything's hungry and it'll be cleaned up within hours."

"If he's a big guy, then he'd be able to carry bodies from one place to another." Kane pulled to the curb outside Miller's Garage. "Unless he has his killing field close to the mine shafts. As there are many in that area, it would be easy to use a ton of them scattered across a small radius to hide the bodies."

The forests seemed to be psychopathic killers' playgrounds. In her time as sheriff, Jenna had witnessed many atrocities that had happened in the forest. "That idea would make sense, as we don't have anything else to go on at the moment."

"It's below freezing outside, so smell wouldn't be too much of a problem." Kane scratched his chin. "If this is the case, I would say the killer is waiting for the snow. With the melt three or four months away, it would give him plenty of time to move on to another area without arousing suspicion. If this guy moves around like we assume, it wouldn't take him too long to establish another comfort zone."

Jenna nodded and indicated a tow truck parked alongside

the road. "That has to be Oakley's truck. All of George Miller's tow trucks are red. You go and check the tires, and I'll go inside and have a chat with him." She pushed open the door and a blast of wind froze her cheeks.

Hurrying into the office, Jenna smiled at Mary Jo Miller, George's daughter. "Hi, Mary Jo. Can you point out Matthew Oakley please? I need to have a word with him."

"He's a big guy, dark hair. He's working on a white Toyota truck in the workshop." Mary Jo smiled. "He's hard to miss."

Leaning on the counter conspiratorially, Jenna lowered her a voice to just above a whisper. "Has he been here all day?"

"No, he came in from a job over at Blackwater." Mary Jo paused for a beat and tapped her long painted nails on the counter. "He lives out that way and usually cruises the highway back and forth, looking for work. You'd be surprised how many people need the auto club when they're traveling on the highway."

"Okay, thanks." Jenna pulled open the door and reluctantly stepped out into the arctic wind.

The front of the garage workshop had been rolled down to keep out the cold. Bright fluorescent strip lights shone down over a line of vehicles on hoists being repaired by mechanics wearing dark blue coveralls. The smell of oil, gas and rubber filled the air. As Jenna reached the door Kane caught up with her and they walked inside. "Did you find anything?"

"Yeah, he has run-flat tires too." He shrugged. "I must have started a trend. The problem I have is that it's a tow truck, single cab. It would be difficult to carry a body inside or on the back."

It wasn't too difficult to recognize Matthew Oakley from the other mechanics. She walked to the front of the vehicle and got his attention. "Mr. Oakley, do you think we could have a word, please?"

"Sure." Oakley put down a wrench and wiped his hands on an oily rag. "Do you have a problem with your vehicle?"

Imagining Kane allowing anyone to touch the Beast, Jenna shook her head. "No, the truck is fine. We're looking for people who move between Blackwater and Black Rock Falls on a regular basis. I believe you cruise the highway looking for breakdowns and you may have seen something pertinent to our current case." She pulled out her notebook. "Were you in the vicinity of the Triple Z Bar and Black Rock Falls late on Monday night or between Stanton and Pine between five and eight on Wednesday evening?"

"I was at the Triple Z Bar on Monday night." Oakley smiled and his intense gaze drifted over her. "Dropped by to play pool with a few old buddies. Wednesday evening... hmm I was around town on that day. I think I had dinner at Aunt Betty's Café. Can't swear to it, the days run into each other when I'm busy."

"Do you recall being anywhere near Broken Wolf Forest in Blackwater last Friday night or anytime this week, especially Wednesday?" Kane gave him a long look.

"It's possible, I move around all the time. Ask around. People notice me. I'm hard to miss." Oakley looked at Kane as if sizing him up. "I figure you have the same problem. Am I right?"

Oakley moved his gaze back to Jenna in a slow caress. He was very sure of his attraction to women, and Jenna could feel Kane tense beside her. Ignoring the male bravado, she lifted her chin and gave him a dismissive stare. "Do you know or have you met anyone by the name of Maisy Jones."

"No." Oakley leaned against the side of the Toyota truck and folded his arms across his chest looking bored.

"Billy Stevens?" Kane stepped closer to Jenna. "Or the Bridger family?"

"No and no." Oakley shook his head. "Never met them."

Jenna scanned her notes. "What about Ginger Vaughn?"

"That one I know." Oakley smiled. "She is some looker. Red hair down her back and green eyes."

"How do you know her?" Kane's expression hardened.

"I don't *know* her. I know *of* her. Her face is on flyers everywhere. She's an artist and holds exhibitions at the town hall." Oakley wet his lips. "That's where I first saw her and since then I've noticed her around town in Blackwater. She's a little hard to miss, you know."

"Well, not lately." Kane narrowed his gaze. "Seems like she's gone missing."

"Well, I haven't got her." Oakley laughed. "Although. She's the type I like: small and slim with beautiful eyes." He looked at Jenna. "Like you, Sheriff."

"Well, I'm afraid the sheriff is taken." Kane shrugged. "Tough luck, huh?"

"Never say never." Oakley grinned at Kane. "That's my motto." He blew out a sigh and checked his watch. "The owner of this truck will be coming by to collect it soon. Is there anything else I can do for you?"

Jenna nodded. "Yeah, do you own any property apart from your home?"

"I have a cabin out at Troubled Creek but I only use it in summer." Oakley sighed. "I like to go fishing there. It's peaceful apart from the brown bears. Seems they like to fish there too. I figure that's how the place got its name. If you fish there, you'll get into trouble."

"Yeah, well the bears were there first." Kane cleared his throat and turned to Jenna. "Is that all, Sheriff? We need to be moving along."

Unable to get a vibe from this man, Jenna handed him her card. "Thank you for your time." She paused and turned back to him. "Did you happen to see an old beat-up truck alongside the road not far from the Trible Z Bar when you left on Monday?"

"Can't say that I did." Oakley stared at the card and then

back at Jenna. "I'll be sure to call you if anything else comes to mind."

Suddenly wishing she'd asked Kane to hand over his card, Jenna hurried back to the Beast, oblivious to the sleet pelting her jacket. She climbed inside and looked at Kane, who was observing her with interest. "What?"

"That's the second man to hit on you this week." Kane looked confused. "You used to bite back when men were suggestive and now you ignore them. Why is that?"

Trying not to laugh, Jenna patted his cheek. "Well, we weren't married before, so I stuck up for myself."

"So, what's changed?" Kane frowned. "I didn't just stand by before and allow men to disrespect you, did I?"

"No, but you've changed. It's subtle, but you're a little possessive, and I'm not opposed to that because I'm a little possessive of you too." Jenna smiled at him. "Now, if they hit on me, it's like I have a silverback standing beside me ready to tear off their heads, so I just ignore them. One look at your expression and they know I'm in a no-touch zone." She waved her hand displaying her wedding band. "I have a ring of confidence. As soon as people know I'm your wife, this acts like a brick wall." She glanced at her watch. "Okay, next on our list is the plumber, Lance Barker, out of Hatchett Street. That's near Maple."

"I'd like to make a few notes before we move on." Kane started the engine. "We'll drop by Aunt Betty's for lunch and give Duke a walk. We don't know if Barker is out on a job. I'll call him and find out where he is at the moment."

Jenna smiled at him. "That would be nice. I'm sure feeling the cold. My bruises seem tenfold right now." She leaned back and stroked Duke's head. "And Duke looks like he's wasting away," She burst out laughing. "Hurry now, before they sell all the cherry pie."

TWENTY-NINE

Blackwater

Jo Wells' teeth chattered as they edged their way along the perimeter of the forest surrounding the substantial cabin owned by Ginger Vaughn. Ice cracked under her boots. Sleet ran down her neck and cut into her cheeks. It was a miserably cold day in Broken Wolf Forest and the last place she wanted to be. They moved slowly toward the cabin with Carter in the lead scanning the area. Out front was the vehicle registered to the missing woman, but something didn't look right. The garage doors stood wide open and plainly visible inside was a crated picture with the number six prominent in red paint. Water ran in rivulets into the garage dangerously close to the picture. "An artist wouldn't go to the trouble of crating up a painting and then leaving it out in the elements. Something is wrong."

"Yeah, I figured the same, and if that's the painting she brought home to sell to a client, the sale obviously didn't go through. Maybe she decided to drown her sorrows and now she's sleeping it off. I can't see anyone lurking about. I figure we're good to go." Carter moved onto the porch and pounded on the door. "Only way to find out for sure is to see if she's inside."

Jo jumped from one foot to the other as icy cold wind wrapped around her legs. In the forest, branches cracked, sounding like gunshots. Keeping her back to the wall, she scanned the forest, seeing no one. Not a sound came from inside the house after Carter's pounding. "Maybe the garage leads inside?"

"We'll take a look." Carter led the way down the steps but froze mid-stride when he came to the garage doors. "Look here in the mud. It's the same tire marks found where Maisy Jones went missing. This could tie in the disappearances between both counties." He crouched down. "I'll take some shots before the sleet washes them away." He pulled out his phone. "Check and see if that door is locked."

Jo stepped around him, aware the garage might be a crime scene and made her way to the door. She removed her warm gloves and replaced them with examination gloves and turned the knob. The door swung open without a sound. "FBI. Miss Vaughn, are you here?"

Nothing.

"We'll take a look inside." Carter followed Jo into the house. "It doesn't look lived in, does it? No ashes in the hearth or a half-filled coffee pot. This place looks as if it's been cleaned. As if she's already packed up for winter."

Jo opened the refrigerator. "Apart from condiments it's empty. She wasn't living here, that's for sure. Let's check the rest of the cabin. I don't think anyone is here. The only thing I can smell is paint. If someone had been killed here, it would stink."

They moved around the cabin and cleared all the rooms, but apart from a few paintings draped with white cloths, the rest of the place appeared unoccupied. "It looks as if she painted here through summer and was in the process of moving back to town. She has a place in town, and once the snow comes, this cottage will be isolated."

Jo led the way back through the garage. "Maybe we should move the picture before it gets wet?"

"I'll take some shots of it first. It might be significant to the case." Carter pulled out his phone. He bent and picked up the painting. "Open the door, Jo, and I'll place it in the kitchen."

Standing to one side as Carter maneuvered the picture inside the door, she looked out into the sleet. "We'll need to check her truck."

"Okay." Carter pulled the door closed behind him and smiled at her. "I'll go. Your teeth are chattering. Maybe you should wait here, and when I'm done, I'll go and get the cruiser?"

Shaking her head, Jo followed him out of the garage and to the truck. "There's no way that I'll risk waiting here while you head off alone. There could be a serial killer watching everything we do. That forest is so dense I'm surprised Vaughn wanted to live here. I sure as heck wouldn't." Shivering, she turned her back to the wind as he searched the truck.

"Car keys." Carter held them out like a trophy. "She left them in the ignition. This means whoever abducted her came just after she'd gotten home. There's nothing else in there. No purse. Maybe she didn't carry one." He sighed. "No signs of a struggle. It's not looking like an abduction to me."

Jo analyzed the situation. "Maybe not, but if she left the keys in the ignition, she didn't intend to stay either." She looked at Carter. "Apart from the painting, it's all too neat. I think she knew this man."

"The information we have is that she was delivering a picture to a client." Carter popped a toothpick into his mouth and moved it across his lips thinking. "If that's the painting in question, why didn't he take it?"

Jo folded her arms over her chest to ward off the swirling sleet-filled wind. "She'd have a record of the sale. It's probably back at the gallery. If he'd taken the painting, then we'd have the name of the client. Think about it. Taking it would be pointing a finger at him as her abductor. This guy is smart. He could say he was held up, tried to call her and got no reply. Even an abductor could do that right? If he has her, he has her phone. No blood at the scene and no sign of a struggle. All we have are the tire tracks."

"Seven people missing between both counties." Carter slipped the keys into an evidence bag and pulled down his Stetson against the sleet. "If any of Jenna's cases tie in, we have a problem and it's growing real fast."

Jo let out a long sigh and, bowing her head against the driving sleet, followed Carter back to the cruiser. "I'll call Sheriff Nolan and then we'll go and see if she left her sales records at the town hall. If we find anything, we'll go and see the buyer. If not it's Joshua Sage, the IT tech out of Hollows Ridge"—she gave him a hopeful look—"can we stop for something to eat along the way? I'm starving."

"Me too. After visiting the gallery, we'll drop by the diner." Carter swung open the door to the cruiser and Zorro was on his feet, stumpy tail wagging. "He looks better already."

Jo laughed as she slid into the passenger seat. "He was just cold, but you should take him for a checkup. It will put your mind at rest."

"Yeah, it will." Carter headed the cruiser back down the dirt road. "I'll call Joshua Sage when we get to the diner as well. He might be in the store in town. It will save us time hunting him down. Don't worry, I won't scare him off. I'll make some excuse about a computer problem just to see if he's in town."

Jo frowned. "That sounds like entrapment."

"Nah." Carter grinned at her. "It just so happens I do have a legit question about computers to ask him. My laptop is getting slow, so he might be able to give me some suggestions to speed it up."

Jo shook her head in disbelief. "I guess that's okay, but it doesn't sound like an emergency. Maybe you should call Kalo to suggest something?"

"Sure." Carter grinned at her. "Like everything he does is legal."

The town hall had signs leading to the exhibition and they showed their badges. The person on the door pointed out Ellen Cartwright, Ginger Vaughn's assistant and the person who'd called the sheriff earlier. The young woman was surrounded by people asking questions. Jo glanced at Carter. "She looks a little stressed."

"I'm not surprised." Carter took the toothpick from between his lips and sighed. "Her boss has vanished and it looks as if she's trying to hold the fort."

Catching the young woman's eye, Jo held up her cred pack and tipped her head toward a door with the sign STAFF ONLY. Ellen Cartwright gave her a nod, smiled at the people around her and made her excuses. She hurried over and pushed open the door to a room leading to a loading dock.

"Is there any news about Miss Vaughn?" Ellen looked from one to the other with an expectant expression. "Please say you've found her. It's been a nightmare here this morning. I can't sell any of her pictures without her approval. All I can do is make a list of the clients' offers."

"No, we haven't located her yet." Carter straightened. "It would help if we knew the name of the client she was meeting last night. Do you have that information?"

"No, I don't. She never mentioned his name." Ellen pushed her long hair over one shoulder. "I know the client was a woman. I took the call on Miss Vaughn's phone. I overheard some of the conversation—not that I was listening. There was a problem about collecting the picture. Apparently, the client's husband drives right past the turnoff to Miss Vaughn's cabin out at Broken Wolf Forest on his way home from work, so she arranged to meet him there at six last night. I had Tim, one of the assistants, help crate up the picture and load it into her pickup. She left after that and I haven't heard from her since."

"Does she keep a record of her sales here at the gallery?" Carter looked around the room. A computer sat on a nearby desk. "On that perhaps?"

"No, that shows us when the deliveries are due for pickup." Ellen sighed. "Miss Vaughn kept everything on her iPad and she gave out hard copies of receipts. She photographed them and kept them on a file in her iPad as a backup. She took both of them with her when she left last night."

Jo frowned. They'd found nothing in Miss Vaughn's vehicle. "Did she have only the one painting with her? Would she have another crated up at the cabin?"

"Not that I'm aware." Ellen shook her head. "No, I'm sure. The pictures at the cabin were unfinished and she only took one from here. It was in a crate with a bright red number six painted on it. That represents the number in the catalog."

"Did she have her purse with her?" Carter raised one blond eyebrow.

"Yes, she carried one. It was black leather with a medallion-type clip on the front." Ellen's face had become distraught. "Something bad has happened to her, hasn't it? I mean, you're the FBI. You must be here for a reason."

Jo kept her voice calm and her face expressionless. "Due to the explosion on the highway, the sheriff is busy right now and we were in town. We have no idea where she is and we're just following clues. She might be staying with friends. Do you know any of her friends, apart from her boyfriend?"

"She didn't socialize. I think *boyfriend* is the wrong term to use. As far as I know, they went on casual dinner dates. He is an artist as well. She never mentioned him as the love of her life or anything." Ellen folded her arms over her chest. "She was a little remote. Her work was everything to her and she seemed to be unaware of anything else around her. We wouldn't see her for six months at a time when she was out at the cabin, but she always called and never missed a day during an exhibition. It was how she made her living and she wouldn't risk missing a sale." She lifted up her arms and dropped them. "This is why I called the sheriff. Not being here and not answering a call from the gallery just wouldn't happen."

After exchanging a meaningful look with Carter, Jo nodded. "Okay." She handed Ellen a card. "Call me if you hear anything and, of course, if she shows or calls you. We'll keep searching for her. Thank you for your time." She led the way out through the gallery and back to the cruiser.

"What do you think?" Carter tossed a toothpick into his mouth and looked at her.

Jo pulled open the door and looked at him over the top of the cruiser. "From the evidence, this is another abduction."

THIRTY

Maisy Jones paced up and down, the words of the Smiling Man ringing in her head like an earwig. She hadn't slept, even though the new room he'd given her was clean and fresh. Set away from the rotting corpses, the room resembled a backpacker hostel. She had a clean bathroom, a bed with pillows, linen and blankets. Clean clothes, a small refrigerator stocked with food, even a coffee maker. He obviously didn't have any qualms about her throwing a pot of hot coffee over him to escape. She sat on the bed chewing her nails. After seeing him wheel a young woman with long red hair into the makeshift morgue, her life had suddenly changed.

"What does it feel like being my accomplice?" He'd grinned at her and, clasping her arms behind her, had pushed her out the door and along the passageway to her new room. "I appreciate what you did to help me, but I want more. This room proves I keep my word. Help me one more time and I'll set you free. This was just a test."

Maisy had stared at him uncomprehending. "You made me lure that poor woman to her death. What else do you expect me to do?"

"I want a child." He'd opened his arms wide. "I've seen the perfect one. They go to the supermarket every second day and allow the kids to run riot. She has two, and I want the boy. All you have to do is to distract the mother and I'll do the rest."

The plan surged through her mind. They'd actually discussed tactics. She'd listened to his plans and even suggested an alternative. Her task would be to steal the baby and he'd distract the mother. Oh, yeah, she'd agree to take the baby to get away from him, but then she'd run straight to the cops. He'd seen straight through her as if she'd written the idea on her forehead. Yet he'd promised her that once he had the child, she'd be free to go but he'd reminded her, he had proof she'd made the call. He had her fingerprints on the phone and he'd make sure to leave evidence to incriminate her. Overnight the implications of what would happen if the Smiling Man was caught dominated her mind. The cops would find the bodies and he'd cut a deal and give them her name. She'd be as guilty as he was because, in fact, she had lured the redhaired woman to her death.

Pushing back tears, she flopped down on the bed and stared up at the ceiling. Her heart pounded when her gaze settled on the front of an air-conditioning vent. It was industrial size and big enough for her to climb through, but how would she open it? She stared at the two spoons on the counter. They were all he'd given her to eat with and she might be able to use one to pry open the front of the vent if she could reach it. She pushed the chest of drawers over a foot or so and, using the chair as a step, climbed on top, spoon in hand. To her surprise, at closer inspection she found the front of the vent wasn't screwed down at all. It swung open on hinges like a door and was probably left unlocked for cleaning. She used the end of the spoon to reach high enough to push it wide, but the opening was too high to reach. She tucked the spoon inside her pocket and, taking a deep breath, she stretched her fingers as far as she could reach and jumped. Her fingers gripped the edge and, using the molding around the wall for leverage, she pulled up and slid inside.

Panic gripped her as she stared ahead into the darkness. The once shiny aluminum surface was thick with dust and animal scat. Anything could be living in there, snakes, spiders or rats. Her skin crawled at the thought of them running all over her, but she had to get away. Edging forward, she moved her hands slowly, feeling ahead into the musty air. The thick coating of dust and grime made it hard to breathe and cobwebs hung down everywhere. She moved slowly, inching her way into the smothering darkness. It was so tight her back rubbed the top and she couldn't lift her head. The duct went straight for a time and then, to her horror, turned sharply to the left. Squeezing around the bend would be her worst nightmare. Claustrophobia swamped her, and she fought down waves of panic. *I can do this.*

She sucked in stale air and tried to concentrate. Rolling onto her side, she jackknifed her body and, using the rivets in the metal, pushed with her feet and slid around the bend. Darkness closed in around her but a tiny spot of light in the distance shone like a beacon of hope. She moved onward but ahead the vent narrowed. The joints between the sections had been reinforced with metal surrounds. She collapsed in despair. There would be no going back now. It would be impossible to shuffle feet first all the way back to her room. Breathing rapidly, she fought for control and rested her head on her arm. Sweat trickled down her back and thirst tore at her parched throat, but she lifted her head and pushed one arm through the hole. Her head went through next and then she wiggled until her shoulders slipped through. She pushed forward but couldn't move. Stuck against the reinforcement and desperate to escape, she wrenched her body forward and realized that her shirt was caught on the screws. Terrified of dying alone trapped inside a metal coffin, she swallowed a scream of despair and panting, rolled onto her side and eased one arm back to untangle her shirt, and then dragged her body forward. The tiny light grew bigger and soon she could make out the outline of another grate.

The dim light pushed her on. She dragged her body through each narrow section until she finally reached the grate and peered into an empty room. It was the same as the one she'd left but dust and remnants of plastic and old newspapers littered the filthy floor. She must be in a room farther down the hallway outside the makeshift morgue. Excited, she pushed on the grate, but it didn't move. Panic had her by the throat and in desperation. She thrust her fingers through the vents and pushed. With a whine of rusty hinges, the door moved an inch. Using all the strength she could muster, she pushed hard, willing the door to open. Inch by inch, she forced the door and stuck her head outside. She breathed deeply and shook the cobwebs from her hair. It was a long drop to the floor and there was nothing to climb onto. She couldn't turn around to drop down feet first and lay flat, panting not knowing what to do. Going out headfirst wasn't an option. She'd likely break her neck. *Think, there must be a way.*

Staring at the hinged door, she sucked in a deep breath and reached up with one hand to grip the top. Taking a firm hold, she eased out her shoulders and grabbed the top with the other hand. She turned and sat on the edge and then pushed out and dropped down her legs. Metal cut deep into her palms as she hung in midair, suddenly too afraid to let go. It looked such a long way down. Her sweaty dust-covered fingers slipped and she fell, hitting the floor and biting her tongue. As the metallic taste of blood spilled across her mouth, she staggered to her feet and stumbled to the dirt-encrusted sink. She turned on the faucet and waited for the rust to clear. After washing her hands, she cupped her palms and drank. Turning toward the door, she wiped her mouth on the back of her hand and moved closer.

She'd made a noise when she fell, and if the Smiling Man was close by, he'd have heard her. Trembling with the fear of being caught, she pressed her ear against the gap beside the hinges and listened for a few minutes. Hearing nothing but her own ragged breathing, she slowly turned the handle. "Nooooo!"

The door was locked.

THIRTY-ONE

Inside Aunt Betty's Café, the smell of pumpkin soup filled Jenna's nostrils. She inhaled deeply and sighed. As she raised a spoonful of the delicious nectar to her lips, a shadow crossed the table and beside her Kane stiffened. She raised her attention from the bowl of soup and looked straight at the black microphone held by the news anchorman Troy Leman.

"Sheriff Alton, are the reports about the local artist Ginger Vaughn, correct?"

Jenna lifted her gaze, annoyed a camera was pointed at her, invading her privacy. "What reports are you referring to, Mr. Leman?"

"The Blackwater sheriff alerted the FBI after Ginger Vaughn went missing. She didn't show for her exhibition at the gallery in Blackwater. Do you believe this case has anything to do with the people who are missing from Black Rock Falls?"

Jenna kept her expression neutral. "Mr. Leman, my jurisdiction ends at the border of Black Rock Falls. I believe you should direct your questions to Sheriff Nolan." She cleared her throat. "Before you ask, I have nothing further to add on the missing persons cases or the explosion. Please direct all your enquiries about the latter to the Helena auto forensic team." She stared at him. "Now, if you'd allow us to eat our meal in peace, we can continue to do our jobs." She raised both eyebrows and stared at him.

"Come on now, Sheriff." Leman pushed the microphone closer to Jenna's lips. "Everyone knows you're tight with the FBI from Snakeskin Gully. Are you working together on these cases?"

"That's enough." Kane pushed back his chair and stood. "In future direct all your questions to Deputy Rio. He is our public relations officer. Sheriff Alton will only address the public if the need arises. At this point in time, there is no development in any of the cases. Should that change, you will be the first to know." He walked toward Leman with one arm extended until they all backed out of the diner.

Shaking her head, Jenna watched as Kane walked back toward her. "That has to be a first. I know these reporters need to get a story, but he could have waited until we'd finished eating."

"It's the nature of the beast." Kane shrugged and sat down. "How's the soup?"

Jenna laughed. "As soon as I can get a spoonful in my mouth, I'll tell you."

Twenty minutes later, they arrived outside a neat log-built cabin on Hatchett. Jenna climbed out of the Beast and headed up the gravel pathway. Alongside the house sat a black truck with advertising along one side. She waited to one side of the stoop for Kane to examine the truck and then knocked on the front door. A few moments later, a man came to the door and she looked up at him. "Lance Barker?"

"Yeah, Sheriff, what can I do for you?" The tall thick-set man leaned against the doorframe and folded his arms across his chest.

Jenna indicated to the black truck parked in the driveway.

"Is that your truck?" She watched his expression as his gaze moved past her and then back again.

"Yeah, that's my girl." Barker grinned at her.

"Do you by any chance use run-flat tires?" Kane pulled out his notepad and had a bland uninterested expression.

"Yeah, I do, but there's no law against that is there?" Barker's lips curled up at the corners in an amused grin. "I figure I'll be changing them for snow tires pretty soon." He looked up at the sky. "The snow is light so far this year but it's gonna be nasty later. It's always a very harsh winter when it's late in the year and usually lasts right up to March or sometimes April."

"We didn't come here to talk about the weather, Mr. Barker." Kane gave him a long hard stare. "We're hunting down anyone who might have been between here and Blackwater over the time a few people went missing. As you move around some in your work, we figured you might have seen something."

Jenna pulled out her notebook and refreshed her memory. There were so many victims, she'd lost count. "I believe you travel between here and Blackwater for work? Have you done any work for Mr. Bridger out of Paradise Falls, Blackwater?"

"Nope, can't say that I have." Barker scratched his cheek. "I was working out at Blackwater on Thursday and Friday."

"Did you do any work around Broken Wolf Forest?" Kane raised both eyebrows.

"Yeah, I was out that way. I cleared a toilet for an old lady out at Parker's Way, Mrs. Darlington. I have her number if you want to speak to her." Barker pulled a phone out of his back pocket and scrolled through the contacts. He gave them the details.

The man wasn't acting suspicious and was co-operating with them, but Jenna wanted to push a little harder. "During the time you worked around Broken Wolf Forest, did you happen to see a young woman walking a group of dogs?" She waited a beat when he didn't answer. "Her name is Jenell

Rickers and she runs the Doggie Daycare Center in Blackwater."

"Yeah, I saw her. She was walking down Main and heading toward the forest. That would have been Thursday morning around eleven. She crossed the road right in front of my truck and gave me a wave for stopping for her." He shrugged. "I'd finished my job with Mrs. Darlington and was heading to Black Rock Falls."

"Were you in the vicinity of the Triple Z Bar late on Monday night or near Stanton on Wednesday around six?" Kane looked up from his notes. "We're looking for anyone who might have driven past a beaten-up old truck sitting on the side of the road on Stanton about five minutes' drive from the Triple Z Bar."

"No, I'm sorry I can't help you." He scratched his belly lazily and yawned. "If that's all, I'd like to get back to watching the movie on TV."

Jenna exchanged a glance with Kane and when he shook his head, she pulled a card out of her pocket and handed it to Barker. "If you think of anything or hear anything about the things we've spoken about, please give us a call."

"I surely will." Barker stepped back from the door and closed it in their face.

"I don't think it's him." Kane stepped off the porch and crunched his way along the gravel driveway back to the Beast.

Jenna climbed into the passenger seat and turned to look at him as she clicked in her seat belt. "What makes you so sure?"

"He seems like a regular Joe to me." Kane shrugged and started the engine. "He gave over information freely and willingly and didn't ask too many questions. Then there is the tires. I took a good look at them when we walked past, and the tread on them doesn't match the pattern of the truck we found near where Maisy Jones went missing. Run-flat tires are expensive, so I can't imagine he would change them on a whim. He doesn't know that we found tire tracks at more than one crime scene. It's not him."

Jenna stared at the house for a beat and then sighed. "Okay, I guess we go back to the office and regroup. I'd like to know if Kalo has found any dirt on anyone on our suspects list." She pulled out her phone. "I'll give him a call."

"Kalo."

Jenna leaned back in her seat. "We're not making much headway. Have you found anything interesting on any of our suspects?"

"No priors, as in jail time—a few fines, but basically, they're clean. All of them are smart. Nothing really of interest. Matthew Oakley, the mechanic, was a choirboy, never married and he owns a cabin out of Troubled Creek. Wiley James, the realtor in Blackwater, studied for the priesthood and left. He married and divorced, which I found strange for someone so supposedly devout. Barker, the plumber, used to ride with a biker gang and was involved in a ruckus in the Triple Z Bar about six years ago. He owns his house and a cabin at Bear Rock. That's the place where all the crazies hang out, right? You might need to watch him."

Jenna glanced at Kane who shrugged. "We've just spoken to him and he seems harmless enough, but we'll keep that in mind." Checking her watch, she frowned. "Have you heard from Jo and Carter?"

"Nope."

Jenna pushed the hair from her face and sighed. "Okay. We're heading back to the office but we'll be heading your way soon. We can work out what's next when we update the files. Catch you later and thanks." She disconnected.

As they drove through town, snowflakes dusted the sidewalk and turned the park a patchy white. She stared out of the window at a group of townsfolk hanging fairy lights around the covered shelter that was used each year for the Nativity scene.

As the Beast slowed in the traffic, she could pick out the statues inside. Each year different organizations donated their time to decorate the display. She smiled. Every time they'd passed by, they had completed a little more. She glanced at Kane. "What do you want for Christmas this year? I can never decide what to give you."

"I have everything I want." Kane smiled at her. "I'm a contented man."

Jenna returned his smile. "Yes, but I want something to put under the tree for you. Can't you give me a little hint?"

"Nope." He chuckled. "Whatever you decide will be perfect. I love Christmas shopping and we have a ton of gifts to buy. Don't forget, we'll need extra for the people living in the shelter over Christmas. I'm sure warm clothes and some personal items will be welcome. Father Derry can hand them out for us. Apart from our beliefs, for me, helping those less fortunate is the true meaning of Christmas."

Jenna squeezed his arm. "That's one of the things I love about you, Dave. You're always thinking of others."

THIRTY-TWO

Blackwater

Carter leaned back in his chair in the Blackwater Diner and waved to the server for more coffee. The Blackwater Diner could hardly be called more than a greasy spoon. Instead of the wonderful aromas of fresh-baked pies or the sauce on barbecue ribs he enjoyed at Aunt Betty's Café, this place smelled like old cooking oil. The coffee was tolerable but even the atmosphere inside was lacking. He'd decided to take Jo's advice and contact Kalo about a computer problem and pressed his phone against his ear. "Can you do something to my laptop remotely that an IT guy could fix it a few seconds?"

"Just how bad do you want it? A complete breakdown or just the inability to get into files?" Kalo sounded amused.

Carter growled deep in his throat. "Come on, man, you're the expert. Think of something."

"Okay, what about an app that you can't close? Will that do?"

Carter looked across the table at Jo and grimaced. "Yeah, and be quick about it. I'm calling the guy now."

"*Sure, sure. There it's done.*" Kalo chuckled. "*If he can't fix it, I guess you'd better call back and ask me, but you'd better be nice.*" He disconnected.

He called Joshua Sage and the IT expert picked up in a few seconds. Carter explained the situation. He mentioned being an FBI agent and needing to access his laptop. "It's an emergency. I'm in the diner in town. Can you come by now?"

"*Yeah, no worries. I'll be there in a few minutes.*" Sage disconnected.

"How are you going to bring the conversation around to our missing persons cases?" Jo peered at him over the rim of her coffee cup. "He'll get suspicious if you just start right in with questioning him."

Carter took a spoonful of the apple pie and pulled a face. "Dining at Aunt Betty's Café has ruined my taste buds. Everything I eat in this place tastes like it's made from cardboard." He pushed the plate away and reached for his coffee. He looked over as the bell over the door rang. "This has to be him." He indicated with his chin to a man carrying a small case and waved him over. "Joshua Sage?"

"Agent Carter?" Sage smiled. "This is the first time I've worked for the FBI. It will look good on my page."

Carter pushed his laptop across the table. "Maybe not. Sit down. I can't close the app on my screen, which means I can't get into any of my files, and as I'm on a case at the moment, it's important that I do."

"Okay, let me see." Sage hit a few keys and a box came up. He selected the app in the box and closed it. It took him all of six seconds. "Just a second. I'll access the app again and make sure it doesn't get stuck on the page. It's very unusual for something like this to stop responding." He hit a few more keys and then nodded. "Yeah, it's all good now."

Carter pulled out his wallet. "What do I owe you?"

"I don't think I can charge you for six seconds' work, Agent Carter. It wasn't a callout. I was driving by." Sage pushed the laptop back toward Carter and went to rise.

Carter held out his hand. "Do you have time for a cup of coffee and something to eat? My treat?"

"Sure." Sage sat down and smiled at him. "What brings you to town?"

Unable to believe his luck, Carter bit back a smile and exchanged a knowing glance with Jo. "We're hunting down people who live in Blackwater and move back and forth between here and Black Rock Falls."

"I move between the two towns all the time." Sage ordered a burger and fries from the server and then turned back to Carter. "Is there anything I can do to help?"

"Before you go on"—Jo stared at Carter, lifted one eyebrow and then tipped her head toward Zorro sitting beside the table in his FBI coat—"I think Zorro needs a walk. As you're busy, I'll take him across to the park."

Hoping that Zorro would go without him, he looked at the dog and pointed at Jo as she got to her feet. "Go with Jo. Play-time." He handed Jo the dog's leash. "Call me if you need help."

Zorro was looking at him and tipped his head from one side to the other as if trying to make out exactly what he was asking him to do. Going with somebody else was a new command. To Carter's surprise, when Jo tugged on the leash, Zorro stood, shook himself and wiggled his backside in a happy dance. Carter watched with interest as Jo led him out the door. On the sidewalk, she paused beside an SUV with the sign IT-FIX-R-US, pulled out her phone and took images of Joshua Sage's ride and tires. He smiled to himself. Jo never ceased to amaze him. He turned back to Sage. "Yeah, maybe if I ask you a few questions, you could help me track down the people we're looking for? They're not criminals. They've been reported missing recently."

As Sage ate his meal, Carter went through the list of missing persons and asked if Sage had worked for them. When Sage replied in the negative, he moved on to the areas where the missing persons had vanished. Sage hadn't been anywhere near Paradise Falls or Broken Wolf Forest in the last few days, but he had noticed a beaten-up old truck on Stanton on Tuesday morning when he drove into Black Rock Falls. He mentioned being there late on Wednesday as well, when Billy Stevens went missing. "So, you would have driven past Pine when you were heading back to Blackwater on Wednesday afternoon?"

"Yeah, it was late, around six-thirty." Sage stared into space for a few seconds and then snapped his fingers. Come to think of it, I do recall seeing a truck crawling down Pine as I went past. I saw a young guy with a backpack heading in the same direction and I figured the guy in the truck knew him and was slowing down to give him a ride."

Pulling the notebook out of his pocket and searching for his pen, Carter leaned forward on the table and looked up at the man. "Can you describe the truck?"

"It was just a glimpse and I only saw the back. Dark in color, maybe blue, black or green. I didn't see who was driving. They'd already turned the corner by the time I passed. The young guy was carrying a backpack and I assumed he might have been a student from the college. Although, now as I think it through, he didn't seem to know the truck and wasn't hurrying toward it as if he was expecting to get a ride."

Interested, Carter smiled at him. "That's very valuable information, thank you. Did you happen to see what happened next? Did anyone get out of the truck?"

"No, I was way past it in a few seconds." Sage shook his head. "Like I said before, it was just a glimpse. Although, I do recall the truck was a pickup with a tall metal cover over the tray and it was the same color all over." He drained his coffee cup and let out a contented sigh. "If you're done with me, I really need to get back to work. Thanks for the meal."

Carter smiled. "Thanks for fixing my laptop." He pulled a card out of his inside pocket and handed it to him. "If anything else comes to mind, give me a call."

"Yeah, I will." Sage stood, picked up his tool case and walked out of the door just as Jo was heading back in.

"Did he have anything interesting to say?" Jo handed him Zorro's leash and sat down opposite him. She nodded when the server came with a pot of fresh coffee and waited for her to refill the cup. "I took images of his truck."

Carter rubbed Zorro's ears. His dog looked absolutely normal and had a sparkle in his eye. "You know, you're the first person I've allowed to take him for a walk? I've been easing Dave into working with him just in case anything happens to me. He seems to be well settled with Duke. Even left to his own devices on their ranch, he would survive just fine. He knows how to find the doggie doors and the food and water."

"That's good to know, but what did Sage say?" Jo removed her gloves, pushed them inside her pocket and wrapped her hands around the hot coffee cup. The end of her nose was red and her cheeks rosy from the freezing cold.

Carter explained. "I didn't read anything into Sage, but you can see things in people that I miss. If he is telling the truth, then we have a timeline for Billy Stevens' disappearance. We have a basic ID of the truck. Now, we know it's a dark-colored pickup with a covered tray." He laid his palm open on the table. "Let me look at your phone." He scrolled through the images of Sage's truck. "He's not running run-flat tires. I figure we can take him off the list."

"Or is he as smart as a whip?" Jo sipped her coffee and sighed. "Imagine if you had abducted a ton of people and you ran into the FBI. How would you react? We know psychopaths are smart and can think on their feet. The information he gave you would have some elements of truth to make it believable, but if he is the abductor, then it might be the complete opposite."

Impressed as always by Jo's intellect, Carter shook his head. "You know I'm not a trusting person by any means, but I have to admit that psychopaths' minds work on a completely different level." He let out a long sigh. "I thought I could read people really well."

"That hasn't changed." Jo gave him a sympathetic smile. "Normal people are usually quite easy to read as they show their emotions and act in a certain way. There are no absolute hard and fast examples of psychopathic behavior for any of us to follow. This is the problem we face. Because being a psychopath doesn't mean they're killers. Many have different psychoses as well, in one or in multiples. This makes them react differently to different situations and sets the ones capable of murder aside. The only thing they all have in common is that they are overconfident. The way Joshua Sage willingly agreed to hand over information to you was a red flag to me because most people coming face to face with an FBI agent would be a little nervous. That man was very confident in your presence, which means that he believes he can outwit you."

Carter tipped back his hat, stared at the ceiling and whistled. "You're saying I could have just eaten dinner with a psychopathic killer? Do you think he could have been involved in abducting all those people?"

"Maybe." Jo drained her cup and replaced it on the saucer. "He might not be involved with the abductions but his behavior is suspect. We should keep his name on the back burner should anything else happen in town over the next twelve months or so."

Shaking his head, Carter stood, pulled out his wallet and dropped bills on the table. "Let's head back to Black Rock Falls. I'll see if I can get Zorro to the vet for a checkup. By that time,

Jenna and Kane will be back at the ranch. We need to discuss our information with them. I hope they've had better luck than we've had today."

"Hmm." Jo collected her things and stood. "Joshua Sage's pickup fits the description he gave of the truck he saw last Wednesday night."

Carter frowned. "He wouldn't be that stupid, would he?"

"More like overconfident. If the signs on the side of his truck are the magnetic ones some contractors use when they have one vehicle for both home and work, he could be describing his ride. It would be part of the game to him, to see if you noticed the similarity." Jo shrugged. "He seemed way too comfortable in your presence for my liking." She sighed. "Let's go. I'll call ahead for an appointment for Zorro."

THIRTY-THREE

"Maisy, Maisy, Maisy." The Smiling Man stood in the open doorway staring at her. "What did you think you could achieve climbing through the air-conditioning vent?" He chuckled in that sinister way that sent shivers down her spine. "Surely you didn't believe there would be any possible way of escaping this building—did you? I know this place from top to bottom. You're not the first person I've kept here for a time. Do you have anything to say to me? An apology after I've been so darn nice to you?"

Terrified of what might happen next, Maisy pressed her back against the wall. She understood being nice was just his way of taunting her. He needed her cooperation to finalize his plans but the way his dead eyes moved over her face, nothing he could say could hide the evil behind the smile. She searched her mind for something reasonable to say to him but deep inside she knew no matter what she said it wouldn't be a good enough excuse. "I needed some fresh air. I wanted to see the sky and see if it was snowing outside. It will be Christmas soon and it's the best time of year, with the town decked out with decorations. It doesn't matter what town you're living in, every one of them is the same."

"I like the holidays too." The Smiling Man leaned against the doorframe. "When I was a kid it was the only time of the year people were nice to me."

Trying to forge a connection, Maisy nodded in agreement. "I know how that feels. Why do you figure I came all this way to work in Black Rock Falls?" She sighed. "I've seen pictures of the town over the holidays. It looks like a Christmas card and everyone joins in the celebrations. Did you know that every year they all get together and build a Nativity scene in the park and sing Christmas carols around it?"

"Yeah, I know." The Smiling Man gave her a long look. "The problem is they change after the holidays. Don't you know that people are not who they seem to be?"

He'd changed in that second. Maisy stared at him, hardly believing her eyes. The man who had walked into the room looked almost normal but this man was a predator. His eyes had hardened as they looked at her, and his posture had become rigid as if he was trying to contain the monster within. She nodded. "Yeah, I understand. Many people are nice to your face and then plan to stab you in the back as soon as you turn around."

"Exactly." He suddenly laughed maniacally and turned away from the door, leaving it wide open. "They look all milk and honey on the outside, but inside they're rotting."

Confused, Maisy walked to the door and peered into the hallway just as he disappeared through the double doors into the makeshift morgue. The next door along the hallway was wide open. Nervous, she made her way slowly toward it, frightened at what she might find inside. It was as if he'd given her a warning. Edging her way toward the open door, she peeked inside. It was the room she'd escaped from and nothing had changed. She turned back and looked both ways up the passageway. He would be busy with his bodies for a time and it was her only chance to discover the way out. The stink of death oozed out of the morgue as she passed by, hurrying to the door at the end of the passageway. She turned the knob, pushed hard on the door and choked back a cry of anguish. If she'd made it this far, she wouldn't have escaped. The door, like all the others, was locked.

Disappointed, Maisy walked slowly back to her room. She dragged clean clothes out of the drawers and carried them to the bathroom. After locking the door, she peeled off her filthy rags and climbed into the shower. There could be only one way of escaping this man. She had no choice but to go along with his plan. Pressing her forehead against the tile and letting the hot water run over her, she allowed the tears to come. If she wanted to be free, she must give him the innocent life of a child.

THIRTY-FOUR

SUNDAY

Noisy conversation hummed around Jenna's kitchen table as everyone spoke at once, discussing the case and the interviews they'd conducted the previous day. The room filled with the delicious aroma of crispy bacon and maple syrup as Kane served up yet another stack of hotcakes for the hungry group. As she refilled everyone's coffee cups, Jenna listened with interest about the potential suspects. All of them were still *potential* because no bodies had been discovered, nor had actual proof or circumstantial evidence come to light, which left the team chasing their tails. The list remained the same, and although Kalo had done an extensive search to discover any other potential suspects in the area, he'd come up with zip.

"We have evidence that doesn't lead anywhere. It seems a ton of vehicles have run-flat tires, and that's only circumstantial evidence, at best. We do have the partial footprint, but all the men we've interviewed are around the same size. It could be any one of them." Carter leaned back in his chair and sighed. "We haven't received any ransom requests or found any bodies and I can't even suggest what next steps to take. We've done everything possible. It's like chasing smoke."

After a lengthy discussion with Kane the previous evening, Jenna had reluctantly come to the same conclusion. The thought that people might be out there in the cold and in danger worried her, but without one single lead to find them, there was nothing more she could do. She nodded. "I figure we should let the investigation sit until Monday. It will be Christmas in a few days and we haven't even got our tree up yet. I'm sure that Jo would like to go home for the day to see Jaime, and as the stores are open until late, I wouldn't mind taking some personal time to buy Christmas gifts."

"I hope you're all planning on staying over for Christmas this year." Kane pushed plates piled with bacon and hotcakes onto the table. "I have enough festive food here to feed an army for six weeks." He smiled. "The roads will be cleared from here to town if the snow comes and we can go into town on Christmas Eve and watch the carolers. It's a lovely atmosphere with all the townsfolk joining in the celebrations."

"Jaime would love that." Jo beamed and then shot a glance at Bobby Kalo and her face dropped. "If you have room for all of us?"

Jenna caught the glance and smiled at her. "Yeah, I'm sure Bobby wouldn't mind moving into our spare room for the holidays." She stared at him. "Oh, unless you're planning to go back home to your family, Bobby?"

"There isn't a back home." Kalo shrugged. "So yeah, I would love to stay. Would I be able to tag along with you guys when you go into town today?"

"Sure." Kane slapped him on the back. "I'd enjoy the company. Once Jenna gets into town around this time of year, she's like a whirlwind running through the stores." He chuckled. "It doesn't take me too long to buy what I need and then I usually just sit in the Beast with Duke and watch her run around."

"Okay, then I'll check the weather report to make sure we

can fly back to Snakeskin Gully." Carter pulled out his phone and scrolled through the pages on the screen. "Yeah, we're good to go." He looked over at Jo. "I'll do my preflight check. I'll need to refuel at the airport. Can you be ready in thirty minutes?"

"I'm ready now." Jo grinned at him. "While you're doing your preparations for takeoff, I'll just take my time over breakfast and clear the table so Jenna can leave."

Grateful for her generosity, Jenna smiled. "Thanks."

The white dusting of snow covered the lowlands and in the distance Jenna made out the heavy white blanket over the Black Rock Fall's mountain range. Snow might be light on the ground in town, but the skiing season was in full flight up in the mountains. As they turned into Stanton and headed along the highway to Main, Christmas decorations adorned many of the outlying houses, and pine trees in the front yards twinkled with fairy lights. As they reached the signpost to Black Rock Falls, Jenna pointed to an inflated snowman attached to the post, with one arm waving back and forth. "That's new. The townsfolk have gone all out this year. Isn't it pretty?"

"It would look even better if it snowed harder." Kane smiled at her. "Are you planning on closing the office over the holidays?"

Jenna stared out of the window, admiring the displays of reindeer pulling sleighs and Santa Claus figures hanging from rooftops. Other houses had Nativity scenes in the front yard. "If we solve this case, we'll be running a skeleton staff for ten days to take in New Year's Day." She glanced back to him. "We'll hang a sign on the door on Christmas Day and New Year's Day to call 911 in an emergency, but Maggie has volunteered to open the office every other day. We'll take turns answering any emergency callouts over the time. With any luck we'll have a nice peaceful holiday."

"Okay, where do you want to go first?" Kane smiled at her. "I'll do my shopping and we'll all meet back at Aunt Betty's."

He glanced over one shoulder at Bobby Kalo. "Does that work for you?"

"I'll just tag along with you if you don't mind." Kalo pulled a woolen hat down low over his long hair and pulled up his hoodie. "I need some advice on what to buy."

"Sure." Kane turned back to Jenna. "Here okay?" He indicated to a space alongside the curb close to Aunt Betty's Café.

Jenna nodded. "Sure." She kissed Kane on the cheek. "I'll call you if I need any help carrying anything." She waited for him to stop at the curb and then climbed out of the Beast.

Dragging her list from her pocket, Jenna hurried from store to store. She'd planned out her trip and had completed all her purchases before heading back to the Beast to dump her shopping. Her next stop was the supermarket to pick up a special order of Scottish shortbread she'd purchased especially for Kane. She went to the checkout to speak to the cashier and waited for the right person to be called. They'd asked her to wait in Cakes and Coffee, a small enclosed area inside the store, and someone would attend her. As she made her way through the aisles, a little voice squealed and she turned to see Rowley's wife, Sandy, with the twins, Vannah and Cooper. The one-year-olds had started walking at ten months and were wobbling around everywhere. Keeping them contained in a stroller was proving to be a tough time for Sandy. "Hey, there you are." Jenna grinned at her godchildren and looked at their slightly frazzled mother. "Coffee?"

"I thought you'd never ask." Sandy grinned. "The twins can play and wear themselves out. There is a playpen in the corner with colored balls inside and the twins love it. If I wasn't so afraid of someone stealing one of them, I'd leave them in there while I did my grocery shopping."

They ordered coffee and dropped the twins into the playpen and listened to the shrieks of delight as they mingled with the other toddlers. Jenna sat down at a table and smiled at

Sandy. "This is a great idea." She glanced at two men hunched over their phones. "Having a place to sit down for the guys to wait if they don't want to do the shopping and for exhausted mothers is wonderful. Although, this isn't part of my day at any time. Apart from the odd quart of milk and fresh fruit and vegetables, the kitchen is Kane's domain and he's taken to ordering everything we need online in bulk. A delivery truck comes by once a month. It makes life so much easier."

"Hmm, a dream come true." Sandy sighed and smiled as a server brought the coffee. "Now I'm not working, our income doesn't stretch to monthly orders." She pushed a hand through her hair. "I tried to go back to work, but the salary they offered me wasn't worth it after paying for childcare. I tried it for a month to see if they'd offer me overtime, but they didn't and the twins turned into monsters."

Wincing internally, Jenna had been so busy of late time seemed to slip right on by. She made a mental note to give Rowley the promotion he deserved. He'd also worked long hours and had never applied for overtime. She could and would do something about that for both her deputies. The mayor had organized the financing for the new office and extensions to the sheriff's department and supplied all the new equipment. The funding for her department had tripled this financial year due to the town's prosperity, and the mayor spared no expense to keep the town safe. She could easily have employed another two deputies without putting a dent in the budget. She looked at Sandy. "It came to my attention that Jake and Rio haven't once applied for overtime. I have Bobby Kalo staying in my cottage at the moment and he's offered to estimate what we owe them. I'll be speaking to them later today to ensure they file their overtime. I know we're all friends, but we make enough sacrifices in this job without missing out on our entitlements."

"Oh, that would be wonderful." Sandy flushed and stared at

her. "I hope you don't believe I was asking for a raise for Jake. He'd be mortified."

Smiling, Jenna shook her head. "Not at all. I'd planned to ask Bobby to look into it for me. He is always asking for things to do. He seems to be able to do so many things so fast. It's not all hacking. He's a very smart kid."

Out of the corner of her eye, she noticed a tall man staring at the children. He had his hat pulled down low and stood arms folded across his chest and feet apart like a sentry. She flicked a glance at him. Assuming he was an overprotective father, she sipped her coffee and chatted with Sandy about the twins. The sound of Cooper's distinctive "Dadeee, Dadeee, Dadeee." The little boy was calling for his dad, Jake Rowley. Expecting Rowley to walk into the eatery, she glanced up. Horrified, she sprung to her feet. Cooper was over the shoulder of the stranger, arms waving. As they headed for the exit, Cooper's face crumpled and he wailed. It had happened in seconds. She glanced at Sandy, who was on her feet with one hand pressed to her mouth. "Stay with Vannah."

With no time to waste, Jenna pressed her tracker ring. The alarm would bring everyone running to her position. She leapt over the enclosure around the eatery and ran, dodging shopping carts, children and old people with walkers. She made it to the checkouts as the man disappeared into the crowd milling slowly along Main. She raised her tracker ring to her face as she ran. "A man wearing dark clothes, six-four, black Stetson, has abducted Cooper Rowley from the supermarket. I'm in pursuit on foot but he's moving fast."

Kane would hear her and so would Wolfe, Rio and Rowley. In the distance she could only make out the man's hat as he walked swiftly through the crowd. For one moment he stopped and then turned and walked across Main. Jenna stared in disbelief. He was no longer carrying Cooper. In desperation, she searched the crowd and raised her voice. "Cooper, Cooper."

"No! No! Dadeee." The high-pitched call for help pierced the sounds of the busy town.

Jenna ran, pushing people mercilessly out of her way. Heart pounding and gasping for breath, she stared at a young woman heading toward the curb, holding the squirming, kicking Cooper. Breathless, she gained on the woman and pulled her weapon. "Put the baby down and stand away or I'll shoot. I'm not fussy where I hit you right now. A headshot, maybe your knees, but I will shoot. Put. The. Baby. Down!"

A huge black truck roared up the middle of the road. For one second, Jenna thought it was Kane driving the Beast, but when it slowed and the young woman started toward it, panic gripped her. It wasn't Kane. She holstered her weapon and ran toward the woman. As the woman paused to avoid an oncoming vehicle, Jenna reached her. She drew back her arm and using all the force she could muster, punched her in the side of the head. As the woman staggered, Jenna grabbed the screaming Cooper, wrenching him from her arms. The woman swayed and then gathered herself and pushed hard at Jenna and ran toward the black truck. Horns sounded but Jenna, arms wrapped tight around the little boy, fell backward clutching Cooper to her chest.

In a sickening thud, she hit the sidewalk hard on her back and all the breath exploded from her. In the distance she could hear sirens and realized her team had sprung into action. People crowded around her, all grasping at her to help her to her feet. Trying just to breathe, she held the little boy tightly and rubbed his back, speaking nonsense. The next moment, Kane pushed his way through the townsfolk. She looked at him. "He got away. His truck is like the Beast."

"Which way did he go?" Kane's voice was smooth and calming as he ran his hand over Cooper's head and smiled at him and then stared from one end of Main to the other.

Breathless, Jenna sucked in air. "Toward Blackwater. He's long gone and there's a young woman with him."

"There's nothing to see here, folks." Kane waved the crowd away. "We're dealing with it. Go on your way. Happy holidays."

Rowley's cruiser screamed to a halt and he leapt from behind the wheel and ran toward her with Rio close behind. Jenna handed Cooper to his father. "He's fine, just a little shaken. Sandy is in the supermarket."

"Hey." Wolfe arrived with Dr. Norrell Larson and, from their flushed faces, they'd been running. "Cooper will have evidence all over him. This has to be the same guy who abducted the others." He stared at Kane. "He's only five minutes ahead of you, is all. The Beast will catch him. Go for it. I'll need to make sure Cooper is okay." He looked at Rowley. "We'll take a nice quiet walk back to the store. He'll settle once he sees his sister and mom." He sighed. "My truck is parked nearby. I'll grab a forensics kit along the way."

Jenna turned to Rio. "Drive the cruiser to the supermarket and wait for Rowley." She turned and followed Kane to the Beast. "Let's catch this guy."

THIRTY-FIVE

Kane handed Duke's leash to Kalo. "Head down to Aunt Betty's Café. We'll meet you there later."

"You can't come with us. It's going to be a rough ride." Jenna smiled at him. "Take care of Duke." She strapped in and turned to Kane. "Do you think we can catch him?"

Trying to control the rush of anger welling inside, Kane dropped into the zone. He'd need every ounce of concentration to catch this man, and when he did, he'd need every ounce of control not to tear him limb from limb. He started the engine and hit the lights and sirens to get through the traffic. He needed help and turned to Jenna. "Carter is heading this way. He called me just before. Jo asked Wolfe if Jaime could stay with his daughters while we worked this case. As all three of them are at home at the moment with his housekeeper, he was more than happy to have her stay for a few days. Jaime is over the moon to be able to see her friends again."

"That's great." Jenna was gripping the side of the seat. "If you're trying to talk to me to keep me calm, don't worry, I'm fine. I'm used to your driving and flying along the highway at incredible speeds."

The Beast's engine roared as Kane accelerated along Stanton. Traffic moved to the side of the highway to allow him to pass. As they reached the on-ramp toward Blackwater, he glanced at her. "Contact the airport and ask them to radio Carter. You know his call sign. Tell them to inform him that you are texting Agent Jo Wells. When you get a confirmation, send a message to Jo with the description of the truck we're chasing down. Carter will be able to get ahead of me faster than I can drive and be able to send us the coordinates. It will be the only chance we have of catching him. He could have taken any of the side roads to parts unknown in the time he's been gone."

Minutes later Jenna confirmed that the message had gone through to Carter. As they sped along the highway, the Beast passed vehicles as if they were standing still. Kane kept his gaze on the road ahead, hoping to see the black truck in the distance. They had been traveling for about ten minutes when the FBI chopper flew above them and took off in the distance. Ahead, a line of eighteen-wheelers traveled in a convoy. Kane slowed the Beast but kept a good distance from the last truck. He would need room to accelerate the moment the road ahead became clear enough to overtake the convoy. Beside him he could hear Jenna's sharp intake of breath as he slammed his foot down on the gas and the front of the Beast lifted. In a roar of precise mechanical engineering, his black truck responded and they pulled out to pass the convoy. In a *whoosh, whoosh, whoosh* as they passed each one, Kane had the sensation of flying. Ahead on their side of the road, vehicles were heading in their direction. Slowing down now would be suicide. He slid his hand down to the nitro switch. In a blast of power, the Beast took off at high speed and seconds later they had passed the trucks and moved back onto the right side of the road.

"The truck has left the highway." Jenna was staring at her phone. "He's heading out across the flatlands. Take the next exit."

This was part of Black Rock Falls that Kane had never visited. He slowed the Beast and they shot down the off-ramp. "What's out this way?"

"Not much." Jenna kept her gaze on her phone. "Many years ago there was a prosperous mining town here, but they closed the railroad loop that serviced it and it became a ghost town."

Kane flicked her a glance. "The railroad is still there. The track runs from Helena and all the way through to Washington."

"Yeah, it does, but long ago many little offshoots were closed during the Depression. Towns died. Not all of them though. Some of them are doing well." Jenna read another message. "It looks like he is heading for the ghost town. See the signpost that says MINER'S END. Take that road. It's straight all the way and crosses the railroad track. He must be holed up in one of the abandoned buildings."

Kane stared out across the lowlands and in the distance he could make out a small speck moving away from them. "That has to be him. Please tell me that we're still in our jurisdiction."

"Yeah, the border is miles away." Jenna went back to her phone.

Considering the threat, Kane turned to her. "Give me a description of this guy."

"He's big and muscular. I didn't see a weapon but he moved easy." Jenna looked at him. "He could be any one of our suspects but I'm leaning toward Joshua Sage or Matthew Oakley. Both these men have the right build and are young enough to walk in that smooth way, like the way someone trained to fight walks. Like you do."

The anger Kane was trying to suppress filtered through again. As Cooper's godfather, he kept a place in his heart for the little boy, the same as his sister. He doted on Cooper and the thought that someone had snatched him while he was in town made him as mad as heck. "Good, then it will be a fair fight."

"Dave, this is so not like you." Jenna squeezed his arm as they tore along the straight road at high speed. "We'll take him down and find out what he's done with the other people. If this is him. He might not even be involved in the other abductions. You can't just beat him up for taking Cooper."

Kane flicked her a glance. "I have one rule I live by, Jenna. One sacred rule that can never be broken. All the things I've done in my life, all the orders I've carried out. I've killed because it was my job, and I did it for my country or to protect people. I'm a trained killing machine but I know what's right and what's wrong, so I obey orders. To be able to do this without a conscience, I live by one simple rule: nobody touches what's mine."

A message signaled on Jenna's phone. She said nothing to him but glanced up, her eyes troubled. "There's a freight train coming. Jo says he is heading straight for the crossing and not slowing down. She figures he's going to try and outrun it."

Kane nodded. "Maybe he's seen the chopper? I can't see it now. It must be above us somewhere. Ask them." He waited for Jenna to send a message and seconds later a reply came back. "What did they say?"

"No, they said since the get-go they've been high and just observing so they didn't spook him." Jenna stared at her phone. "They said they'll be right there the moment you need them."

In the distance the freight train and its endless boxcars went on forever. They'd never make it in time. The only choice they had would be for Carter to follow the other truck and see where it was going. Kane shook his head. "We'll be stuck on this side of the track. Tell them to watch at a distance. We'll follow and take them into custody when we can. Then we'll need his assistance for backup."

"Copy that." Jenna blew out a long breath. "I'll message

Rio, he should start heading this way as well. We can't carry prisoners in the Beast."

Kane barked a laugh. "Not Wolfe?"

"You won't kill him." Jenna leaned back in her seat. "You'll want to find out about the others just as much as I do." She sighed. "Believe it or not, I agree with your rule. If anything happened to me, it's comforting to know you'd avenge me. I sure as heck would avenge you."

THIRTY-SIX

The long wheatgrass flashed by in a streak of golden brown as they hurtled toward the railway track. The road had seen better days and Kane weaved around potholes and tumbleweeds but hardly slowed the breakneck speed. They had gained on the black truck and could see it clearly ahead of them. Jenna's heart skipped a beat at the sight of the train. It was moving at high speed and ahead in the distance the railroad-crossing lights flashed, but the black truck didn't slow down. "He's trying to beat the train." She held her breath and stared in disbelief. "He's not going to make it."

The train driver had seen the truck heading toward the crossing. A loud whistle issued a warning, but the black truck increased its speed toward certain death. The sound of screaming metal blasted into the air as the train hit the brakes. Sparks flew from the metal wheels as they slid along the tracks in a trail of flames. The next second, an explosion shook the ground, sending birds flying into the sky as the train obliterated the black truck. The screeching, torn wreck was dragged hundreds of yards along the track. Twisted metal and glass flew into the air, peppering the ground over a wide area. The earsplitting squeal of brakes went on forever as the train came to a slow stop. Kane drove alongside the tracks and parked some distance away from the wreck. Horrified, Jenna stared at the remains of the truck. It had been ripped in two. The front was gone completely and the back had spun away and sat nose down in the long wheatgrass. The back half appeared almost untouched. The sight sickened her. "Sweet Jesus. There are two people in that truck."

As the chopper dropped into sight and landed some ways away, Jenna climbed out of the Beast. She pulled out her phone to call Wolfe and explained the situation. She stared at Kane, who was walking along beside the train, checking under each boxcar from the crash site and all the way to the front of the train. From the bloody carnage spread all around her, the driver hadn't survived. She headed for the back section of the truck to search for any survivors and was met by Carter. "What a mess. Why did he do this? Do you think it was suicide?"

"Nah, from the speed, he figured he'd make it." Carter moved a toothpick across his lips. "It's a common error. People can't estimate the speed of a locomotive." He indicated to the chopper. Jo is staying in the chopper with Jaime. It's best she doesn't see the wreck." He blew out a long breath. "Let's take a look at the remaining section. You mentioned he had a young woman with him." He stopped walking and removed his hat. "Well, I'll be..."

Jenna stared in the same direction. The backdoor of the truck opened slowly in a creak of damaged metal and a young woman came out and collapsed in a heap. "That looks like the woman who had Cooper."

"There are body parts all over the track and under the boxcars." Kane came up behind them. "There's an arm just over yonder. We might be able to identify him by his prints. Kalo mentioned a couple of our suspects had been arrested for a misdemeanor." He stared at the young woman. "Is she alive?"

"Could be, she climbed out easily enough." Carter headed toward the wreck. "I'll go see." When he reached her, he bent and checked for a pulse. "Yeah, she's alive and I recognize her. This is Maisy Jones."

Amazed, Jenna went to his side and kneeled down beside the young woman. Maisy's eyes flickered open and she looked at Jenna but said nothing. "Where does it hurt?"

"I think I'm okay." Maisy wiggled her fingers and toes. "My head hurts but when I realized what he was doing, I lifted my legs across the back seat." She sat up slowly, holding her head. "That man kidnapped me and kept me in a room with corpses. I tried to escape."

"What were you doing with him in town, and if you were in danger, why didn't you go for help?" Kane glared at her. "You must have been waiting on the sidewalk for him to come along with the baby. You helped him, didn't you?"

"You don't understand." Maisy brushed away tears. "He'd never let me go. I had to make a bargain with him. He would have found me and taken me back and killed me. He is insane. He collects dead people. He murders people."

"You helped him kidnap a baby and you knew he planned to kill him." Kane's face had drained of color. "You stood by and allowed this to happen. You're as guilty as he is." He shook his head. "You disgust me. All you thought about was saving yourself."

"There's a warrant out for her arrest in Idaho." Carter stared at Kane. "She's wanted for the murder of Zander Hastings." He bent and cuffed her and then dragged her to a sitting position by the back of her jacket. He bent down close to her face. "When the Black Rock Falls Sheriff's Department has finished with you, you're mine."

Shocked, Jenna rubbed both hands down her face. Both Kane and Carter were walking a very fine line and she needed to take control. She walked away from Maisy and beckoned them to follow her. She lowered her voice. "Stand down, both of you. She's innocent until proven guilty, and you darn well know it. That was my godson too, Dave, and I'm as mad as you are, but we follow the rules to the darn letter. Right now, because of our relationship to Cooper, we need to step away. Rio will be here soon and he'll take over the case or she'll walk on conflict of interest."

"Maybe for her part in the kidnapping." Kane hadn't taken his eyes off Maisy. "It's not a conflict of interest where the abductor is involved. I'm sure as heck not walking away from finding the other people he's taken."

This was Jenna's first trainwreck and she would need to contact various local departments to deal with it. Turning to Kane, she waved a hand at the train. "The train can't leave. Can you go and speak to the driver and make sure he's okay? He must be in shock."

"I'll go." Carter stared toward the front of the train. "We'll need the details for a report. Maisy seems to want to talk, maybe she'll tell you where he was keeping the others." He shrugged. "You can keep it off the record. No harm, no foul."

Unsure, Jenna frowned. "I guess I can't stop her talking."

"I'll call the disaster and emergency services coordinator. They'll send out all the appropriate people." Kane pulled out his phone and scrolled the contacts list. "Wolfe is on the way, so we have that area covered. He'll collect what's left of the abductor and hopefully identify him by his prints. I'll run his plates. We might find him that way."

Keeping her eyes averted from the carnage alongside the track, Jenna walked back to speak to Maisy Jones. Glass sparkled in the grass and she sidestepped bits and pieces of twisted metal. The body of the abductor was spread over a wide area, but she decided not to look too closely at the debris around her. She sat down beside Maisy and pulled out her notebook to take down information. She looked at the young woman. "You don't have to say anything to me, but if you have any idea where the other people are being held, I will put in a good word for you with the DA."

"I don't know exactly where he was keeping them." Maisy rubbed her cheek on her shoulder and dropped her gaze to her knees. "He blindfolded me until we got to the outskirts of Black Rock Falls."

Jenna nodded. "Can you describe what type of building it was?"

"I figure it was an old hospital or an asylum." Maisy lifted her head and turned to Jenna. "Inside was all tile, like hospital wards or operating theaters. That's the only part of the building I was able to see. At first, he kept me in a small room that led to a bigger room with those double doors you see at hospitals. The room I was in was more like a private room, but it was filthy and old. Everything in there was old. The gurney he gave me to sleep on looked as if it was made in the 1950s."

Listening intently, Jenna gave her a sympathetic look. "You mentioned something about corpses?"

"Yeah." Maisy shuddered. "In the main room he brought in different people all the time. I recognized the first three. You see, my truck broke down after I left the Triple Z Bar. It was a little after midnight and I had to walk back along Stanton to the motel. This guy in a big black truck pulled up and offered me a ride. It was so cold and, as the motel was only a few minutes away, I decided to take the risk. He locked the doors and when I turned around there were three people sitting in the back seat and they were all dead. He covered my mouth with something that stunk and I don't recall anything else until I woke up inside the small room the next day."

Making fast notes, Jenna stared at her. "That first morning, what did you see?"

"The place stunk of death and he kept me locked inside with dead bodies." Maisy looked at her wide-eyed. "I was so scared, but I went into the other room to look for a way to escape. The bodies of the people—a man, a woman and a young boy—were hooked up to a machine that drained out their blood into buckets. The same thing happened all the time. Bodies would disappear overnight only to be replaced by others."

Appalled, Jenna swallowed hard. "He drained their blood?"

"Yeah and pumped them full of some other stuff." Maisy shrugged. "You know the stuff that smells like a funeral parlor? He used that. The blood came out and that went in."

Jenna stared at her in disbelief. "Then what did he do with them?"

"I don't know." Maisy sniffed. "He wheeled them out of the room and in the morning, there were more in their place."

In her opinion, Maisy appear to be well-fed for someone that had been missing for a week. "I assume that your abductor kept you alive for a reason. What was that? Do you know?"

"Yeah, he wanted me to call an artist and make arrangements for him to go and collect a picture out of Broken Wolf Forest." Maisy shrugged. "I was hungry and he offered me food to do it. I didn't know he was going to kill her."

"You knew he was going to kill the baby, didn't you?" Kane was standing right behind them listening.

"No." Maisy burst into tears. "He promised he'd let me go free."

"I'll call Kalo. Maybe he can locate any old hospital buildings close by." Kane pulled out his phone. He looked at Carter as he walked toward them. "We're going to need you to help sort out this mess, especially if we have to stand down. Can you take Jaime to Wolfe's house and come back?"

"Sure." Carter looked at Jenna. "Is that okay with you, Jenna? I'll be at least thirty minutes."

Trying to process the information that Maisy had given her, Jenna nodded. "Yeah, sure. Did you get anything interesting from the driver of the train?"

"Nope." Carter shrugged. "He tried to stop, but it was impossible with the number of boxcars he was haulin'. He's shaken but seems okay. There are two men in the locomotive, both are fine. It was fortunate we didn't have a derailment. Once this mess is cleaned up, he'll be able to be on his way if Wolfe considers him fit. It's not the first time someone drove in front of him." He indicated to the chopper. "I'll be back soon." He ran to the helicopter.

Jenna stood and walked away to where Kane was speaking on his phone to Kalo. "What's up?"

"Rio was at Aunt Betty's Café when I called, and Kalo and Duke are with him." He removed his hat and scraped a hand through his hair. "Rowley is on his way as well. Sandy's mother is with her and he figured we'd need him here."

Jenna shook her head slowly. "I should have promoted him years ago."

THIRTY-SEVEN

It seemed like hours before Wolfe and the others arrived. She dispatched Rio with Maisy Jones as soon as Wolfe had examined her. The disaster and emergency services coordinator had everyone organized and doing their jobs. Wolfe and his team were collecting body parts, and after a time, Wolfe came to her side. She looked at him. "I don't envy you, your job today."

"Well, at least I have some good news at last." Wolfe frowned at her. "The driver was the owner of the truck. The prints match Matthew Oakley, the auto club mechanic out of Winding Alley." He watched her reaction. "Was he on the suspects' list?"

Jenna recalled the handsome man who had hit on her at Miller's Garage. To think he'd ended up in pieces made her stomach churn. He'd been the overconfident, typical type for a psychopath. Overconfident to the end, it seemed. By trying to beat the locomotive, he'd not only killed himself but had taken his secrets to the grave. "Yeah, we interviewed him. He was working at Miller's Garage." She raised her eyes to Wolfe. "I wonder what he did with the others."

"You'll find them, Jenna." Wolfe smiled at her and turned back to his team.

She walked over to Kane. "We have an ID: Matthew Oakley, the auto club mechanic. I'm surprised he hit on me. Seems he preferred to play with dead bodies."

"Yeah, he did stink." Kane stared at the evidence bags piling up in the back of Wolfe's van. "I figured it was really rank body odor."

The FBI chopper landed a few yards away from the Beast. Before the blades had stopped spinning, Jenna, Kane and Duke headed toward it, grabbing Kalo on the way. With Kalo's information on the local towns, they needed Carter to fly over the ghost town to hunt down an old building that could be a hospital. They climbed inside and he took off. From the air, Jenna could see exactly how much damage had occurred in the trainwreck. Debris was scattered in all directions on both sides of the train. In the distance she made out the outskirts of a dusty old town. The railroad track still existed but had been disconnected from the main line. The chopper circled the town, going back and forth. In her headphone she could hear Carter speaking with Kane.

"That has to be the hospital." Carter's voice came through her headset. *"Down there on the right. I can drop the chopper in the park opposite. It's not too far to walk from there."*

Jenna glanced at Kane. "Maisy said he kept the doors locked. How are we going to get inside?"

"They haven't made a lock I can't open." Kane grinned at her. *"I'd have made a great thief."*

When the chopper landed, they all climbed out, including the two dogs. Jenna stared along the deserted, dusty sidewalks. The hospital still had the signage out front but some of the windows were broken. Alongside, storefronts still held advertising in the windows. It was as if whoever had been in this town had just walked out and left it to rot. She followed the others across the road and up the front steps to the hospital entrance. To her surprise, the doors swung open easily. Inside was a front counter, behind that, hallways leading in different directions. She turned to Kane. "Which way?"

"I figured from what Maisy said, we should be looking for the operating theaters." Kane went to a list displayed on a notice board beside a map of the building. "This way."

As they headed down the passageway, the terrible stench of death greeted them. Mottled light came through the dusty windows but the passageway gave Jenna the creeps and she instinctively reached for her flashlight. The first three rooms they peered into were empty. It was obvious no one had been in there for a very long time. They followed the stench of death and came to a locked door, but outside on a hook was a bunch of keys. "We can't be that lucky, can we?" She stood to one side as Kane tried each one in the lock.

Inside, they found what Maisy had described: the large tiled room, a line of gurneys against one wall and a small room that looked lived in. They split up and searched every nook and cranny. No bodies. All Jenna found was an old gas generator set up in the middle of the room. She met up with the others in the hallway. "Tell me you found something."

"The equipment is there, just as Maisy described it." Jo raised her eyebrows. "It's a typical embalming set up. I've seen similar used by undertakers. They could have had a morgue here at one time and I would say this was some of the equipment that was left behind."

"One other thing, there is a bath in one of the rooms that's been used for something, a chemical maybe?" Carter held up an evidence bag. "I've taken samples of the residue in the bottom of the tub. Apart from that, we found zip."

"Same here." Kane looked all around. "I figure whatever he was doing here he'd finished up before he tried to abduct Cooper. He was probably planning on moving on. I guess we take a look around the outside of the building, just in case he's buried the corpses." He turned to Kalo. "Do you recall if there is a crematorium around here anywhere?"

"Even if there was, it wouldn't have been any use to him." Kalo shrugged. "It takes a ton of power to run a crematorium, and as far as I can see, there hasn't been any connected here for years."

Jenna listened with interest to the discussion. "I figure we go and search his house. He lives out at Winding Alley in Black Rock Falls." She looked at Carter. "We'll go and pick up the Beast and meet you in town."

"Sure." Carter rubbed his belly. "Make it at Aunt Betty's. Breakfast was a long time ago. We'll grab something to go."

After, they walked around the town searching for any disturbed patches of ground and found nothing. Even the old churchyard was dilapidated and neglected. They climbed into the chopper and headed back to the crash site. Jenna walked up to Wolfe to get an update. "What's happening?"

"The track has been cleared." Wolfe rubbed the back of his neck. "We've collected all the body parts and I've cleared the driver and his assistant as healthy. They are both in good shape and I also tested them for alcohol and drugs. They both came up clean for the usual things. I figure they're good to go. The crash investigation team and all these other people are doing their own thing. I have no idea how long they plan to be here, but sometimes these things can take weeks, so you have to hand over to the person in charge and just walk away. They'll send you a report when they're done." He smiled at Norrell, who was standing beside him looking as fresh as a daisy. "It was great having Norrell with me today. We had a jigsaw puzzle of bone fragments and she managed to fit them together at the speed of light."

"That's just what I do." Norrell smiled at Jenna. "But it's really great to be appreciated. In my line of work, the cases are usually so cold most of the relatives of the victims are deceased."

Jenna laughed. "Yeah, well being a forensic anthropologist would be intriguing. I know Wolfe's daughter Emily is very interested in your specialty."

"One step at a time." Wolfe narrowed his gaze at Jenna. "I don't want Emily to run before she can walk."

"I've just spoken to the coordinator guy and he'll be here for days." Kane moved to her side. "We're meeting Carter and Jo in town and then heading out to search Oakley's house. Just in case he keeps the victims hidden there."

"We'll be right behind you." Wolfe removed his examination gloves. "Call me if you find anything."

Jenna stared at the wreck and shook her head. "I still can't believe Maisy Jones walked out of that alive."

"Some people are just lucky." Kane stood beside her shaking his head. "Or maybe, fate stepped in so we had a witness. She wants to save her own skin, so she'll talk. It will be interesting to see what Jo can get out of her."

Sighing, Jenna turned toward the Beast. "Yeah, it will, but I hate being on the outside of this one, but then I do trust Jo to get to the truth." She glanced at Kane. "The thing is, was she telling the truth or does she know where he's stashed the bodies?"

THIRTY-EIGHT

Carter followed Jo into Jenna's office to get an update. Maisy Jones was cooling her heels in the interview room and had been given a meal. Bobby Kalo had decided to wait with Rio and Rowley. "Don't you want to come with us?"

"Not this time." Kalo grimaced. "Searching houses for dead bodies isn't in my job description. I'll wait here until you're done."

"I'll be back to interview Maisy Jones." Jo looked at Rio. "I'll need you to sit in as you're the lead officer on her case now. It would save time if you went in to see her and mirandized her. Turn on the recording device as it's your word against hers in there. If she wants a lawyer, you'll be able to arrange one before we get back. If that's the case, explain the warrant for her arrest in Idaho." She frowned. "You're on your own but we'll be back soon. Rowley can't go near her or Jenna and Dave. If you can, call in old Deputy Walters, it would be an option."

"Yes, ma'am. I've already informed Idaho she's in our custody. They mentioned starting on her extradition and I told them she'd be going through our system first. We have her for the abduction of Rowley's son, and with the sheriff as a witness, she isn't leaving here anytime soon." Rio shrugged. "Maisy hasn't said two words to me. She is very subdued. I wouldn't like to leave her alone overnight. She might try and take her life."

"That won't happen." Jo snorted. "She used Rowley's son as a bargaining chip to save her life. Don't worry. Wolfe has checked her over. She's fine."

Carter pushed back his Stetson. "As soon as we've charged her, she'll be heading for county. She'll be out of your hair by dinnertime. We'll leave you to it. We're meeting the sheriff in town." He looked at Jo. "We'll walk alongside the park so Zorro can have a run. He's been sitting to attention all day."

"When I called the vet, he said to bring him in tomorrow." Jo rubbed Zorro's ears. "He asked me the usual questions and from my answers he figures he just doesn't like the cold weather. He suggested you get him a thicker coat." She smiled at him. "Duke has a ton of them. We walk right past the general store. You can get him something warmer there. It will only take a minute or so."

Carter checked his watch. "Okay." He followed her to the door. "Jenna and Kane will be arriving in town soon. We don't want to keep them waiting."

After selecting a thick winter coat for Zorro and two spares, Carter dumped two of them in the cruiser, and replaced the one Zorro was wearing and then hurried across Main to meet up with Jo. She was watching a few of the townsfolk scatter straw over the floor of the pergola they'd transformed into a Nativity scene. He smiled at her. "A little more snow and it will be perfect. He looked skyward. "I don't think it will be long. It's been clouding up all day and it's so darn cold, I can't feel my feet."

The moment they walked through the gate to the enclosed area of the park, Zorro quivered in excitement. He loved to stretch his legs and was just waiting for the order to go and have some fun. Carter looked down at him and unclasped his leash. "Playtime."

The Doberman ran around in circles, his mouth stretched wide open in obvious bliss. As he circled closer toward the people moving a Christmas tree to one side of the pergola, he skidded to a stop and turned toward them, baring his teeth. When the hackles raised around his neck, alarm bells went off for Carter. He placed two fingers in his mouth and whistled. The urgent command usually attracted an immediate response from his dog, but this time Zorro held his ground. Carter took off at a run as terrified townsfolk backed away, eyes wide with shock. One man drew his pistol and took aim. Holding up both hands, Carter raised his voice. "FBI, lower your weapon. FBI K-9, drop your weapon. He won't attack. He's warning you to keep away from immediate danger." He stood between Zorro and the weapon, realizing in his rush to change coats on his dog he'd neglected to include the FBI cover. "Don't move. Stay where you are and I'll clear the area." He sighed with relief as the man holstered his gun.

Zorro's continuous barking concerned Carter. He touched Zorro's head. "Stand down."

The dog sat beside him but his low growl continued through his bared teeth. As Jo ran up beside him, flashing her creds at the startled people, he turned to look at her. "Something is obviously very wrong here. Move the people away from the area. I don't want to scare everyone, but you know what Zorro's specialty is, and if someone's planted a bomb close by, then we're all in danger."

"Okay." Jo held her cred pack in the air and ushered the people to a safe distance. "The dog is trained to detect imminent danger. Move along and we'll let him do his job."

Carter crouched down beside Zorro. "What is it boy? What

do you smell?" A quiver went down the dog and he barked again and then whined.

Not having seen this type of behavior before, Carter gave him the order to seek but Zorro just walked round in a circle and sat down by his feet. He clipped on his leash and walked with him slowly inside the pergola. The dog's hackles rose and he barked at the mannequins dressed to resemble a Nativity scene. They all had long flowing robes and headdresses. Carter stared at them, looking for any sign of a suicide vest hidden under the robes, but his dog wasn't signaling an explosive device. He was acting irrationally. "What the heck is wrong with you?"

With care, he lifted the flowing headdress from the mannequin sitting on the floor beside the empty straw-filled manger. The waxen features with expressionless painted eyes stared blankly ahead. He moved the long red hair to examine the back of the figure for explosives and a bolt of horror ripped through him. Not a bomb but a thick purple mark cutting deep into the neck. The hairs on the back of his neck prickled as he moved his gaze over the other figures: one older man, one younger and a boy, two women. Sickened, he stepped away, backing out of the pergola and waved Jo to his side. "Take a look in there but don't touch anything. We'll need to hold everyone who was working on this today for questioning."

"Okay." Jo frowned. "What am I looking at?"

Carter met her gaze. "You'll see." He pulled out his phone and called Jenna. "I'm at the pergola in the park where they're building the Nativity scene. I've found the victims."

"What all of them?" Jenna sounded astonished.

Carter nodded. "Yeah, all of them.

"Are they alive?" Jenna had the phone on speaker and he could hear the roar of the Beast's engine in the background.

Trying to push the vacant staring eyes and pale faces from

his mind, he shook his head and turned as Jo came out of the pergola. He stared at Jo's horrified expression and swallowed the rising bile. "No, they're very dead." He cleared the lump in his throat. "The sick freak has turned them into wax figures. They're part of the Nativity scene."

THIRTY-NINE

Jenna couldn't speak for a few moments as the horror of the situation hit home. She took a deep breath and then let it out slowly. "Is there a baby in the manger?"

"Nope." Carter sounded remote. "I figure he'd selected Rowley's kid. He'd have been out tonight hunting down a replacement, if he'd missed the train."

"Our ETA is ten minutes." Kane flicked on lights and sirens to clear the road ahead. "Rowley should be back at the office by now, we'll call him and get him down to your position to secure the scene. Wolfe was still at the trainwreck when we left him. We'll need his team here to sort this out. This is way out of our league."

Processing all the information, Jenna tried to ignore the overwhelming rush of grief toward everyone caught in this nightmare and swallowed hard. "Are the victims identifiable?"

"Yeah. Their eyes have been painted. So, I figure he closed them and painted the eyelids to make them look like mannequins. The features are very pale but it's easy to see they're the people on our missing persons list." He blew out a long sigh. "I only got up close and personal with the figure kneeling beside *the crib. She has to be the artist, Ginger Vaughn. Zorro went ballistic, so I was checking them for explosive devices and noticed ligature marks on the back of her neck. After I took a better look at the others it was pretty obvious who they were."*

Trying to force her mind through the procedure for a multiple homicide, Jenna's training dropped into place. "Okay, if you can call Wolfe for me, I'll get Rowley down there as soon as possible."

"Copy that." The line went dead.

Jenna turned to Kane. "Stop at Aunt Betty's. I've ordered coffee and a box of takeout. We're all dead on our feet. We won't be searching Oakley's house today. We'll have enough to do writing this up."

"You won't get an argument from me." Kane turned onto Main and slowed to park outside the diner. "I'll go. You get Rowley on the job."

Jenna nodded and made the call. She'd disconnected as Kane pushed the box of takeout onto the back seat. The aroma of coffee filled the Beast and her stomach growled. She turned to Kane. "I'll ask Jo to go back to the office so that she can start Maisy's interview with Rio." She sighed. "Maybe we can drink the coffee on the run."

"That sounds like a plan." Kane sighed. "I'm sure glad that Wolfe has Norrell to assist him. She was a great choice and they seem to be getting along really well. I know Emily is at home, but I figure she'll want to assist as well."

Trying without success to analyze the mind of a psychopath, Jenna stared at the people gathering alongside the park. The word had already got out that something had happened. "I'm sure Wolfe will call her if he wants her involved. It's going to be a horrific crime scene. Who could possibly have a mind so twisted that they would do something like this?"

"There must have been something from his past that triggered the episode." Kane hit his siren to move people away from the path to the pergola. "Unless he left something in the house to give us a clue why he did something so disgusting, we'll probably never know. From what Maisy Jones was saying, he didn't discuss what he planned to do with the bodies. Maybe Jo will be able to give us an answer?"

Pulling on examination gloves, Jenna climbed out of the Beast and answered the tirade of questions from the townsfolk with a "no comment." She followed Kane as he cleared the way ahead to where Carter was standing with Jo. "What have we got?"

"It's not pretty." Carter walked beside her to the pergola. "You'll need to prepare yourself."

Surprised the smell of death was missing, she walked inside. Throughout the pergola, incense burned in small pots, sending small streams of smoke curling into the air. Underfoot, the thick coating of fresh straw added a barnlike fragrance. Beside her, she heard Kane's intake of breath as he moved along the display of mannequins. She turned to stare at them and using her flashlight examined each one carefully. "This must be about the most bizarre crime scene I've ever attended. There are no obvious causes of death. Well, apart from the fact that Ginger Vaughn appears to have been strangled."

"Don't y'all concern yourself with the cause of death." Wolfe had walked in behind them without making a sound. "We'll take photographs and then get these people back to the morgue." He sighed. "I figured it's going to be a long night and maybe drag into the next few days." He glanced around. "Who was first on scene?"

"That would be me." Carter hovered at the doorway. "I lifted the headdress of the red-haired woman. Zorro alerted me and I was searching for explosives. Darn near turned my stomach when I saw the ligature marks on her neck." He frowned. "I didn't touch anything else but there were people in here when we arrived. We have them waiting over yonder."

Jenna turned to Wolfe. "Maisy Jones is in a holding cell at the office. I need Jo and Carter to go and interview her with Rio. Rowley is on his way to handle the crowd, but if we mention a possible bomb threat, they'll hightail it out of here fast enough. Do you need us here to assist you with processing the scene?"

"Nope." Wolfe smiled at her. "My team can handle it and Em is coming in to assist with the autopsies. I'll leave the investigations to you guys."

"Thanks." She indicated to the Beast. "We have food and coffee in the truck if you need anything."

"We're fine." Wolfe picked up his forensics kit and waved his team inside. "I'll call when I have anything." He glanced at the crowd. "Saying a potential bomb threat is a good idea. We'll need to keep the truth of what happened under wraps. As the killer is dead, it won't go to court and the details need to be suppressed to protect the families and those people who worked here. It's better they don't know the mannequins are corpses. A shock like this for all those good people must be avoided at all cost. I'll be able to remove the bodies without anyone seeing us, but the sooner you disperse the crowd over there the better. You'll need the details of the people working on the Nativity scene, but then let them go to save them any distress."

Jenna nodded. "Not a problem. So, when do you want me to inform the next of kin?"

"When I have completed the autopsies, I'll make them ready for formal identification." Wolfe sighed. "I'll need information from their relatives, so you can leave the notification to me if you want. It will take a couple of days. I handle things a little different than you, as in, 'We found a body. It might be so and so. Are you willing to come in and do a formal ID?'"

Staring blankly into the pergola, Jenna shook her head slowly. "Okay, but call me if you need me to do anything."

"Well, I will need a list of their next of kin." Wolfe turned back to his work.

Jenna smiled at him. "Not a problem." She pulled out her phone and sent a message to Kalo to hunt down the next of kin.

"We'll head back to the office." Jo stared at the Beast. "I lost my appetite when I walked into the pergola, but I'll grab some food. Carter's stomach is starting to growl like Kane's. I'm sure once we've walked for a time, we'll need something to eat."

"It's open." Kane tipped his head toward the Beast. "It only locks the doors and sounds the alarm if you try and drive it."

"Thanks for the tip." Carter signaled to Zorro and they strolled through the onlookers and toward the Beast.

Jenna headed toward the small crowd of people waiting to be interviewed. She had devised a faster way of gaining information by asking people to produce their identification and then photographing it using her phone. Using the recording app on her phone, she asked them to give their name before interviewing them. It seemed that they were parishioners from various churches in the area who gave up their spare time to create the Nativity scene. They did the same thing every year, but this year instead of using the small plaster figurines, the mannequins had started to appear over the last week or so. Each morning another mannequin would arrive and the small incense burners had been lit. They'd never seen the mysterious benefactor and just worked on decorating the outside of pergola. She agreed with Wolfe and made a point of not telling them the mannequins were actually dead bodies, as that information was so horrific and would disturb them. Instead, she'd just informed them that suspicious objects had been found in the pergola, which would be removed.

After collecting a list of the other people involved, Jenna sent them on their way. Some of them were very distressed, and Kane suggested building a second Nativity scene in the children's playground. In there was a covered area that was used for children's parties over summer. He informed them that once the suspect materials had been removed, they would be able to collect their decorations. With everybody in a better mood, Jenna followed Kane back to the pergola.

"I'm sorry to say it"—Rowley came to her side—"but I figure Matthew Oakley got what he deserved."

"Don't be sorry." Kane fell into step beside them. "Looking at what he did here, some people would call it divine justice."

Jenna slowed and looked at the crowd. It was so cold Duke's teeth chattered like castanets. She couldn't understand why people wanted to stand around watching the medical examiner. With his van backed up to the entrance of the pergola, nothing could be seen going back and forth. She turned to her deputies. "Spread out and disperse this crowd. We need to get back to the office. We might not be able to be involved with the Maisy Jones case, but I want to be outside listening when Jo interviews her."

"So do I." Rowley wiped his mouth with the back of his hand. "I just thank God that you got there in time, Jenna. One thing's for darn sure, we're never going to let those babies out of our sight again."

FORTY

Snow dusted the hood of the Beast as they headed along Main, and by the time they pulled into their space outside the sheriff's office, snow had built up on the wipers, leaving wet streaks across the windshield. Jenna climbed out just as a blast of freezing wind rolled down from the mountains, chilling her cheeks and seeping through her clothes. As Kane grabbed the box of takeout, she unhooked Duke from his harness and headed up the steps to the office. It was good to be inside in the warm again and she smiled at Maggie, standing behind the counter wearing a Santa hat. Since they had left, she had decorated the front counter with red and green fairy lights. "Did Maisy Jones ask for a lawyer?"

"She did indeed." Maggie rolled her eyes skyward. "Mr. Samuel J. Cross is in with her now. I figure he drew the short straw." She shrugged. "I called that new guy and his secretary told me he'd already left for the day."

Jenna frowned. "New guy? What new guy?"

"His name is Jeremiah Ash. He came here to settle from Butte. So the DA told me." Maggie pointed to the stairs. "The FBI agents are in your office."

"Thanks." Jenna followed Kane up the stairs and into her office.

"Nothing much has happened since we last spoke to you." Jo stood and took the box from Kane's arms and placed it on the desk. "Sam Cross has been with Maisy since he arrived. Rio is waiting in the hallway outside the interview room for him to finish. If we're lucky, we'll have the time to grab a bite to eat before we start the interview. If he decides to allow us to interview her."

Jenna looked into the box and pulled out a bagel with cream cheese and one of the to-go cups of coffee with her name written on the top. "That's good. I was hoping to at least drink a cup of coffee as I walked around interviewing the people in the park, but there just wasn't time."

"I'm wondering what motive Oakley had for doing this." Kane dropped into a chair and bit into a sandwich. "Have you given it any thought yet, Jo?"

"Yeah, it's been on my mind since we discovered the bodies." Jo sipped her coffee. "I need to know more about his background and it's imperative that we search his house to find some clues. I'm intrigued to know why he did this and the reason he didn't kill Maisy. It seems very strange to me that he abducted her from the side of the road, allowed her to see the dead bodies in the back of his truck and yet negotiated with her. Psychopaths don't negotiate or make friends with strangers they don't trust. There was no way he planned to let her just walk away. What she was telling you about him, Jenna, goes against every pattern of behavior I've documented to date."

Exhausted, Jenna sank into her office chair and leaned back with a sigh. She took a bite of her bagel and a sip of coffee to wash it down as she considered Jo's conclusions. "When we interviewed him at Miller's Garage, he came over as a player more than a killer. He actually tried to hit on me with Kane standing right there beside me." She sipped her coffee and looked at Jo over the rim of her cup. "He was overconfident and overbearing. Although I have to admit, he did come into the tall, dark and handsome category, so I guess it was his way of getting what he wanted."

"Or trying to keep the conversation away from the topic." Jo nibbled on an egg salad sandwich. "They often do that, you know. They believe they can use charm to control which way the conversation is going. You have to remember that he was trying to obtain information too. He needed to know what you'd discovered. Asking you out on a date wasn't to kill you, it was more likely to get you on his side so he could constantly use you for information. They like to keep one step ahead if possible."

"Well, he sure did." Carter tossed a bunch of fries into his mouth, chewed and swallowed. "He was way ahead right up until he crossed the railroad track." He shook his head. "Man, I'm sure glad he didn't derail the train." He looked straight at Kane. "Seems his truck didn't have the advantages of the Beast. I figure your truck would have made a mess."

"I'm not so sure." Kane cleared his throat. "Just in case this is leading to you asking me to try some type of crazy experiment, it's never gonna happen."

"Hmm." Carter grinned. "That truck of yours is stronger than it looks. I examined it for damage after Jenna was thrown onto the hood during the explosion and there isn't a mark on it. I'm starting to wonder if the Beast is made from the same material as those UFOs that came down at Roswell." He chuckled.

"Nah." Kane shrugged. "Just American steel, is all."

A knock came on the door and Rowley poked his head inside. "Wolfe and the team have finished in the park. He said that they did a forensic sweep and found nothing of interest. The ground is frozen all around, and as it's a public place, nothing would have been admissible evidence." He took a breath. "They'll be starting the autopsies as soon as possible. There is so much information on the file Kalo sent him about the missing persons, it shouldn't take too long at all to get IDs. He'll call you if there's anything interesting to report."

Relieved that Wolfe had everything under control as usual, Jenna smiled at Rowley. "Head on home and don't forget to put in for overtime. We'll be tying up loose ends for the next day or so. If you need a personal day before Christmas to go shopping, I'll make sure we can arrange one for you."

"Thanks, but I'll work all the overtime you want without pay for the rest of my life if you need me. I can never repay the debt I owe you for saving my son." Rowley touched his hat, turned and headed toward the stairs.

Emotion gripped Jenna and she sprang from the desk and ran after him. "Jake. Wait up."

"I meant it." He gave her a somber look. "I've lived through so many emotions today. I can't imagine losing my boy. I couldn't stand it."

Tears streaming down her cheeks, Jenna hugged him. "Me neither. Look, it's over. The man is dead and we'll never have to think about him again. Go home and kiss Sandy and hug your kids."

"Okay." Rowley stepped away, his neck red. "I meant it about the overtime."

Jenna smiled. "We owe you a ton of overtime, and you and Rio will be getting it before the holidays, that is nonnegotiable. There is one other thing I need to speak to you about, but with all the commotion, it slipped my mind." She met his suddenly concerned gaze. "I sent the paperwork to the mayor last night about your position here."

"You're going to fire me... at Christmas?" Rowley dropped his gaze from her face and he drew in a deep breath.

Laughing, Jenna took him by the shoulders and gave him a little shake. "Heaven's above, no. It's a promotion. You're no longer a rookie, Jake. Go home and tell Sandy. The increase in salary is substantial."

"Thank you." He removed his hat and tossed it into the air and caught it with a yip of excitement. "I'll be back first thing in the morning."

Jenna watched him go and walked back into her office. She'd just pushed the last piece of bagel into her mouth and swallowed when the desk phone rang. It was Maggie.

"Sam Cross is ready for you to interview Maisy Jones."

Jenna stood. "We're on our way." She looked at the others. "Showtime."

FORTY-ONE

Staring at the two-way mirror outside the interview room, Jenna turned to Kane. "I really want to be in there asking the questions."

"If there's something you need to ask her, we can always send in a note." He pulled up a chair and handed her an earpiece to listen to the interview inside the room. "We know most of what she knows anyway. I doubt she'll come up with any surprises."

Jenna listened as Maisy recounted what had happened from the time she left the Triple Z Bar, until Matthew Oakley pulled up in his truck and offered her a ride to the motel. Jo was asking for detailed information. Had she seen the man at the bar during the time she'd worked there? Was there anything suspicious about him before she climbed into his truck?

"*No, I didn't see him at the bar and he seemed like a regular guy when he stopped to help me. He told me he'd been hunting and his truck was stinky.*" Maisy's voice was tinny through the intercom but clear. "*It wasn't until I got inside the truck that I noticed it was real bad. The doors locked as soon as I sat down. When I turned around to look into the back seat, I could see three obviously dead people through a Perspex screen. I opened my mouth to scream and was trying to get out of the door when he thrust a stinky rag into my mouth. I blacked out and woke up on a gurney in the place I told you about."*

"You mentioned that the bodies were there in the adjoining room." Jo was all business. *"Did you attempt to escape at this time?"*

"Of course I did, but the doors were locked." Maisy looked exasperated. *"How did you think I felt being locked in a room with three dead bodies? All I could hear was a drip, drip, drip of their blood splashing into the buckets. It was a nightmare."*

"When exactly did he next speak to you?" Jo leaned forward and made notes on a legal pad on the desk. *"Was he acting normally? Did he threaten you?"*

"He never acted normally." Maisy looked at Sam Cross and he gave her a 'keep going' motion with his hand. *"He said if I didn't do what I was told, he'd turn the lights off and let the rats eat me overnight. I was kept in the light twenty-four hours a day. I didn't know what time it was, but he did bring me a meal. I don't know how long I'd been there when he made me a proposition. He said he would give me a better place to live if I made a phone call to a woman to arrange the collection of a painting. I needed to get out of the room with the corpses. Surely you understand? I figured there may be a chance to escape from a different room, so I agreed to pretend to be his wife. I spoke to a woman called Ginger Vaughn, a local artist in Blackwater, and arranged for him to go by her house at Broken Wolf Forest to collect the picture."*

"Okay. How did he persuade you to help him kidnap Cooper Rowley?" Jo's face was expressionless.

"He told me that the call to Ginger Vaughn was a test, and if I assisted him with the little boy, he would let me walk free. I agreed because I would be in town and could grab the kid and run straight to the cops." Maisy reached for a glass of water on

the table and sipped, as if trying to get a short break from the questioning.

"The sheriff was right there when the handover happened. All you had to do was stop and give her the boy and explain, but you didn't, did you?" Jo hadn't looked up from her notes.

"There were a ton of people on the street and kids all over. I didn't see it was the sheriff." Maisy lowered her eyes to her bound hands.

"When the sheriff grabbed Cooper Rowley from your arms, you had the chance to run away or ask her for help. Instead, you pushed her over to get away, didn't you? You could have run in any direction and yet you jumped back in Oakley's truck." Jo's hard gaze drifted over Maisy. "Can you see why I'm finding it difficult to believe what you're saying?"

"I did try to escape. I was terrified of him. His eyes changed in a second. I could see that he was crazy." Maisy grasped her hands together on the table. "You don't understand. I was in fear of my life. I even climbed through an air-conditioning duct to escape, but it just took me back to another room and that door was locked as well."

"So, if you were as terrified of this man as you say, it makes no sense at all that you didn't ask the sheriff for protection. She was right there, carrying a weapon, and yet you jumped into the back of his truck. Why was that? Did you miss him?" Carter was leaning forward with both hands palms down on the table glaring at her. "You were home free. You're lying now, just the same as you're lying about killing Zander Hastings."

"We're not here about the Zander Hastings case, Agent Carter." Sam Cross leaned back in his chair and tipped back his light brown Stetson. "It's not your case."

"I beg to differ." Carter straightened and leaned his back against the wall, arms folded across his chest. "We were brought into that case by the Nampa Police Department."

"Maybe, but I've been made aware that investigators from

Idaho will be here shortly to interview my client." Cross was making copious notes on his legal pad. *"If we could just stick to the kidnapping, and the abduction of my client."*

"Is there anything else you can tell me about Matthew Oakley." Jo looked up from her notes. *"Did he, by any chance, explain to you what he was doing with the bodies?"*

"No, but he did tell me a few things." Maisy kept glancing at Sam Cross as if to get his permission to continue. *"He said that the only time people were nice to him was over the holidays."* She thought for a beat. *"He sang Christmas jingles when he was working on the bodies."*

"Anything else he said or did that was unusual?" Jo sighed and leaned back in her chair, twiddling the pen in her fingers.

"Yeah, he said that people were nice, but were like peaches and cream or something on the outside and rotten underneath." Maisy stared at Jo. *"Does that mean anything?"*

"No." Jo looked at Carter. *"I've finished the interview. Do you have any questions?"*

"Nope. I'm done here." Carter straightened. *"Agent Carter has left the room."* He headed for the door.

"I've spoken to the DA. Your client will be formally charged and sent to county jail." Rio stepped forward. *"Charges include conspiracy to commit murder, in the case of Ginger Vaughan, kidnapping of Cooper Rowley and assault of a law enforcement officer during the execution of their duties."*

Jenna pulled out the earbuds as Carter walked into the hallway. "That was harrowing. I wonder how the jury will see her reason for taking Cooper."

"There's no excuse for using a toddler as a bargaining chip. She'll be in jail for a long time, whatever the outcome." Carter looked at Jenna. "He was referring to the wax figures, wasn't he?"

Sickened, Jenna nodded. "Yeah, each one of those figures probably represented someone in his life who had been nasty to him at one time or another. All bright and shiny on the outside and rotting flesh in the middle."

"I'm wondering how many times he's done this before in different states." Kane rubbed the back of his neck. "Covering real people with wax and making them look like mannequins took some skill. I don't believe this was the first time he's done this. The problem is proving anything. We all know what happens to decorations after the holidays. Most of them end up in landfill, and if the bodies weren't discovered, that's where they'll be, never to be seen again. One thing's for darn sure, Matthew Oakley almost committed the perfect crime."

FORTY-TWO

MONDAY, WEEK TWO

Snowfall had arrived at Black Rock Falls overnight in abundance, coating the landscape like frosting on a cake. Snow fell slowly and it turned the view of the cottage that Kane had once called home into a setting inside a snow dome. Jenna touched the long icicles dangling from the gutter around the front door and headed down to the gym. She stripped to her workout clothes and started on her usual exercise routine. This was usually followed by an extensive workout with Kane, but now that Carter was staying with them for the holidays, she was content to watch them try to kill each other. The thumps and groans that came from the mat made her smile. Both of them regarded the other as a punching bag. One thing for sure, neither of them had lost his edge. The workout was brutal and she had to call time and insist they head for the shower. "Come on, guys. I know Jo has offered to cook breakfast this morning but I don't want to be late getting into the office. Wolfe would have worked most of the night and I would like to know what he's doing this morning. If he is conducting autopsies on the victims this morning, I want to be there." She grimaced as Carter landed a punch and danced away.

"Just let me swat this fly and I'll be right along." Kane swept Carter's feet and grinned. "There, that didn't take long." He offered Carter his hand and pulled him to his feet. "You'll need to take the cruiser if you're planning on dropping Jaime back at Wolfe's house for the day."

"Not a problem." Carter reached for a towel and wiped his face. "As long as I don't freeze to death running back to the cottage."

"Nah, you'll be fine." Kane grinned. "I used to do it all the time. It was like coming out of a sauna and rubbing yourself with snow. I hear it's good for the heart."

"Right." Carter shook his head and pulled on sweatpants and a sweater. He grinned at Kane and placed one hand on the doorknob. "Tomorrow you're going down, man."

"It will never happen." Kane flicked a towel at him and grinned at Jenna. "What?"

Jenna waited for Carter to leave and ran her fingers through Kane's hair. "Nothing. I just love you is all."

An hour later, they arrived at the office. Jenna and Kane worked with Rio and Rowley to update the files. Maisy Jones was locked away in the county jail. The findings of the wreck on the highway were still in the preliminary stages, but from the information released to them, the accident was caused by the driver of the tanker using his cell phone. Dash cameras revealed the tanker plowing into the eighteen-wheeler before spinning out of control and overturning in the ditch. The explosion that followed was caused by sparks igniting the inflammable liquid leaking from the damaged tanker.

Jenna emailed the file to everyone concerned and gave Kane a brief outline about what had happened. She glanced at her watch. "Wolfe said he would be starting the autopsies at ten. We have time to go and take a look at Matthew Oakley's house.

It would be interesting to discover if he kept trophies. It might give us some indication of how long he's been murdering people and coating them in wax."

"As Jo and Carter have taken Zorro to the *v-e-t* for a checkup, we should take Rio and Rowley with us. It will save time." Kane glanced at Duke in his basket. "I'm glad he hasn't learned how to spell yet."

Jenna finished her cup of coffee and stood. "Me too. With his phobia of the *v-e-t*, it's better he lives in ignorant bliss."

They pulled on their coats, gloves and hats and then headed downstairs. After informing Rio and Rowley to follow them, they headed out the door, leaving Duke pretending to be asleep in his basket in Jenna's office. The snow outside was getting heavier and snowplows and salt sprayers chugged up and down Main. Kane had already fitted the snowplow attachment to the front of the Beast, and Jenna had faith that it could get through just about anything. They headed to Winding Alley and found Oakley's house without any problems.

It was a neat, red brick, older-style home with a front porch that leaned a little to one side. The wooden steps creaked as Jenna stepped on them. She wondered why someone would keep a neat yard and yet neglect to paint or maintain the house. She knocked on the front door and they waited, not expecting a reply, but in truth they didn't know if Oakley lived alone. After knocking again and getting no reply, it didn't take Kane long to pick the lock on the front door. Jenna pushed it wide open and they both peered inside.

"Rio and Rowley are here." Kane looked toward the road.

Jenna nodded. "We'll wait for them and then decide who is searching what area. I noticed there isn't a garage. If we're going to find anything it's going to be here inside the house."

With Rio and Rowley as backup, they moved inside and went into the mudroom. The house smelled of cooking with an overtone of mold. Jenna turned to her deputies. "You take downstairs and we'll look at the bedrooms. Don't forget to look at places that could conceal things, like under loose floorboards or inside books, secret drawers in desks. You know the deal. If this guy has been doing this for some time, he could have things hidden all over. Take your time and check every corner of this place. Make sure you're wearing gloves." She snapped on a pair of examination gloves and handed a pair to Kane.

"Copy that." Rio pulled out his Maglite and followed Rowley into the family room.

Jenna headed for the stairs with Kane on her heels. Upstairs, they found three bedrooms. One was obviously used for sleeping. Of the other two, one was dusty and obviously unused and the other contained cartons, each marked with dates and the names of towns throughout the USA. On a desk sat a computer and a printer set up to print glossy photographs. She turned to Kane. "I'm not sure I want to look in those cartons. If this is what I think it is, Matthew Oakley has been a busy boy."

"Oh, man." Kane ripped open the nearest box and lifted out a bag containing hair. "There are a ton of these in here." He held one for her to see. Written on each one was a date, and place. He held them up shaking his head. "It gets worse." He pulled out a pile of photographs. "These are before and after shots." He turned one over. "The names of the victims are on the back, the date he killed them and where he put them."

Horrified, Jenna stared at the gruesome images. "We'll hand all this over to the FBI. Apart from what happened in Black Rock Falls, all these people are spread across the country. I suggest we leave everything untouched and they will call in a specialized forensic team to deal with it. Right now, Wolfe has enough to deal with."

"Okay." Kane pulled out his phone. "I'll record everything in this room and we can send them a copy. I'll take photographs of everything in the box I disturbed."

Once they were done, they went downstairs to see what the others had discovered, but it seemed that Matthew Oakley had kept everything in the one room. Jenna turned to Rio and Rowley. "This is to be treated as a crime scene. Seal the front and back door with crime scene tape, and the front gate as well. We don't want anyone coming in here and contaminating the scene. When you're done, you can head back to the office, unless you want to attend the autopsy with us?"

"Not me." Rowley pushed his hands into the back pocket of his jeans. "Seeing those poor folks in the park was enough for me."

"Do you want me to report this to the FBI headquarters in DC, as it's nationwide?" Rio tipped back his Stetson. "Or do we leave that to Carter?"

Jenna nodded. "Yeah, leave it to Carter. We'll need to run this past him first or he'll believe we're going over his head. I'm sure this is way too big a deal for a local field office. Can you imagine the resources they'll need to sort through those boxes in there? There must have been a hundred or more images in the first carton that Kane opened." She pulled her woolen cap down over her ears as the cold wind bit into her cheeks. "Carter will know who to contact." She hunched against the snowfall and headed back to the Beast. As her boots crunched on the small patches of snow-covered ice, she leaned toward Kane. "I sure hope this day improves. It sure takes the ho, ho, ho out of Christmas."

FORTY-THREE

It had been a relaxing distraction for Wolfe to have breakfast with Dr. Norrell Larson, the forensic anthropologist who had recently joined his team. They'd worked until late into the night removing wax from Matthew Oakley's victims. After a few hours' sleep, they'd decided to meet up at Aunt Betty's Café for breakfast. He sat back in the chair, sipping his coffee and admiring the woman opposite him. It had been a long time since his wife had passed, a long and lonely time, during which he had never so much as looked at another woman. He could never replace her, but Angela had insisted he move on and find someone else rather than spend the rest of his life alone. She was wise beyond her years and her advice often ran through his mind like an earwig. In truth, he hadn't been attracted to anyone else at all, but Norrell was a very special woman. They had so much in common and he found himself spending hours just talking to her. Not only about their mutual interest in forensic science, but so many other things as well.

It didn't take him too long to discover that Norrell enjoyed reading a wide variety of subjects. He liked that she showed a deep interest in his children and when around them had listened to their constant chatter and never seemed to get bored. She was a homebody like him and eating a meal surrounded by family was something that she enjoyed. At first, he'd believed that his eldest daughter, Emily, who was currently working on her degree to become a medical examiner, might not get along with the extremely intelligent Norrell, as she was only ten years her senior, but the opposite had proved to be true. They had become fast friends, constantly discussing topics including body farms and forensic anthropology cases that Norrell had worked on over the last few years. Julie and little Anna treated her like one of the family and had no qualms about seeing her with their father.

Wolfe rubbed his chin. He'd met his wife in high school and the modern dating game was very new to him. He admitted the same to Norrell and she'd just smiled and squeezed his arm, saying that she was happy to take things one day at a time. That suited him just fine. He'd always been the slow and steady type —old-school, as Kane would have said. It had worked well for Kane, so he'd enjoy Norrell's company and hope she didn't get bored with him.

"You seem distracted today, Shane." Norrell placed her cup on the saucer and frowned at him. "I think most of the cases that we're looking at today are almost self-explanatory. Is there anything of concern?"

Shaking his head, Wolfe smiled at her. "I'm a little distracted, is all. In fact, I'm distracted every time I'm with you." He waved a hand absently around the room. "I like this. You and me sitting here eating breakfast, chatting about our day. It seems kind of right."

"I agree." Norrell took a strip of crispy bacon from his plate, grinned and then popped it into her mouth. "I've felt comfortable with you since the first day we met. Men hit on me and become pests. These days, no one wants to take things slow and be friends. Allowing a relationship to grow is something I want, and I believe this is what's happening between us. I feel as if I've always known you. Perhaps we knew each other in a different life or something?" She sighed. "Sorry to change the subject but it's getting late. Are you holding back the autopsies until Jenna and the guys arrive?"

Nodding, Wolfe waited for Susie Hartwig, the manager of Aunt Betty's, to refill his cup and then looked back at Norrell. "I try to keep the autopsies at the same time each day unless something comes up, so they know to arrive around ten. As Colt Webber is a badge-holding deputy, he usually stands in for the preliminaries, so when Jenna and Kane arrive, I've determined a provisional cause and time of death. I go over the findings with them and then they decide if they have time to watch the entire process."

"Then I guess we had better finish our meal and get back to the morgue." Norrell glanced at her watch. "It's twenty after nine."

Wolfe shrugged. "Take your time, Emily and Weber are both doing the final preparations. I can rely on them to have all the X-rays on file and have collected any results from the samples we've taken. The team runs very smoothly even if I'm not there. Emily has been a great help to me during her studies. Sometimes in this town there's not very much time to think, and now being called out to cases statewide at all hours of the day and night isn't making life any easier."

"It will help when my team is in place." Norrell finished her meal and then looked up at him again. "I have funding for three assistants and can always rely on the local college to send out students if I need more in the field. I'm honestly not expecting to be doing too many digs here in town. When I'm not out digging up bones, I'll always be more than willing to assist you, and my team will be available as well." She sighed. "Unfortunately, none of them will be here until the new year, so until then it's just you and me delving into unsolved crimes and mystery." She grinned. "I think that is what drives me, you know: the story behind what happened, who the people were and why they were murdered. I've always loved mysteries and in this line of work I'm right in the middle of it. I believe it takes someone who can take the information they find and expand it to create the small section of time just before a person died."

This is why he liked her so much. They were on the same wavelength. "Yeah, I'm the same. I like to speak for the person on my examination table and bring whoever murdered them to justice by using whatever instruments I have at hand." He pushed away his plate and stood. "I guess we'd better make tracks. I hope you're staying for dinner tonight? My housekeeper is making pulled pork."

"I wouldn't miss it." Norrell pushed to her feet.

They arrived back at the morgue a little before ten. Wolfe smiled as Emily came down the hallway toward him, her rubber-soled shoes squeaking on the tile. "Everything ready? I figure it's going to be Jenna, Kane, Jo and Carter today."

"Yeah, they're ready." Emily frowned. "I've placed Charlie, Clare and Gavin Bridger in examination room one with Billy Stevens. Your notes mentioned that you consider they are all victims of carbon monoxide poisoning, so I figured they should be placed together." She indicated with her thumb toward examination room two. "The two strangulation victims, Ginger Vaughn and Jenell Rickers are in two. Where will you be starting first?"

Shucking his coat, Wolfe went to the alcove outside the examination rooms, removed his sweater and pulled on scrubs. He took one of the large plastic aprons from a pile on a shelf and wrapped it around himself. He turned to Norrell. "Where would you like to start today?"

"Carbon monoxide poisoning." Norrell pulled on scrubs. "The sooner we can release that family to their next of kin the better."

Wolfe raised one eyebrow at Em. "One it is. Have you heard from Jenna? I missed them earlier this morning when Jo dropped by with Jaime." He smiled. "That child slips into our family as if she belongs there."

"Yeah, she is an angel and it's so great for Anna to have a friend stay over for the holidays. They can do so much together. Oh, and Jenna messaged me before. She figured you'd be sleeping late today after pulling the graveyard shift." Emily grinned. "I told her you grabbed a few hours and took a late breakfast. She'll be here at ten."

Before Wolfe had the opportunity to reply, the back door to the morgue slid open and Jenna came inside with the others close behind. He waved at them and indicated to examination room one. "I'll meet you inside when y'all are ready."

FORTY-FOUR

The temperature inside the morgue seemed warmer than usual as Jenna removed her coat and hung it on a peg outside the examination rooms. She glanced at her reflection in the mirror above the sink and a rosy-faced, red-nosed person looked back at her from under a thick woolen cap. The temperature outside had dropped considerably since they'd left home, and just walking back and forth from the Beast, had frozen her feet and hands. The odor inside the morgue hadn't changed, but the smell of candle wax mingled with the usual smell of chemicals and death. She waited until the others had removed their outer clothes and replaced them with scrubs. She looked at Jo's serious expression and took her to one side. "A kid is involved in these murders. If you want to miss this one and wait in Wolfe's office, I'll come get you when we're done."

"I appreciate your concern, but I've attended autopsies with kids many a time." Jo adjusted her face mask. "Just because I'm a mother, it doesn't stop me working on juvenile crime scenes." She turned to look at Kane. "After looking at the images you discovered at Matthew Oakley's home, I called Kalo to do a deeper search into him. I figured there's more we need to know about that man."

"Yeah, something triggered him, but not having him around makes it difficult to discover a motive for his killing sprees." Kane pulled on examination gloves with a snap. "There has to be something in his background we've missed. Maybe he was adopted or has changed his name at one time or another."

Jenna waited for Kane and Carter to take the dogs into Wolfe's office. It was warm inside and he always had water and a bowl of food waiting for them. As Carter walked back, she touched his arm. "You went to the vet this morning. Is Zorro okay?"

"Yeah, he's fine." Carter's eyes danced with amusement. "The vet figures that now he's getting older he feels the cold and maybe has the start of a little arthritis, although his X-rays look okay. So I need to keep him warm...well, warmer. I figured the coats he had were just fine, but now he has puffy coats, and if he needs boots in the snow, I have them as well. Although he wasn't too keen when I tried them on him. He walked as if I had tied blocks of wood to his feet."

"We keep a blanket in the Beast for Duke, and blankets at the office with his basket." Kane shrugged. "There's a difference between the two dogs, although they both suffer from the cold weather. Duke makes a conscious decision if he wants to come with us or not. If he decides to stay at home, he just sticks his head under his blanket and ignores us. Zorro is on duty twenty-four/seven. He doesn't make up his own mind, he follows orders. Maybe when he refused to get out of the cruiser the other day, he was rebelling."

"Hmm, you sayin' that hanging around with Duke is giving him bad habits?" Carter's eyebrows rose.

"No, I'm saying he's just being a dog." Kane led the way to examination room one and flashed his card across the scanner.

Jenna followed them inside, glad she had used the mentholated balm under her nose. The smell inside the examination room was overpowering. She stood with her back leaning against the counter and folded her arms across her chest, not wanting to get too close to the uncovered bodies on the gurneys. Although skin covered them all, the rose-red hue on their skin resembled burn victims. Kane moved to her side and leaned a little against her in a show of solidarity. She glanced up at him and met his troubled gaze with a nod.

"Okay, now you're here I can save you time by running over the preliminary examination of all of these victims, but first I'd like to bring your attention to the images on the screen of the vehicle after the trainwreck." Wolfe moved to the array of screens. "Y'all know that the back half of the truck survived intact. It may have slipped your notice, but after examining the interior, I discovered a Perspex divider between the front and back seats. Oakley had completely sealed the interior, even going as far as installing new seals around the windows and doors. I also found an inlet pipe running from the exhaust to the back seat. The mechanism is incomplete due to the wreck, but we have to assume he persuaded the victims to get inside the back of the truck and once he had started driving, he turned on the flow of carbon monoxide." He ran his gaze over the team.

Astonished, Jenna stared at him. "Jo and Kane both said that he was an organized psychopath, and this proves it beyond reasonable doubt. What else do you have for me, Wolfe?"

"The victims were posed and then painted with numerous coats of wax. After the first layers had been completed, the bodies were painted and then further layers were added." Wolfe moved from one body to the other. "Apart from the obvious physical signs of a deep red, flushed skin color, which is a significant indicator of carbon monoxide poisoning and completely different from the application of hot wax on live tissue, the blood samples we analyzed from all the victims in this room show high levels of carboxyhemoglobin."

"The family hasn't suffered any significant injuries, but Billy Stevens put up a fight." Kane moved along the line of bodies. "He has defense wounds to his forearms and hands."

"Yeah." Wolfe rolled the body of Billy Stevens onto his side. "He was struck from behind, but I believe his first injury is consistent to an elbow to the neck. This tells me he approached his killer, so maybe Oakley was on the ground and Stevens went to assist him and was attacked. Once inside the back of Oakley's truck, he didn't stand a chance."

Stomach clenching, Jenna's attention moved over the small body of Gavin Bridger. "Did he suffer?"

"Fear at being abducted." Norrell moved to her side, placed a hand on her arm and squeezed. "Once inside the back of the truck, he could have had a headache or felt nauseous, but with the high concentration we found in the blood, it would have worked fast." She met her gaze. "No other injuries on any member of the family. No sexual assault."

"Not so for Matthew Oakley." Wolfe raised one blond eyebrow and looked at Jenna. "He wasn't killed on impact. From my inspection of the locomotive, he was thrown from the truck on impact and caught under the cowcatcher on the front of the locomotive and cut to pieces." He walked back to the screen array and displayed blood results. "He wasn't under the influence of drugs or alcohol. I have what's left of his body parts if you'd like to see them?"

Jenna shook her head. "No thanks. I've already seen them in situ."

"I'll be completing tests on various organs, but in my opinion and Norrell's, the Bridgers and Billy Stevens died from carbon monoxide poisoning. Their time of death can't be calculated because all the bodies have been embalmed using formaldehyde, but we must assume from Maisy Jones' statement that they died shortly after they were abducted." Wolfe glanced from one to the other. "Any questions? No? Well, we can move to the next room."

FORTY-FIVE

It was good to walk into the hallway for a short respite, not only from the smell but the aching tragedy inside. Fighting down the human revulsion at seeing the tragic loss of a complete family and a young man, all innocently going about their daily lives, Jenna removed her mask and went to the alcove to replenish the mentholated salve under her nose. Those people would never see another Christmas, never reach their full potential. One man destroyed all that, and the fact he had died might seem like justice for many, but to her it meant he took his secrets with him. How many more bodies of innocent people were out there? How many people waited by the phone in the hope their loved ones would someday contact them? The idea made her sick to the stomach. She straightened and followed the others into examination room two. Her gaze moved over two bodies covered with white sheets, their feet exposed and each attached with a toe tag.

"You, okay?" Kane leaned into her. "You're sheet white."

Jenna nodded. "Just angry we didn't get the chance to inter-rogate Matthew Oakley. Where are all the others he killed? We need to know."

"Don't concern yourself with them, Jenna." Carter stood beside her. "The DC HQ has taken over the case. They'll have all their best teams hunting down and identifying the victims. If they're out there, they'll move mountains to find them."

Nodding, Jenna met his gaze over her mask. "Thanks, that's reassuring. Will you be involved?"

"Only with the Blackwater victims." Carter folded his arms across his chest and leaned back against the counter. "I'll send in a report of the trainwreck and the Black Rock Falls victims, but as the perp is dead, they'll be no need to follow up."

"These two are different." Wolfe uncovered the women's faces. "Jenell Rickers was attacked from behind, with what we assume was a dog's leash. Oakley wasn't too concerned about removing trace evidence. She had dirt under her fingernails, which we assume happened during the attack in Broken Wolf Forest. I'm running samples to see if they match the immediate area. We can assume she walked the dogs to the exercise yard in the forest and was somehow lured away by Oakley and then attack from behind and strangled. There's a fire road running through that part of the forest and no doubt he left his vehicle there. It's in a secluded area and it would have been easy for him to carry her to his truck without being seen."

"The attack on Ginger Vaughn looks brutal." Carter shook his head. "Blunt force trauma to the head and then he garroted her. He really hated this one."

"Yeah, so it seems. She must resemble someone he particularly disliked." Wolfe indicated to the X-rays on the screen. "He hit her so hard he fractured her skull."

Trying to see any sign of a pattern, Jenna shook her head. "There are so many differences here. If I hadn't captured Maisy, we'd have never suspected this guy."

"Yeah, we did. He was on our list." Kane shrugged. "It was only a matter of time. He made his first mistake by recruiting Maisy to help him."

"Any signs of sexual assault?" Jo moved closer.

"Nope, none at all." Wolfe covered the first body and indicated to Webber to return it to the refrigerated drawer.

"I'm trying to figure out his motive." Jo glanced at Kane. "I'm seeing different types of people, different ages and sexes. This is so out of character for most of the psychopaths I've researched or interviewed previously. They usually always have their own preferred types."

Thinking over Maisy Jones' statement, Jenna looked from Jo to Kane. "I think you're missing something. Maisy mentioned people were only nice to him over the holidays, so maybe he committed these crimes over all the holidays throughout the years. I think the emphasis is on people. So he collected a random selection of people. Perhaps all those who looked like those who had been nasty to him during the year in one way or another."

"Or how he remembered them from a traumatic childhood." Jo let out a long sigh. "I hope Kalo finds something in Oakley's background to give us more insight into why he killed so many people."

"Why the need to display them?" Carter stared at Jenna.

The whole horrific picture fell into place and Jenna lifted her chin, confident she had the solution. "For whatever reason they hurt or bullied him, I figure by displaying them, in his twisted mind, he was showing everyone how bullies can appear to be nice on the outside and rotten inside."

EPILOGUE

CHRISTMAS EVE

Snow had fallen heavily overnight, and Jenna had woken to a winter wonderland. The blanket of white was thick on the ground and frosted the trees all the way from the ranch up into the mountains. Her house was full to bursting with happy people. They had spent the day preparing a feast and decorating the Christmas tree. It now stood proud in the corner of the family room with gifts piled up to the first branches. They had spent a short time at breakfast discussing the case. Maisy Jones had pleaded guilty to assisting Matthew Oakley in the death of Ginger Vaughn and the attempted abduction of Cooper Rowley. Her case was held over for sentencing until the new year. She would spend time in the state pen and once her sentence was complete would face murder charges in Idaho. The Nampa PD had a convincing case against her, after finding a bottle of liquid heroin with her fingerprints on it in her garbage. One small mistake would cost her any hope of freedom, but then they all make mistakes in the end.

Bobby Kalo had discovered some information on Matthew Oakley's past life. He had spent time in the foster care system as a child but had been adopted at the age of ten into a family that had been involved in a cult and later arrested for neglect of their six children, who'd been kept in appalling conditions and tortured. His name had been changed once more, and he'd worked his way through college. He'd become an auto club mechanic, moving from town to town. It was during this time, going on the FBI cold cases matched to his photograph collection, that Oakley had started his deadly campaign. The whereabouts of the victims would be under investigation for a long time.

"Hey, no more thinking about cases." Kane pulled on his boots and stood. "This is our time now. Time with our friends to make memories to take with us into old age."

To Jenna, he looked so fine, not dressed in his usual black, but in blue jeans and a dark blue sweater that matched his eyes. His hair combed just right and wearing cologne. He rarely wore cologne on the job in case the bad guys smelled him coming. She smiled and went to him. "Okay, I promise. I'm so glad Wolfe is bringing Norrell to dinner. It wouldn't be the same without him and the girls. Rio, Cade and Piper will be here as well. Oh, and Rowley is bringing Sandy and the twins over in the morning for a spell. I know they want to spend Christmas with their families, but I so want to see the twins' faces when they open the gifts, Jaime's too."

"It was a fun time for me and my sister too." Kane pulled her close. "We're lucky we have friends, although I like being alone with you. Someone asked me why we spend all our time together, and I told them because we're best friends as well as spouses."

Jenna giggled and hugged him. "Well, I have Sandy, Jo, Em, Julie, Rio's sister Piper, and now Norrell to go on a girls' night out if the need arises." She grinned. "And you guys prefer to go fishing and visit the rifle range before sneaking into Aunt Betty's."

"Oh, we don't mind a night of playing cards and pool at the

Cattleman's Hotel either, but with Carter it's sometimes diffi-cult to enjoy ourselves."

Jenna stared at him. "How so?"

"Carter seems to attract an entourage of women when he's not with Jo." Kane shrugged. "They find him attractive, I guess. Wolfe can look at them and they keep away, but they seem to figure if we're out on the town, we're available, which is fine for Carter but not for me or Rowley."

"What about Rio?" Jenna frowned. "He's single."

"Nah, he has his sights set firmly on Emily." Kane chuckled. "He makes excuses and walks away." He pushed her hair behind one ear and kissed her. "Ready?"

Jenna sighed. "Yeah, let's go."

They left the dogs asleep, in front of the fire, and headed out to town along the freshly salted roads. The moon had peeked through the clouds, sending a blue hue across the lowlands. It was in these times, when fresh snow had just fallen and the clouds had parted to reveal stars twinkling in a blue-black sky, that Jenna found peace and contentment. As they arrived in town, they could see people bundled up against the cold, heading toward the hastily erected Nativity scene in the park opposite Aunt Betty's Café. The local band was playing and braziers with red hot coals sat along the edge of the park to warm everyone. As the choir burst into song, Jenna stood surrounded by friends and joined in singing loudly along to all her favorite carols.

Jenna and Kane had celebrated their own special Christmas earlier in the day. They'd wanted a private moment to exchange their gifts. Jenna fingered the diamond snowflake earrings that matched the necklace Kane had given her the previous year. He had been thrilled with his gift. It was a silver belt buckle with his initials around the outside and, in the center, a rearing black stallion like his horse, Warrior. Jenna had it made for him by a friend of Atohi Blackhawk, their Native American friend. She snuggled into him and sang off key, making him laugh. She smiled at her friends surrounding her and looked up at Kane. "You know, Dave, it doesn't get more perfect than this."

"Yeah, it will." Kane grinned at her. "Our story together has just begun."

A LETTER FROM D.K. HOOD

Dear Reader,

Thank you so much for choosing my novel and coming with me on another of Kane and Alton's chilling cases in *Now You See Me*.

If you'd like to keep up to date with all my latest releases, just sign up at the website link below.

www.bookouture.com/dk-hood

I say "chilling" because I always follow the seasons in the stories, and you'll find Jenna and Dave celebrating the holidays in the middle of winter. It is the season I personally love the best because I get to see my family. I've made this a special time for Jenna and Dave as well... albeit laced with the usual thrilling murder and mayhem. So, what's next for Kane and Alton? Let me see. It will be spring by then, with wildflowers in the forest and fresh beginnings. Everything looks so peaceful, but you just know someone is out to spoil everything. Who will be the puppet master this time? Who will decide the fate of the next victim in Black Rock Falls?

I guess I'd better start writing so we can all find out.

If you enjoyed *Now You See Me,* I would be very grateful if you could leave a review and recommend my book to your friends and family. I really enjoy hearing from readers, so feel free to ask me questions at any time. You can get in touch on my Facebook page, Twitter or through my web page.

Thank you so much for your support.

D.K. Hood

http://www.dkhood.com
dkhood-author.blogspot.com.au

 facebook.com/dkhoodauthor
twitter.com/DKHood_Author

ACKNOWLEDGMENTS

Many thanks to my Facebook friends for the inspiration behind some of the names and places in this story, including Stacy Skelly Streicher, Kim Bradley Blalock, Miriam O'Brien, Luanne Rice and David Kentner.

Special mention goes to Joanne Hurley—thank you!!

As always, to my editor Helen Jenner and the fabulous #TeamBookouture, which works so hard to make sure every book is as good as it can possibly be.